FADED GENES

FADED GENES

Searching for a Cure and Finding Home in Altamura, Italy

A Novel and Screenplay by

Patrick Girondi

Skyhorse Publishing

Dedications

I dedicate this book to the people of Altamura.

To my three sons; the Skyhorse Publishing team; and Megan Euker, my agent: thanks for the confidence and support.

Special thanks to the musicians in the Orphan's Dream band, past and present:

Marco Abbattista

Massimo Allegretti

Renzo Arbore

Peppino Barberio

Ken Barnard/Street
Factory Music

Mimmo Basetta

Antonio Benedetto

Salvatore Centoducati

Roberto Chietera

Giuseppe Chiefa

Michele Ciccimarra

Paolo Clemente

Luca Debonis

Nicola Dibenedetto

Antonio Francia

Farelive

Ronny G. and the
Ultimate Concept
Band

Sergio Langella

Mino Lionetti

Luigi Lovicario

Enzo Matera

Giordano Mazzi

Enzo Melasi

Eustachio Montemurro

Francesco Pontillo

I Pooh

Antonio Sansone

Michele Santarcangelo

Alessio Santoro

Arturo Sanzo

Giuliano Scavetta

Nanni Teot

Contents

Chapter 1

Hubble Rubble

A short, somewhat stout forty-seven-year-old man sits at a cluttered desk. Pittsburgh Penguins ticket stubs are stacked in a corner on top of a music CD that reads "PatG." Dozens of pages from insurance policies are sprinkled about in apparent disorder. In the middle of the desk rests a Styrofoam bowl containing a plastic spoon and an empty packet of crackers, its insides dyed red from chili. At the top of the desk is a trophy with a picture of the man resting against it. He is holding a baseball bat with 2022 engraved on it. Hanging on the wall above him is an insurance license bearing his name, Daniel Hubble. He rubs his balding head while analyzing the papers in his hand.

Danny's is the last family-run insurance business on the Hill and one of the few left in Pittsburgh. The office is small, with linoleum floors and brown steel furniture.

Irene, his sixty-one-year-old secretary, enters. "Good morning, Mr. Hubble."

"Morning," he says without looking away from the papers. "Who paid old man Schmidt's policy?" he asks.

"I did," Irene responds.

"I told you not to pay policies with our money unless you tell me first," Danny says.

"I did tell you," Irene responds.

"When did you tell me?"

"Wednesday."

"Wednesday . . . What was I doing?"

"You were talking to Marsha."

"Marla," Danny says, then hesitates. "Don't talk to me when she's here."

"Yes, Mr. Hubble."

"And tell ole Schmidt to settle up. With his heart condition, Farmers Insurance is just itching to cancel, and if they find out we paid, they'll cancel me."

"Yes, Mr. Hubble."

1

Irene walks out. Danny puts on his jacket and follows her, passing her desk, which is in a tiny room connected to his office. The floor is the same linoleum as Danny's, and the furniture is made of the same brown steel. Irene's desk faces a large glass window with "Hubble Insurance, since 1969," written in red.

It's a beautiful Pittsburgh day, and Danny walks out and heads down Federal toward Jefferson. He saunters another fifty feet and heads into Rui's Chili House, which occupies a thin slice of a dilapidated building at the bottom of the Hill.

Rui's has been around forever. There are five wooden booths along the wall, a few small tables with red and white checkered tablecloths, and a bar with thirteen stools that predate any of Rui's customers.

Danny grabs the newspaper and one of the chrome stools at the counter. A dark-skinned Nicaraguan, fifty-ish, cleans sugar from the countertop with his hand, and pours it into a large, deep chili pot resting on the grill. Rui then pours a cup of coffee and places it in front of Danny.

Danny looks at him and raises his eyebrows. "They're going to close you."

"Why?" Rui asks, in a heavy Nicaraguan accent.

"'Cause you throw anything in there. Someone said you put lighter fluid in it the other night."

"Rumors. Old Man Flaherty spilled some while refilling his flint striker, but I cleaned the counter before I scooped the crumbs . . . I think."

"Why do I do this to myself?" Danny shrugs and gently shakes his head.

"My chili's more nutritious than Heinz ketchup." Rui picks up a ketchup bottle. "Monosodium sorbate, I put in coffee. Sulfate potassium 3, I put in donut crumbs. Glucuronic acid, I put in . . ."

"Okay, okay," says Danny.

"Besides," Rui says, "I'm Number One." Rui points to a framed newspaper article hanging on the wall. "Rui's Chili," it reads. "Number One in Pittsburgh!"

Danny takes a swig of coffee, glances at the newspaper article, breathes in, rolls his eyes, breathes out, and then looks back at Rui.

"The college kids line up on Friday and Saturday night to eat my chili!"

"I don't know why, it never tastes the same," Danny says.

"Bingo! You hit it on the top. I give America what it wants."

Danny smirks, "and just what might that be?"

"Diversity," Rui beams.

"I've never seen you eat your chili," Danny counters.

Rui lines his right index finger to his nose. "I'm not American."

Danny stands up and walks toward the door. Rui's coffee was horrible, but Danny was a victim of habit and Rui was a nice guy.

"Hey Danny," Rui calls after him, "I wanted to ask you. You educated man. Is antique spelled 'ea' like a freak or 'ee' like a peek?"

Danny puts two dollars on the counter and doesn't answer. The door closes, and Rui pours what's left of Danny's coffee into the chili pot.

Danny returns to his office. At noon, he sends Irene out for sandwiches, and continues a typical day, shuffling claims and waiting on the phone to speak to insurance companies and delinquent clients. With online insurance, he knows his time is limited, but he hasn't the faintest idea what he'll do when he closes shop. Still, for now, it paid the bills for him and his mother.

At five thirty, Danny stands up and puts on his jacket. There's a softball game he wants to watch at six thirty. He yells into Irene's office. "Did old man Fratto bring my mother's tape?"

"Yes, he did, Mr. Hubble. He says that you're the only people renting DVDs left in the whole United States. Most people just download. He says that it would be cheaper for you to buy all the wrestling videos he has left. He'll give them all to you for $50. He also says that your mother has seen 'em all a hundred times."

Danny blows out air as he walks toward Irene's desk. "Irene, have you ever noticed that you say the same thing to me every evening?"

Irene concentrates. "Why yes, Mr. Hubble, but you always tell me to give you your messages word for word," she says, then marches on. "He also told me that he didn't want the two-dollar rental fee. He said that you could give him 10 dollars a month and save 40."

"And you told him . . .?"

"I told him what I always tell him—not that it's what I tell him, it's what you tell me to tell him, I mean." Irene clears her throat. "I told him that if he didn't take the two dollars, you'd fire me."

"Good." Danny grabs the DVD and shoves it under his arm with a bunch of office folders and walks toward the door. He knew that Mr. Fratto would be closing in the near future and that he'd have to learn how to get the wrestling matches from Amazon. Danny hated Amazon and hoped this didn't happen anytime soon.

"Have a good weekend, Mr. Hubble."

"Thanks, Miss Irene. Do you have plans for the weekend?" he asks, smiling purposefully.

"Yes, I'm going to pick up a tub of Rui's chili and head home and watch television," Irene answers.

Danny continues to smile, nods and turns to leave. "Good."

"You know, Mr. Hubble, Rui has the best chili in all of Pittsburgh."

Danny turns back, quietly smiles, and exits.

As he heads to his car, Danny passes Rui's Chili House. The place is packed. Danny peers in the window. Rui sees him and winks.

Danny winds up the road past the Allegheny Dwellings, a city housing project. It's the beginning of spring and the trees are budding—a welcome sign after another frigid Pittsburgh winter. He continues up Rising Main and pulls onto his own, Belleau Street.

The road is lined with modest bungalows built after World War II. For decades, Fineview was predominantly German, but in the late 1960s, Italian and Irish folks started making their way into the neighborhood. Like most small communities, it's very close-knit, and news travels like lightning. Danny still lives with his mother, and he parks directly in front of the home that he and his mother own.

He doesn't have a lot of time; he wants to be at Fineview Park by six fifteen. He loves to scout out the new talent and size up the old players. The season began in early April and finished by mid-July so that families could enjoy their vacations. Year after year, Danny noted how players returned with more weight, less hair, or a stronger limp. He noticed every particular; every detail could reveal a man's confidence, response time, and agility. Danny had already promised everyone that this season would be his last and this was why it was so important for him to size up the new talent. His team made the playoffs every year and had won the championship four out of the last ten. It was his strongest desire that this, his last season, would be his best.

There weren't a lot of things to do in Fineview, Pittsburgh's smallest community and an enclave of less than 1,300 residents. Danny was a local celebrity and had become famous for what fans called the "Hubble Rubble." An opposing batter once said, "The ball comes at you like it's been shot out of the ground. You don't know if you should swing or run."

Tonight, the guys from Brighton were playing Perry South—Brighton Park had no lights, so Fineview always hosted them. It was Danny's father who had run the drive to fund the lights sometime in the 1970s, and regardless of who played, the park always filled up.

Danny looks up at the piece of gutter dangling from the white, framed two-story. Old Man Miller had promised to fix it years ago—but, of course, Old Man Miller shouldn't be near a roof or a ladder.

At the end of the gutter sat a squirrel. He seemed to be pondering whether to make the jump to the tree that was at least twenty-five feet away. The squirrel looked down at Danny, seeking an opinion.

"Go ahead, jump. Worst case . . ." Danny starts to say, then hesitates. "If you don't make it, the cats will pounce on and devour you. You only live once," he finishes.

Bridget, Danny's old, white-haired mother, is holding a black cat and gazing out of the second-floor window at him.

Danny pretends not to notice and looks back at the squirrel. Two cats coyly mosey toward the bottom of the tree, wittingly paying the squirrel no heed. The squirrel gazes keenly at them and looks at Danny. Danny nods, and the squirrel returns his gaze to the cats.

Cats are welcome in Pittsburgh: the city has always had an elevated issue with rodents and, according to Orkin, Pittsburgh is among the top ten infested cities almost every year. Most homes have a few cats living in the abode and many people put food out for the strays. The latter is probably not helpful, since the cats won't be chasing many rats if they're not hungry.

Danny's mother notices Danny looking up and speaking. She moves her head and focuses on the top of the window, gazing into the trees. She can't see a thing and can't imagine who or what Danny is talking to, or even looking at. *He was always a peculiar child.*

The squirrel perches on the edge of the gutter; the cats gaze up. The squirrel dives but misses the intended branch and crashes into the arms of the tree, desperately clawing to get ahold of anything that might save him.

Danny stares at the squirrel, mercilessly being yanked down by gravity. He glances at the cats and then back at the squirrel. Within ten feet of the ground, the squirrel clutches at the stem of a leaf. The cats lick their whiskers and move directly under him as his weight tilts the cluster of leaves that are brothers and sisters to the twig that is supporting his life.

The movement stops. The tiny stem resists and the squirrel smiles at Danny, completely ignoring his foes. Danny smiles back. *Sometimes a twig separates life from death.*

Danny walks up the stairs, opens the screen door, and takes out his keys. A calico cat races out as the front door swings inward and Danny drops everything. He kneels to gather his files and picks up the *All-Star Wrestling* DVD. He hides it between the papers.

Shortly after, Danny is sitting in a cluttered kitchen. His mother is smoking as she washes the dishes.

"I'm going to get rid of them cats," Danny says.

"Do you want tea?" his mother asks.

As Danny turns to face her, an ash falls onto a plate. He rolls his eyes and shakes his head.

"The little rats pop up everywhere. I'll give Kenny Hess a few bucks to fix 'em," he mumbles.

"I think he nailed Mrs. Hegel's dog to the tree," Ma responds.

"So do I," Danny says.

Danny turns around and looks at a paper on the table. "The old man's dead. No one buys insurance from someone who smells like cigarettes and has cat hairs all over his clothes."

"Drink your tea," Ma answers as if she is not part of the other conversation.

Danny begins removing cat hairs from his suit.

"You look pale."

"I feel weird," Danny responds.

"Go and get a checkup," Ma says as she wipes her hands.

Danny turns and looks at her. "They'll tell me that I shouldn't be living with someone who smokes." He waves a cloud of smoke away as his mother lights another cigarette.

"Did you bring home my video?" Ma asks.

He points to the stack of papers.

She picks up the DVD and glows. "Hulk Hogan and Lex Luger. You're my best," Ma says.

"I'm your only," Danny replies quietly.

Ma's cigarette ash is about an inch long. "You know, that noise your car makes is getting worse. I can hear you from Rising Main."

"Yeah, I know; PatG's gonna fix it."

"Oh, he's a mechanic again?"

"No," Danny answers emphatically. "He's a singer who fixes cars," Danny says, then adds, "sometimes."

Ma walks into the front room and puts the tape into the DVD. She is jumping and swinging at the wrestlers on the television set. Danny stands and puts his headphones on—PatG's music is finally audible.

"Don't you know 'hind every tree! Don't you know they want to take you away from me!"

Three cats, sitting in various positions—one black, one gray, and one white—watch attentively as Danny heads to his bedroom to change.

The park bleachers are already full when Danny arrives. Several of the spectators notice him and begin whispering among themselves. At 170 pounds and short of 5'5, Danny doesn't make much of an athletic impression. But as far as Pittsburgh softball went, he was tops, and as Freddie Patek so eloquently said, "I'd rather be the shortest player in the majors than the tallest player in the minors."

Danny looks over to Olive's tree. Kevin, an Irish-looking redhead, and PatG, a short, Italian-looking guy, are there. As Danny would expect, PatG's talking to some girl. Most people shunned the tree where Olive hung herself over a Fineview cad some years ago. Of course, time passes and not everyone knows about Olive anymore or what "cad" even means. Kevin could care less about the story, and PatG was a cad and likely felt right at home.

PatG's mother was born in Italy; she married an American, and PatG was born less than a year later. When PatG was four or five years old, his father was diagnosed with a rare nerve disorder. The family lived meagerly as his father could not work. PatG's maternal grandfather, who could barely speak English, took care of PatG while his mother worked. When his mother was home, she responded to her husband's every need. PatG's father was already difficult to put up with. His sickness made him worse. His mother; however, never said a cross word to his father, that PatG could remember. Before PatG's father died, he asked his wife to never remarry. She promised to honor his wishes. PatG was eight years old and never saw his mother with another man. PatG believed that the only explanation for his mother's behavior was unconditional love, whatever that meant.

PatG wasn't really philosophical, but he noted that in modern times, men and women love until the relationship becomes inconvenient. Sometimes, he believes that maybe he's searching for a woman like his mother. He also realizes that each time he finds a woman who he suspects might love him unconditionally, he runs for the hills.

He and Danny have done everything in life together—First Communion, Little League—never even having one argument.

Kevin is Fineview's largely unrecognized sage. Most just say he's a drunk but Kevin reads in between the lines of the daily paper, hears the message that the networks are trying not to tell you on the news, and quickly understands the truth in almost any conversation. He's well versed in almost any subject on the planet and can line up complex situations in an organized way within moments. When he spent time in prison, many of the inmates consulted with him as if he were an attorney. Before any of their times, an old radio program called *Amos 'n' Andy* featured a smooth-talking lawyer named Algonquin Calhoun, Jr. Some old timer in the prison gave Kevin the nickname 'Cal,' short for Calhoun. PatG was the only person who called Kevin 'Cal.'

Kevin knew a lot about a lot of things, including disease and medicine. There wasn't any logical explanation. Kevin hadn't made it out of grammar school. But many in Fineview sought Kevin out. Some spoke to him about their symptoms before they went to see their own doctor. Over the years his diagnoses were uncanny.

PatG notices Danny from the corner of his eye. "Danny! We're over here! Hubble Rubble!"

Everyone looks at Danny, who turns red. Many smile, and a couple holler, "Hubble Rubble!"

Danny waves to his fans and walks over to Kevin, PatG, and the girl, watching as the Perry South team takes the field. He believes that by watching an athlete walk out, especially at the beginning and at the end of a game, you can tell a lot about him. You see if he's a hustler, a joker, arrogant, meek, confident, passionate, or just there to eat up a few hours.

The girl smiles, whispers something into PatG's ear, and gets into a red Ford Mustang with West Virginia plates on it. Danny turns away and concentrates on the game. The Perry South Team is slaughtering Brighton, and Danny notes a few hitters whom he will have to be extremely careful of.

Later that evening, in Nick's Club, a dimly lit bar with a small dance floor, Danny and Kevin are watching PatG finish up "Sandra," a song from his latest album. PatG sings blues and rock. He writes all of his own stuff, which likely explains why he's singing at Nick's.

"Yes, folks don't forget. *To stay ahead of trouble, think Hubble.* Our friend Danny Hubble has been serving Fineview and the Hill for over fifty years."

Danny looks at Kevin. "I hate when he does that."

8

"I think that's why he does it." Kevin tilts his head and sips his beer.

"Everyone here drinks. . . . Even if they *do remember*, none of my carriers will want to insure them."

"It's Friday, Danny boy." Kevin again tilts his head and sips his beer. When he finishes, he takes the beer out of his mouth. "Aren't you thirsty?" Kevin asks.

Danny rolls his eyes and turns his head toward the bar. "Get Kev another."

Nick, the owner, uncaps a beer and slides it in front of Kevin.

PatG arrives and puts his arms around his buddies. "Hey, goombahs."

"I ain't your goombah. I'm Irish," Kevin says as he throws back another few ounces.

"Hey Nick, back these guys up. On me," PatG shouts.

Nick looks over at him with a frown. PatG looks back.

"Okay, you're right, get them on you."

PatG grabs the wireless microphone and breaks out into another of his songs, "Tampa Day."

"You know, he's the only guy I know that pays to work," Nick says.

Kevin tilts his beer. "He buys a lot of drinks."

"He loves like no one I've ever known." As he speaks, Danny's staring far away. "He loves like a little boy."

Nick watches. Kevin's silence confirms Danny's soft words.

Danny feels Kevin staring at him, clears his throat, and comes back to the bar. He's got a heart of gold," he says abruptly.

"I hope so. That way, at least his tab will get paid when he dies," Nick quips.

Later, when Kevin walks out of the club, Danny's speaking on his cell phone.

"What are you doing?" Kevin asks.

"I'm going by Marla."

"I'm going by my Marla," Kevin puns.

"Don't you ever get tired of hookers?" Danny asks sincerely.

"Nope. I don't think I could get off if I didn't pay for it."

"What's the going rate, Kev?"

"Two bucks, a fin . . . I remember when some of 'em stopped by just to get something warm in their stomachs."

"Nice."

"A few weeks ago, PatG had the prices jacked. He went with Cherry."

"I don't need to hear this."

"Wait," Kevin interrupts, "big shot finishes and gives her twenty. Word spread, and they all thought they were call girls. He better stay far away."

Kevin stares into Danny's eyes. "I wouldn't pay more than a sawbuck for Marilyn Monroe."

"What if she's there when you get home?" Danny asks.

"She'll get three bucks and half a Philly steak." Staring at Danny, Kevin shrugs his shoulders and adds, "That's all I got."

Danny nods and smiles reverently, "And she gets you. Any woman should be so lucky."

Kevin turns and begins to walk away.

"See you, Kev."

Kevin raises his hand and continues to walk straight ahead.

Shortly after, Danny's on the couch in Marla's apartment. Marla's twenty-five but could pass for twenty-six or twenty-four. She has her head in his lap.

"Danny, do you love me?"

"Watch the film."

"I'm tired. Let's go to bed," Marla responds.

Danny and Marla go into the bedroom and Marla quietly shuts the door. Once inside, they move to the bed. Danny takes his shoes off and Marla does the rest.

About three hours later, Danny tiptoes toward the front door of the apartment. A couple is asleep in front of the TV set. Danny arrives at the door and Marla walks to him, rubbing her eyes. She hugs him.

"Bye, Danny."

"Bye," he responds.

The girl on the floor stirs. "Bye, Danny."

As Danny enters his front room, the first rays of light are sneaking in through the blinds. Ma's snoring. The TV's fuzzy. Danny turns off the television and covers his mother.

She stirs. "Danny, leave money tomorrow."

"Yeah, Ma. 'Night, Ma."

At the same time, a few blocks away, PatG is entering his front room. His mother is on the couch with a rosary in her hands.

"Patti, find a nice girl so I can sleep."

"Ma, women use me for kicks," PatG replies, barely audible.

"You don't give them a chance."

PatG kisses his mother on the cheek and walks into his bedroom.

It's almost noon on Sunday. Danny smiles as he turns into 'Larry's: He's Not Here' bar.

Larry, the owner, is of average height and build. His appearance confirms each day of his fifty-seven years and he is wearing a horrible, light orange-brown wig. The hairs are the same quality as the material you'd find on the head of a five-buck doll.

Five regulars are watching the rerun of a college football game as Danny walks in. They're all from Fineview, and Danny knows them all better than he needs to. Each one of them is married and a blue-collar worker.

"Hey, Danny," Paulie says.

"Hey, Danny Boy. You gonna rock East Al with the Hubble Rubble tomorrow?" Markie asks.

"Boys, I'm not sure if I still got it, and East Al's got some new hitters that blast the ball."

The bar is silent; everyone's eyes are on Danny as he sits on his stool.

"I'll mow 'em down," Danny says.

The patrons smile and Larry slaps Danny's arm. "Hey man, don't be scaring people like that. You know, there's not a lot of things we got left up here on the Hill."

Larry pours Danny a beer and grabs the remote. "A thousand channels and nothing on."

"Go back to that girly film," Paulie says.

"It's Sunday, you ass. Have some respect," Larry rebuts.

Ralphie nods. "Yeah," he says.

Markie raises his beer. "Praise the Lord. Put on rugby."

"Don't Europeans play any real sports?" Paulie asks.

Larry ignores him and wipes the bar off in front of Danny. "Hard-boiled egg?"

Danny nods. "Give me one of them Freakin' Hot Jalapeno Slim Jims too."

"Breakfast of champions," Markie says as he tilts his glass of beer back.

"Out of Slim Jims, Danny Boy," Larry says.

"Okay, give me a bag of bar-be-que chips."

"In training, Danny?" Ralphie asks.

Larry places the egg and chips on the bar. While the others are watching a beer commercial, Larry addresses Danny. "I seen Ma at Schatzel's. I told her to quit smoking or she'd end up like me."

Larry moves closer and whispers, "Damn, chemo's a bitch." He hesitates and rolls his eyes up toward his eyebrows before continuing. "What do you think about the hair?"

Danny smiles, *Rod Stewart . . . I like it.*"

Larry looks at the mirror and raises a closed fist to his mouth. "Maggie, I think I got something to say to you!"

Markie puts his empty beer glass on the bar. "Rod, get me a beer."

PatG is sitting on the steel bleachers as Danny walks toward him, toting baseball cleats and his Fineview Phuckers baseball uniform.

PatG stands, steps out from the bleachers, and walks to meet Danny.

He winks. "You look great, buddy."

"Well, if that's true, then I wish I felt like I look," Danny responds.

A woman stands up on the mobbed steel bleachers. "Danny, get out there and pitch up some Hubble Rubble!"

A man turns to the guy next to him. "Hubble's the best pitcher the Hill ever had. Shoots 'em out of the ground. The batter doesn't know if he should swing or duck."

Danny moves next to PatG.

"How's Marla?" PatG asks.

"Fine," Danny responds. "What did . . .?"

"Got a hummer in the parking lot," PatG whispers.

"Judy?" Danny asks.

"Nah, she's chasing some rap singer." PatG looks at Danny and smiles. His eyes are cringed and his head tilted. "College girl," he says.

Danny smirks. "I remember when they taught science at Pitt."

"I prefer the modern courses, and I'm glad that I'm dark-skinned. I tell some that I'm Spanish. Young girls just gobble up diversity."

Danny pitches the first three innings without giving up a hit. The Phuckers are ahead 8-0 when he pulls himself out. He sits on the bench, studying each and every batter from the opposing team—watching whether they swung wildly, how fast they ran to first, if they got impatient waiting for the right pitch, if they followed their coach's instructions, and what kind of contact they made with the ball. Danny didn't need to take notes. It was all indexed in his mind. He had every player in the league indexed. The Phuckers went on to win the game 11-7.

As the park's emptying out, a woman walks up to Danny. "Danny, how's Ma?" she asks.

Danny turns toward the woman holding onto the fence. "She's . . ." Danny falls to his knees and faints.

PatG kneels next to him. "Give him room!"

Danny's eyes are barely open.

"Someone call an ambulance," PatG yells.

Danny clutches PatG's shirt. "No, I'm fine. Just slipped," he insists and begins to lift himself up. "PatG, get me home."

PatG helps Danny to his feet. "You sure?"

Danny slowly winks.

PatG and Danny are in Danny's bedroom. Danny is laying on the bed.

"I don't like the way you look," PatG says.

"I never liked the way I looked."

PatG is uncomfortable, irritated, and scared. "Cut it out," he tells Danny.

Ma walks in. As she hands Danny a cup of tea, a cigarette ash falls into it. "I'll get more," she says.

Danny shakes his head and lies back down.

Ma goes into the kitchen. "I got to go to Schatzel's for tea. That was the last bag. I thought we had more. You must be drinking more than usual," she says.

She sticks her head back into the bedroom. "Have you been drinking more tea than usual?"

Danny nods his head and Ma leaves.

Danny stares at the window and rubs his cheek. He senses that something's seriously not right. "What's it all about, PatG?"

PatG shakes his head slightly and shrugs his shoulders. "What do you mean, Danny?"

"I mean, what's it all about? What's life about? What's work about? Women? Why are we here?"

PatG looks into his friend's eyes. "Danny, I have no idea. My old man worked like a dog until the day he died. My family's scattered all over the country trying to squeeze out a living."

PatG looks to the side. "I don't know what life's all about, and to be quite honest, I'm not sure I know anyone who does." PatG hesitates and then smiles thinly, "Cal, maybe. You should ask him."

Danny looks at PatG. "I love that guy too, but you, you take it to another level."

PatG smiles broadly. "How can I not? You know what he asked me the other day?"

"No, but I'm sure that you'll tell me."

"The other day," PatG continued anxiously, "he asked me, if feces smelled like roses, would they still call it crap?"

Danny responds with silence. After a few deep moments Danny speaks. "I wish I had a family."

"You do. You've got me . . . and Ma."

Danny nods softly, "PatG, I'm tired. Sing me "Sweet Memories.""

PatG is softly singing to his music, which is playing on the CD player. "*I don't know if you're that strong . . . that you can run from my thoughts all night long . . .*"

Ma has still not returned. Danny's sleeping. The doorbell rings; PatG walks into the front room, opens the window and looks out.

"Marla," he says under his breath, "damn." He closes the window and unlocks the door.

"PatG, I heard about Danny falling. My cousin called and told me. Her boyfriend was at the game."

"Relax," PatG says, "he's fine."

Marla begins to cry. "Is he really?" She dabs her eyes with a handkerchief.

PatG sighs, gesturing for her to come in. They've just settled at the kitchen table when Ma enters carrying a brown grocery bag. She removes the contents and puts them in front of Marla and PatG.

"Lipton is Danny's favorite tea," she says as she opens the cabinet and places it on the shelf.

Ma starts to fill the teapot. Marla looks at PatG.

"Ma, this is Danny's friend Marla," PatG says.

"I have to make Danny's tea," she replies.

"He's sleeping, Ma. Make it later."

"I'll make it now. Danny likes tea."

Ma turns to Marla. "Who are you?" she asks in the nastiest tone she can muster. Marla freezes.

"She's Danny's friend," PatG responds.

"I asked the girl, PatG."

Ma fumbles for a cigarette, lights it and inhales. She stares at Marla, smoke exiting as she speaks. "What do you want with my son?"

Marla smiles timidly. "Hasn't Danny told you about us?"

"Who is this girl?" Ma asks disgustedly to no one in particular.

PatG looks at Marla.

Marla looks from PatG to Ma. "I'm his girl. I love him very much."

Ma moves mechanically and glares at Marla. "*I have to give Danny his tea.*" She turns to PatG. "You should be out fixing cars." Ma hesitates, "Your mother will die without peace."

Ma works herself up and courageously turns back to Marla. "*And you,* I don't know what you should do. But *whatever it is,* you *shouldn't be doing it with my son!*"

The doorbell rings. PatG rises and returns with Irene.

"Talks all over the Hill about Mr. Hubble falling at the softball game. I came as soon as I heard," Irene says.

"He's fine. I'm making him tea," Ma says, as an attorney would if speaking a statement of fact to a judge.

Marla looks over PatG's shoulder and spots Danny, who is standing in his bedroom doorway, clothed in a T-shirt and boxer shorts.

Danny looks at his mother, rubs his hand over his face and looks at Marla. "What are you doing here?" he asks.

Ma stares angrily at her son. "Danny, who is she?"

Danny buries his face in a chair cover. "God, I want to die," he says. "PatG, why did you stop singing?"

"Danny, who is this girl?" Ma asks more forcefully.

PatG, Marla, and Danny move to the front room. Irene has met Marla before at the office and has known PatG for decades—she follows and greets Marla. Danny sits on the La-Z-Boy with the chair cover still over his head.

Irene walks back into the kitchen. "She's a pretty little thing," she says to Ma.

"She's *not* for Danny," Ma says distastefully. "No one will tell me who she is. Who is she?"

"She's very important. . . . When she's at the office, I can't talk to Danny, Mr. Hubble. Did Danny, I mean Mr. Hubble, drink his tea?"

Ma marches into the front room past PatG and Marla. She touches Danny, intending to rouse him for his Lipton tea. "Danny, Danny."

The chair cover falls, revealing Danny's white unconscious face.

PatG is shocked and frightened. "Marla, call an ambulance."

Chapter 2

It Could Never Happen to Me

Twenty minutes later, Danny wakes and sees the face of a man dressed in white. He looks around and sees the lamp and the television—he's still at home.

"What are you doing?" Danny asks the paramedic.

"Hello, sir. I'm Paramedic Sinclair. I'm checking for a pulse."

"I see that, but I'm not dead."

"Yes sir, I realize that, I'm just trying to get your vitals before we take you to the hospital."

"I'm not going to the hospital."

Danny glances around the room. His eyes set on PatG; his face looks abnormally worn and tortured. Danny has never seen his friend more solemn, more engulfed, not even when he was hitting on a hot twenty-year-old. "I pitched three no-hit innings today," he says. "Do you think someone sick could pitch three no-hit innings?" Danny forces a smile.

A tear runs down PatG's cheek.

"I'm tired, that's all," Danny says.

Sinclair interrupts. "All right, sir. I can't force you to get in the ambulance, but your loved ones thought it was in your best interest to call us."

"That's 'cause they don't know what you guys cost." Danny smiles and stands. All eyes are glued on his pale face. "I'm sorry that you came here for a false alarm. Get back on the street, you might miss a call from someone who really needs help."

As soon as the words are out of his mouth, Danny falls face-first to the floor.

In the hospital waiting room, Marla wipes her eyes. PatG takes his head out of his hands and looks down the hall.

Marla reaches over and puts her hand on his sleeve. "Don't worry, PatG. He'll be fine."

"What time is it?" PatG asks.

Marla reaches into her shiny jacket pocket and pulls out a phone. "It's almost midnight," she replies, then looks up as the two hear a commotion brewing around the corner.

"That's Cal," PatG says as he stands and walks. As he turns into the joining hall, he finds Kevin face-to-face with the security guard. "If you want to get socked, just try to stop me," Kevin says calmly.

"Sir, I'm going to call the police. Only family members are allowed after eleven p.m.; I don't make the rules," the security guard pleads.

PatG stops about thirty feet away and watches the scene unnoticed.

"Let me ask you something," says Kevin. "Do you have a cousin or an uncle that you really can't stand?"

The guard is visibly confused. "What does that have to do with anything?"

"Please, just answer the question."

"Sure, I got two cousins and an uncle I'd like to murder."

"Would you go see them in the hospital?"

"Hell no."

"What if someone tried to force you, like your mother. Would you go?"

"No!"

"That's your right," Kev says. "Now, you seem okay. And I love this guy. He's one of my only two friends. I wouldn't force you to go visit a guy you hate, so please, don't stop me from seeing a guy I love."

"You said you're his brother, right?" the security guard asks.

Kevin nods. "We're like this." Kevin shows his two fingers pressed together as one.

The security guard jerks his head to the side. Kevin walks past him and up to PatG. "How's the kid?"

"We don't know much. He fell at the park and blacked out at home. We called the ambulance. He refused to come here, then got up and fell on his face," PatG says.

"I don't like it," says Kevin. "He's lost some meat, looks pale as hell, and I noticed some red spots on his arm and neck the other day. I think he's got leukemia."

"What? Come on, Cal. Leukemia?"

"Well, let's see what the doctors say. I've been wrong before."

PatG stares into Kevin's eyes. "Yeah, when?"

A curtain is drawn around Danny's hospital bed. The tiny compartment is full of machines blinking and beeping at each other. Danny has various gadgets stuck into or hanging onto him. Irene's holding Danny's right hand, and Ma's holding his left hand. Danny's eyes open.

"Oh, Mr. Hubble," Irene begins to cry.

Ma looks down, her eyes watery. "Danny . . . Oh, Danny."

A young doctor in bifocals steps in, reaches into a tissue-sized box, and puts on a pair of blue gloves. He clears his throat as if to announce his arrival, smiles curtly at the ladies, and then turns his attention to Danny, who immediately doesn't like him.

The doctor watches Danny indifferently as he grabs the chart hanging on Danny's bed. Finally, he raises the clipboard to his face and glances at it. "Mr. Huble," he says, smiling tightly.

"There are two 'b's,'" Danny tells him.

"Oh, my mistake, Mr. Hubble. Mr. Hubble, we need to run other tests before we can understand what's happening with you."

Danny purses his lips, and a nurse with a folder in her hand walks in. The doctor looks at her. She nods worshipfully at him. Danny watches as the doctor watches the nurse. The doctor smiles and seems to think, *Not bad looking for a nurse—could make for some interesting recreation later.*

"Sir, I need your insurance information," the nurse says to Danny. "You are insured?" she asks unsympathetically.

"He's an insurance man," Irene blurts out.

"Oh, then I'm sure he's well covered," the nurse offers.

"Yeah," Danny says, "start gouging the insurance company's eyes out. Take the tests you don't need first. That way, you've got a better chance of getting paid for all of them," he jabs.

The nurse forces a smile.

The doctor looks down at her legs. She has cankles, but the rest of her looks appealing enough. "Ladies, say your goodbyes," he instructs Ma and Irene. "Mr. Hu-BB-el needs rest." The doctor offers another mechanical smile, hangs the clipboard on the bed, turns, takes off his gloves, and leaves.

"Sir, what is the name of your insurance company?" the nurse asks.

Danny looks to Irene and his mother. "Girls, you heard the quack. There's no need for you to take part in the sham, and he is right about one thing. I am tired. Ma, hand me my wallet."

Ma gives Danny his wallet and raises a hanky to her face. "I want to stay, Danny. Can't I stay?"

"Yes, Mr. Hubble, your mother should stay with you. I can leave," Irene says.

"No, both of you leave. I need the rest; I'll see you in the morning."

The nurse nods, and Ma and Irene exit and walk toward PatG, Marla, and Kevin.

PatG puts his arm around Ma, who grabs his shoulders and falls into his arms. "Oh PatG, I'm so scared. I tried not to cry in his room, but there's something so, so wrong."

PatG gently rubs her back. "He'll be fine, Ma—Danny's always fine."

Ma raises her head and looks at Kevin. Kevin cowers and looks away.

"Kevin, what's wrong with Danny?"

"I don't know, Ma. How would I?"

Ma buries her head in PatG's chest, crying uncontrollably.

Now Irene begins to cry and Marla comes to her aid.

"I need to sit down," Irene says.

Marla gets her seated. Kevin is trying to sneak away.

"Kevin! Kevin! What is wrong with my Danny?" Ma screams.

Kevin's face is full of tears. He couldn't turn around now to save his own life.

Ma tries to race after him, but PatG grabs her. "Kevin doesn't know anything, Ma. He ain't no doctor."

"Everyone on the Hill knows that Kevin knows—Old Man Crowley, Mrs. Turner, Little Bobby Van Patten. Oh my God." Ma stares at PatG. "Danny's going to die!"

Irene begins to blubber uncontrollably into Marla's shoulder. Tears stream down Marla's face.

Ma is dazed. She whispers, "If Danny was going to be all right, Kevin would have told us. He knows. He always knows. He doesn't want to hurt us. Did he tell you, PatG?"

PatG looks away. "Why? He hasn't even seen Danny since earlier, at the softball game. He just got here. We didn't even have time to talk."

"Look at me, PatG."

PatG looks at Ma and winks. Ma nods. "Irene, let's go home," she says.

The following day, PatG enters Danny's room at nine a.m. Danny's concentrating on the sports news. "The Pirates have a hell of a team this year," Danny says, looking at his friend.

PatG does not respond.

"It's bad, huh? What did our guy Cal say?" Danny asks.

"Let's see what the tests tell us," PatG says.

Danny ignores him. "What did he say?"

PatG doesn't answer.

"It's not good," Danny says, answering himself and looking out the window.

PatG purses his lips and nods. "He thinks it might be leukemia, but let's wait and see what the tests say."

Danny continues to stare out the window expressionlessly. The voices coming from the television are just noise.

"Even if he's right, there's lots of therapy options," PatG says. "You know how many people get through leukemia?"

Danny remains silent. "Tons," PatG continues, "and me and Ma and Kevin and Irene and Marla, we'll be right there with you all the way."

Danny purses his lips, closes his eyes, and nods as if he's made a vital decision. He turns to PatG. "PatG, do me a favor."

"Sure, anything."

"Distance Marla from this. The poor thing—I actually," Danny pauses, "I actually think she likes me." He pauses again. "I can't help the rest of you, but shield her from all of this."

"Danny, she's a good broad. I mean, I can't force her to . . ."

"PatG, promise me you'll try. You'll do everything you can."

PatG nods, just as Irene and Ma walk in.

"You look good, Danny Boy," Ma says.

"Yes, you look good, Mr. Hubble," echoes Irene.

PatG's phone rings and he excuses himself to answer it. "Hey, Marla . . . yes, I'm here. No, he's not awake. I think they gave him something to sleep, a laxative or something. . . . Oh, yeah, that's what I mean. Sure, honey, as soon as he's up, I'll call you." PatG taps the red button and disconnects.

"Do they have Lipton tea here, Danny?" Ma asks in a tone bordering on urgency.

"Yeah, Ma, I tasted it. It's Lipton all right. It's about the only thing they'll let me get down. I got to take some tests on Monday morning."

After a few hours Marla calls, again. "PatG, I'm on my way over."

"He's still out of it, honey," PatG responds.

"That's okay, I just want to look at him."

At about five p.m., Marla opens the curtain and smiles. Ma, Irene, and PatG are present. Danny looks at Marla. "Hi, Marla, I was just chasing these people out of here. I need to sleep."

Marla is confused. She looks at PatG and then at Ma and Irene. Ma looks away. Marla moves next to the bed and takes Danny's hand in her own. There's a line into his vein with white tape securing it.

"Things will be fine, Danny," Marla says.

Ma coughs and makes a repulsed face. Danny moves his hand out from under Marla's.

"Come on, everyone. Let's get out of here," PatG says. "Danny needs his rest, and he's still got more tests in the morning."

Marla stares. Ma and Irene kiss Danny on the cheek and file out. PatG hugs his friend.

Danny whispers in his ear, "Remember, keep Marla out of this."

PatG nods and disappears through the slit in the hospital curtains.

Monday morning, Danny awakes to find himself being wheeled down the hospital corridor by an average-looking, middle-aged nurse. Ma and Irene each have one of his hands and are walking by his side—they've teamed up, and Irene is desperately seeking Ma's approval. Danny's eyes are closed. He doesn't really want to live this part of his life.

"Are you married?" Ma asks the nurse.

"Ma'am?"

"My son's an insurance executive. He's not married. Are you married?"

Danny barely opens his eyes and then closes them tightly.

"No, ma'am, I'm not married."

"Have you ever been married?" Irene asks.

"*No.*"

"Mrs. Hubble, she says she's never been married."

Ma looks severely at Irene.

"I'm Mr. Hubble's private secretary," Irene adds.

"Oh?" the nurse quizzes her.

"He's a fine man," Irene says.

"Irene!" Ma whispers.

"He knows how to use the internet. He doesn't smoke and rarely drinks," Irene continues.

The nurse smiles. "Sounds like a real catch."

"He is." Irene reaches into her purse. "Here's his card. Call or send a computer message. He gets loads of them."

Ma speaks firmly, yet in a low tone so as not to stir Danny, who's awake and hearing every syllable. "*Irene.*"

"Well, it's true. Sometimes women send Mr. Hubble pictures of themselves doing the craziest things!"

Danny's bed arrives at a double door—the end of the corridor.

"Ladies, you'll have to wait here. I'll give you a minute." The nurse takes the clipboard, turns and disappears.

Ma gently touches Danny's shoulder. "Danny."

Irene touches Danny's other shoulder. "Danny, Mr. Hubble."

"He knows his name," Ma says impatiently.

Irene moves her finger to her lips. "Oh."

Danny's eyes open. "Are you two trying to kill me with embarrassment?"

"We're worried, Danny—Mr. Hubble—aren't we Bridget, Mrs. Hubble?"

Ma ignores Irene's babbling. "We'll be waiting for you, Danny."

The nurse arrives and wheels Danny through the white doors.

MRI results can take up to two weeks to coordinate, but already, on Wednesday morning, Danny and Ma are sitting in front of Doctor Terrell, a middle-aged man with glasses and curly gray hair.

"Is everyone comfortable?" the doctor asks.

"I'm comfortable. Danny?" Ma asks.

"Oh, yes, I'm comfortable."

"Good. Do you smoke, Mr. Hubble?"

"Not directly." Danny jumps. "Ouch. What did you do that for?" Danny rubs his leg and looks at his mother.

"Excuse me, honey. It slipped."

"I asked if you smoked, Mr. Hubble."

Danny glances at Ma. "No. But sometimes I'm around people who do." Danny smirks snidely at his mother.

"Mr. Hubble, there's no time for mincing words. It appears that you have a type of leukemia that often afflicts heavy smokers."

Danny's mother covers her mouth with her handkerchief and mumbles to herself, "Leukemia."

"Is it fatal?" Danny asks abruptly.

The doctor seems a bit irritated by Danny's directness. He looks at Ma and smiles tightly.

"Yes," the doctor says.

Danny looks at Ma and then beyond her, out the window at the passing cars. He gently nods his head and turns back to the doctor. "Will I be here for the hockey season?"

The doctor seems a bit jarred—Danny's isn't a normal reaction. He is used to seeing patients grovel and show their underside, desperate for any sign of hope. Like many modern professionals, he entered his camp for economic reasons. The sentiments of many doctors are often stimulated by fat paychecks. Dr. Terrell felt that he was greatly underpaid. He glances at Ma and then stares at Danny.

"I've got season tickets." Danny smiles.

The doctor, openly irritated, clears his throat. "Well, that's hard to say. We must start chemotherapy immediately."

"Doc, I'm an insurance man. What's the name for this leukemia I got?"

The doctor is getting more and more incensed. This wasn't enjoyable. He saw dozens of condemned people each week, and they each treated him as they would their personal savior. He plays with a pen and looks at the results of Danny's MRI. "I have my suspicions, but the tests are not yet conclusive."

"Two minutes ago, you said I have some leukemia that smokers often get."

"Yes, I suspect that, but we still have other exams to conduct and analyze. You see, Mr. Hubble, we need to pinpoint the right therapy to meet *your* needs. We don't just treat patients willy-nilly."

Danny interrupts the doctor. "What do you think I've got, looking at the exams so far?"

The doctor hesitates, not wanting to show his irritation. "Acute lymphoblastic leukemia." He fights but is unable to prevent a smile.

Danny smiles back. "Look, good doctor, I've seen this a dozen times. It's not my choice to spend the last months of my life in agony."

"That's certainly up to you," the doctor replies coldly. "There are choices, *if you'd give me a chance.*"

"You said fatal. . . . How much time?"

"A month or two, maybe six. If you respond favorably to the chemo, it could be considerably longer."

Ma seems to have become conveniently deaf. Her eyes are fixed on a paper clip, but she no longer sees even that.

"What's the alternative to the supercharged X-rays and cocktail sauce?"

The doctor hesitates. "A bone marrow transplant, maybe. . ."

"And then what happens?" Danny asks.

It was far less entertaining to converse with terminal patients who wanted to talk in plain English. Danny was ruining his day.

"Well?" Danny asks.

The doctor didn't respond.

"Well?" Danny screams.

Ma jerks back to life. The doctor looks at her and then back at Danny. "Then it's a dice roll. You beat it or you don't."

"You mean I beat it or I'm dead."

The doctor looks uncomfortably at Danny's mother. Danny looks down and rubs his right hand over his head.

"This is tough. . . . She's my only living relative. Is she too old?"

"DNA compatibility is necessary. We'll do a donor search. We could get lucky . . ."

Danny cups his right hand and shakes it like he's about to roll a pair of dice. He blows into his fist, pushes it forward, and opens it. He moves his head from right to left waiting for the imaginary dice to land.

The doctor looks down at the desk. Then he suddenly looks at Danny. "I have another appointment, Mr. Hubble."

Ma covers her mouth with her handkerchief.

Danny stands up. "Come on, Ma. It'll be all right. . . . I promise."

Chapter 3

Ma's Confession

It's early the following Thursday morning, and Danny is gazing out the kitchen window. There's a squirrel hanging onto the screen. The squirrel reminds Danny of the squirrel from the other day, the one who was saved from death by a twig. Could Danny's life somehow be saved too? *Nah*, he thinks, *that only happens to squirrels*.

Danny turns and pours tea into Ma's cup.

"Ma, drink your tea."

"I have something to tell you," Ma stands and gazes at the squirrel. She moves her hand to touch the screen. The squirrel moves away. "We have to go to speak to a Dr. Winebach this morning," Ma says, still looking out the window.

The squirrel comes back and clings to the screen.

"I told you I'm going alone," Danny says.

"No, please Danny, take me with you. I promise I'll be fine."

Danny looks at Ma. She looks at him. "I promise," she says gently.

Ma turns back to search for the squirrel, but it vanished, along with the urge to light a cigarette.

A few hours later, Doctor Winebach enters his office. "You must be Mr. Hubble and his mother, Mrs. Hubble," he says.

Danny replicates his tone. "And you must be Doctor Winebach."

"Your mother's not compatible," Winebach says coolly.

"Oh?" Danny quips.

"At any rate, people over the age of sixty are at a slightly increased risk for complications during and after donation," the doctor adds.

26

"But I love helping people, Mr. Hubble, if I can. I like my patients to understand their situations. Are you interested in understanding genes?"

Danny glances at the door and then back at Winebach. "Of course," he says, smiling tightly, "and thank you."

"Imagine a gene, G1, gets copied into a different part of the genome, producing G2. Now, another duplication event copies G2, creating yet another copy of G1, *along with some of the new DNA surrounding it.*"

The doctor smiles gently. "Are you grasping this, Mr. Hubble?"

Danny has analyzed enough of his clients' medical records to have an idea of what Winebach is saying. He nods.

Winebach continues. "Since duplicated genes are almost identical to their originals, their pieces often get mistaken for parts of their ancestors that have been assembled incorrectly. They create images—well, frankly, I call them 'faded genes.' They are the geneticist's worst nightmare."

Danny smiles. "Thanks, Doc. What does this mean for me?"

"Well, to start with, you have a peculiar DNA."

"That's me, peculiar."

Winebach looks at Ma and waits for Danny to conclude.

"Faded genes," Danny says.

Winebach nods and takes a deep breath. He looks aside and then back at Danny. "I'm a geneticist, *your geneticist,* and I'd like to help. A relative has the best chance of sharing your genetic makeup. Since your mother is your only living relative, finding an HLA-compatible match will be a challenge."

Ma hastily moves her hand to her chin, turning it like she is trying to open her face. Danny stares.

"What has your oncologist suggested?" asks Winebach.

"Radiation and chemotherapy. I refused."

"Would you consider experimental, nonconventional treatment?"

"The insurance won't cover it, and I don't have the funds."

"There are NIH programs; clinical trials that cost the patient nothing," the doctor added.

"I saw them. None look promising, and Doc, excuse the bluntness, but I'd be helping science with little hope of helping myself. It also means I'd have to move to another city. If my time is limited and there's no real shot at a remedy," Danny looks toward Ma, who doesn't seem to be present, "I want to spend it with my own people."

"Of course, I understand. This is your choice. Come in on Friday morning, though, just to see what the search turns up."

Danny reaches his hand out to Winebach. "Thank you, Doctor."

Danny removes his hand from the doctor's and offers it to his mother. "Madame."

Ma's eyes momentarily brighten. She rises, nods slightly at the doctor, and walks out of his office with her son.

Across town, PatG is heading out his front door wearing a shiny jacket.

"Hows'a Danny?" his mother asks.

"He's fine, Ma," PatG answers.

"They say he's not going to pitch anymore. That doesn't sound fine to me," she bats.

"Ma, he's been saying he's going to retire for years. It had to come eventually."

"Where you gonna sing?"

"I'm at The Club."

"Be careful; they kill people there."

"My singing's not that bad." PatG kisses his mother on the forehead and walks out.

Kevin is at the bar and PatG is already on his second set when Danny arrives. Of course, Kevin is thirsty.

"Danny Boy." He nods.

"What's up, Kev?"

"Same old. You know, I'm starting to like his voice. I'm getting scared."

PatG spots Danny, and Danny shakes his head as if to tell him not to acknowledge him. PatG belts out one more song then says, "Folks, give me two minutes. I'll be right back," and heads over by Kevin and Danny.

"Hey, PattiG, I see that Sheena's back," Kevin says.

"What are you talking about?"

"She's sitting with a few girls at the table over your left shoulder," Kevin answers.

"We're not a thing anymore. She's downing someone else's sausage. I'd say she was someone else's cocksucker, but I don't want to be vulgar." PatG smiles.

"You know, your type of mentality died along with the virgin bride. You should think about changing it," Danny tells him.

"Danny, be careful about changing attitudes. It's just what the soul assassins want," PatG says.

"It's just a thought. You know, with your attitude about women, life could get tough, and pal, I ain't gonna be around much longer."

"Danny, don't talk that crap. It ain't true," PatG says. "Besides, I've always been a gentle man if not a gentleman."

Danny walks toward the bathroom.

Kevin tilts his beer toward the bar, studying it. "Little guy wants us to become liberal thinkers . . . too many thorns in that crown."

"Danny's blue, that's all. You should hear the crazy stuff I say when I'm blue," PatG says.

"Yeah, I remember a few years ago when it didn't work out with Kate Lynn."

"Kaylynn."

"Whatever, but you did say you were giving up the toothless monster."

"That's what I mean. You say stupid stuff when you're down."

Danny rejoins them.

"I got to go to Penn Hospital tomorrow morning to see if the search turned up any matches. Will you come with me?" Danny asks PatG.

"Of course I will," PatG responds.

Danny turns to Kevin. "You wanna come?"

"Nah, you know how I hate hospitals."

"What time tomorrow?" PatG asks.

"We'll leave by 8:00, from my house," Danny says.

PatG nods. Danny continues. "The oncologist called today. He says refusing therapy is suicide. He wants me to see a psychologist."

"Some shrink brought people who attempted suicide to talk at my cousin's drug rehab," PatG says. "After listening to them, he contemplated suicide."

Kevin rests his empty bottle on the bar. "For what they charge, they ought to bring in those who succeeded."

A commotion rises at the end of the bar. The sound of a guy getting slapped echoes through the room.

"Hey! Someone tell her it's happy hour!" Kevin yells.

The owner nods his head to PatG, who picks up the microphone and heads to the small dance floor. He looks back at Danny. "I'll be by your house at 8:00," he tells him.

Nick the bartender grabs Danny's arm and winks. "With ya man."

PatG begins singing "Love that Girl." "*She's got a smile, brightens my day, magnificent file, blue when she's gone away-ay-ay. And I love that girl, yes, I love the girl and someday she'll be mine. . . .*"

The following day, Danny and PatG are standing in front of a smiling nurse at Penn Hospital. A folder with Danny's name is on his desk. "We could check other donor centers," the nurse says.

"At fifteen hundred a pop, there won't be enough to bury me."

"I can get money," PatG says.

Danny shakes his head and looks away.

"I'm really sorry, gentlemen."

PatG and Danny drive out of the hospital parking lot and head home. They reach Rui's and glide up the hill, passing the city projects before hitting the neatly rowed blocks of bungalows that sprinkle the Fineview area.

"Speranza é l'ultima a morire," PatG says to Danny.

"Is that another Italian comment about women?"

"Of course not. This is not the time to be thinking about women. We need to get through this, then we can think about women."

"PatG, I love ya, but in my shape, I'm pretty much done with women. I mean, I doubt that my gear would even . . . that my wheels would even come up so I could take off."

PatG turns away from the road and stares at Danny in a confused way. "Oh, oh, oh . . ."

"Look out!" Danny yells.

PatG swerves the car back over the double line, just missing an oncoming truck.

"If I keep driving like this, we'll both go," PatG mumbles. "But Danny, don't worry 'bout the tires on takeoff. I trust Mick Jagger."

A moment of silence passes. "Okay, Italian philosopher, how long are you going to keep me in suspense?" Danny asks.

PatG smirks. "It's all about the right woman. The right woman, she'll fix your gear. Ever have trouble taking off with Marla?"

"Get back to Jagger."

"You never listen to the words? I love music; I love songs. I know that sometimes a song is 99 percent music, and other times, it's 99 percent lyrics. Like Claudio Baglioni's 'Mille Giorni di Te e di Me.'"

PatG shoves in a CD.

Soft Italian words tiptoe over suave, simple piano music. *Tu che sai la verita, se vuoi se mia tu che puoi, devi crederti non nasconderti. . . .*

(You, who are the truth, if you want you are mine and you must believe, not hide because, it's easy to play hide and seek with ourselves. . . .)

PatG turns, hits a button, and then there's silence. "Danny, that's music, Danny!"

"Are you *ever* going to tell me about Jagger and the plane gear?"

"Oh, well, Jagger, he's English. Poetic?" PatG raises his flat hand, twisting it at the wrist. "He's not Italian."

Danny meets Ma at Floyd's Diner for lunch. Floyd's is just off the hill on Federal, in a brick building in bad need of tuckpointing and adorned with a worn painted sign that's rusted at the corners. Most of the customers are from Fineview and the city projects. Prices are cheap, portions are large, and the quality is what you'd expect when large portions are served at a low price.

Still, Floyd's is a staple in the community. Floyd himself is over 80 years old, but he opens the doors at six a.m. sharp every day except Monday—and that includes Easter, Thanksgiving, and Christmas. Patrons know that no matter how much it rains or snows, whether it's 30 below or 100 degrees, Floyd will be there with his dry sense of humor and dependable smile. Ma and Danny enter and follow another pillar of the community, Floyd's only waitress, to a booth. Angie's thin, blonde out of a bottle, and missing her left hand, which she lost when she got hit by a car when she was just a kid. She doesn't feel sorry for herself and gets incensed when she feels that someone else does. Once she has Ma and Danny seated, she looks to Floyd, who is also the cook.

"Floyd, is that cheeseburger up?" she asks.

"Any longer and you'll be able to stick it in his coke for ice," Floyd responds.

"Give me a break. I've only got one hand." Angie laughs and high-fives another patron sitting at the bar.

"Coffee, Danny?" Angie asks.

"Sure, bring us both coffee," Danny responds.

Angie drops a couple menus on the table and leaves to fetch the coffee and attend to the other customer's ice burger.

Ma ignores the menus—she never looks at them anyway. She stares at her only child.

"Angie," Danny says looking around Ma, "just bring us two specials."

"Two specials coming up," Angie says cheerfully.

"Danny, are there no matches?" Ma asks.

Danny pauses before speaking. "That's right, Ma, and the way Winebach talks, there will likely never be."

Ma unintentionally takes a double breath and gazes over the table as if she's lost something. Danny imagines that she's looking for the right words. He doesn't think she'll have any luck.

The table in front of them is made of hard dark wood. Sixty years of carvings are etched all over it. Ma cups her hands and rests them in front of her, and Danny can't help but notice that her hands almost completely cover a heart with "JT loves SP" carved into the middle of it. She stares down at her hands for a good five seconds before finally raising her head. When she does, her eyes are closed.

"I have something to tell you," she says, hesitating. "It's very important."

Ma goes back to staring at the table.

"Ma, what is it?"

Two or three patrons' heads turn.

"I don't want you to hate me."

"I couldn't hate someone who's cooked for me for forty-seven years."

"I'm a horrible cook."

"That's beside the point."

Angie drops off two glasses of water and the food and speeds away. Ma looks down at her hands and then at the glass of water. She clears her throat. *"Danny, your Dad was not your father."*

More heads turn as Ma continues to stare at her glass.

"Ma, you're watching too much television." Danny whispers, "and keep your tone down; you know nearly everyone in here's from Fineview."

Danny catches a man, Mr. Perisin, staring at them from the bar. Danny stares back and speaks loudly toward him. "Every one of them is waiting for the latest scoop so they can gossip it up around the neighborhood."

The man is a bit shook. He hesitates before he speaks. "I was looking at my car. You know, they steal cars around here?"

"Your car's that way." Danny points out the window at Perisin's beat-up car. "They'd be doing you a favor."

Danny looks back at Ma. "Speak so I can hear you, not the whole joint." He hesitates and lowers his own voice. "Maybe you should start smoking again."

"He's Italian."

"What are you talking about?" Danny whispers.

Ma looks in Danny's eyes and then over at the sugar. "Your father, your biological father, is Italian."

Danny's face scrunches as he looks to the side. He's not understanding or buying any of it.

"That explains why I've got this thing for pasta and clams." Danny grins.

"I'm not kidding," Ma rebuts.

Danny looks away and looks at the cracked wood showing through on the floor underneath the table, where a piece of linoleum is missing.

"I'm 5'5," Danny hesitates. "Dad was 6 foot."

"I was pregnant when I married him," she says. "No one ever knew."

"Are you sure you were pregnant?"

"*I know when I'm pregnant,*" Ma says in a forceful tone.

Heads again turn toward their booth. Danny motions for calm with his hands. "Okay, okay . . . they watch television too."

Ma continues to look at the sugar. "We worked in Nap's bakery. He was stocky with dark puppy-dog eyes."

"Like mine?"

"Exactly."

"So while the bread's in the oven, he skates." Danny hesitates. "Sounds like a real catch."

They're both silent while Angie brings their lunches.

"What's his name?" asks Danny, after she leaves.

"Mimmo."

"This may be hard to take . . . Neemo?"

"*Mee-moh.* It's short for Dominick."

"*Mee-moh* is short for Dominick?"

"I'm going to ask Donald Nap where he lives—they're cousins," Ma says as she looks back at Danny. "Mimmo didn't know about you. He ran from immigration and never came back."

"Dad was great at keeping secrets. His silence saved a lot of people from the insurance companies and a few more from the law. He certainly was smooth, that Mr. Hubble. He never said a word or ever gave me the slightest hint that he wasn't . . ."

Ma interrupts. "He was Danny. He loved you as I love you. Then, as today, we had situations, delicate intimate situations. We dealt with them in the best way we could, privately, intimately. We had pride."

"Yeah," Danny interrupts. "Today there's the internet and Instagram, 'Who's the Daddy?' television shows. We share our personal lives with the world, which couldn't care less, to have those fifteen seconds of notoriety." Danny looks to the side. The leukemia and his mother's news are volatile and making him gush with things he's been meaning to say.

"They have coming-out parties and the media makes a big deal. When did what people do in their private lives become important enough to be the world's business? When did it become possible for people to believe that an elephant was a giraffe because it stretched its neck?"

The tone of urgency in his voice has turned a few heads. A table with two women who seemed to be in a competition to demonstrate who could look more masculine gazed over in disgust. *Another rant from an angry heterosexual.*

But Danny was on a roll, and the words flowed easily. He looked at his mother. "Ma, the ol' man's last wish was that I keep Irene, no matter what it took."

"He was a man—" Ma stops. "Danny, life is about making things fit."

Danny nods. Their plates are almost untouched.

"Let's go, PatG's taking me to my initiation party. Hmph . . . *Mee-moh.*"

Danny takes Ma's hand and winks. "We'll make things fit. Angie, bring the check."

Chapter 4

No Place But Italy

Danny and PatG arrive at the admissions unit to University of Pittsburgh Medical Center's Hillman Cancer Center. Three women and a man are in cubicles, speaking with people Danny assumes are patients. He pulls a number and he and PatG sit down in the waiting room.

"This insurance stuff is crazy. A lot of doctors are beginning to take only cash," Danny says.

"Obamacare," says PatG.

"That's the whipping boy, but I'm not so sure. The insurance companies never needed a reason to gouge our eyes out and they've never made more profit," Danny responds.

"Identify who's getting rich; it's always the same."

Danny nods to PatG. "I guess it's a combination—pieces of Obamacare and health care capitalism. Whatever we're doing, it doesn't work. Everyone in the G20 lives longer, people in places like Italy almost four years longer, and our infant mortality rate is in line with some of the so-called 'third world countries.'"

"That's just bitter insurance man talk; everyone wants to come here," says PatG.

"Almost 10,000,000 US citizens have left the United States and are permanent residents in places like Mexico and Europe," Danny replies.

"Really?" PatG asks.

"We've been taught that lying is patriotic." Danny looks around to make sure no one is listening and then looks at PatG. "But, seriously? I think we lie to keep the masses from revolting."

A half hour passes before a woman rises from one of the cubicles. Danny looks up at the number board and nudges PatG. He and Danny stand and approach the cute dark-skinned girl shuffling papers in Cubicle 4.

"May we?" Danny asks politely.

The girl smiles. "Number 113?"

Danny nods, and for this reason, the woman assumes that Danny is the patient. Danny is thinking that PatG is probably already in love—or, at least, PatG's definition of love. "Please." She points to the two chairs in front of her desk.

"I am obligated to tell the patient that we will be speaking about private, sensitive issues here. Are you sure that you wouldn't rather be alone?" she asks Danny.

PatG remains still but his mind is racing. *She's already pushing me out and doesn't even know my name yet*, he thinks. *I probably won't marry her.*

Danny quickly understands and nods. "Thanks. I'm the patient and there's nothing that we can't discuss in front of PatG." Danny rolls his eyes and smiles. "Now that I'm thinking about it, there's few things about me that he hasn't heard . . . or seen." Danny laughs.

"You're all loosened up, brother. Funny what cute girls can do to a man," PatG chimes in.

"PatG, it's life. I can't change it. I mean, we've got to enjoy 'cause it's always later than we think. Besides, what could there be to hide from a guy who picks up girls at funerals?"

The receptionist raises a hand to cover her smile.

"I'm not kidding," Danny continues. "For a while he carried around the Mass card of a dead girl."

PatG sees that Danny is enjoying himself. It's the happiest he's seen him since the condemnation.

Danny laughs. "He would target a woman, get close to her, and then pull the card out to get her sympathy."

PatG clears his throat. "Interest."

Danny smiles at PatG. The woman is completely focused, and Danny continues.

"PatG, the only unconditional love you could ever have was for a dead person who wouldn't be around to hold your feet to the fire." Danny starts to laugh again, then raises his hand as if to stop the woman from interrupting. There was no chance of that.

"He had the Mass card printed, and the girl's picture was from a magazine."

The woman's face shows signs of curiosity and endless entertainment.

"Danny," PatG interrupts. "I don't think this pretty woman is really interested in this . . . nonsense?"

"Nonsense? This man got all teary eyed telling a new target that the girl was his ex and that they were engaged." Danny hesitates again, and PatG looks down at his shoes. The sound of Danny slapping his leg tells him that Danny is only priming himself to continue.

Danny's raised voice draws the attention of a few of the people waiting for their numbers to be called. "PatG knows some Italian that he learned from his grandfather. He goes up to women, speaks a few lines in Italian and then explains that he doesn't speak English. He goes on to ask for directions or advice. I remember him dating a girl for three months before she figured it out. He's the best."

"Danny," PatG smiles, "I don't think that this sweet thing wants to hear all this."

"Well," the girl tilts her head and lowers her hand revealing a cute smile, "you're both very attractive. What's your name?" the girl asks.

"PatG."

"She means me, you troglodyte," Danny says. "I'm the patient." He looks at the receptionist and smiles. "Danny Hubble. Daniel Hubble."

She types into her computer. "I see. Mr. Hubble, we have all your information. You could have just gone up to the appointment. Do you know where that is?"

"Yes, I do," Danny says. "We take a left to the elevators and then go to the third floor."

Danny and PatG hesitate; neither is in a hurry to leave the presence of this bubbly woman.

"Forgive the bluntness, but I studied Plato, and in the interest of not wasting precious time," PatG says, "are you married, engaged, or appropriated?"

Danny looks up at PatG and then back at the girl. "Father Carlo always said, 'growing old is mandatory; growing up is optional.'"

The girl smiles and then nods slightly. "I'm none of the above."

PatG grins. "I knew it was going to be my day."

Danny tugs at his sleeve. "Come on, lover boy."

"Don't be upset, Danny. If we get married, you'll be our best man."

PatG turns and begins walking toward the open corridor.

Danny hesitates and looks at the smiling receptionist. "Thank you so much. I've got to go, but you're really sweet."

"*Thank you,* Mr. Hubble."

Danny rushes to catch up to PatG. "Hey, Mr. Philosopher, what did Plato say?"

"The same thing you said, 'It's always later than we think.'"

Danny stares at PatG, having forgotten that this was the phrase he had just used. "It's always later than we think," he mumbles.

Danny slept in the hospital. He was stuck with more needles than he'd liked to remember. The following morning at eleven o'clock, PatG arrived to drive Danny home.

"I'm not going to do this anymore."

"No one can force you, Danny," PatG says.

It's raining, and on the way home, PatG and Danny are stalled in bumper-to-bumper traffic.

PatG breaks an uneasy silence. "You know that Marla is really stuck on you. She calls every day, sometimes five times a day.

Danny remains quiet. He nods his head and looks out the window.

"You know, Danny, you could come out of this and maybe not have her anymore. Wouldn't that be a sin? I mean, sometimes it's not that we don't understand what we've got but that we think we'll never lose it, so we don't even care to investigate. . . . She really seems to be the one, Danny Boy."

"Keep your eyes on the road, and you're probably not the right one to give relationship advice. Would you like me to remind me of some of your lines? Don't you always say that the last letter in the word relationship should be 't'?"

"You listen to all that crazy stuff I say? I'd give anything to find someone like Marla. She's smart, pretty, and nuts about you."

"I don't want to make this any worse on her than it has to be," Danny says.

"Is it that you don't want to make it worse on her or that you don't want to make it worse on yourself?"

They begin winding their way up the hill. While passing the Allegheny City Housing Projects, Danny speaks. "Seems nothing ever changes," he says.

"That's a good thing. I like things the way they are," says PatG.

"Yeah, but think of those kids born in the housing project. Everyone should get a shot." Danny stares out the window as they pass Schatzel's Grocery. "Today it seems that more people get shot than get a shot," he says. "What kind of chance do those kids have?"

"Yeah," PatG says. "They got it tough." He pulls up in front of Danny's house.

Danny gets out and looks up at the hanging gutter, hoping to see the squirrel. He hears PatG pull away and waves as he stares at the back of his friend's car. For as long as Danny can remember, PatG has always had a rosary around his rearview mirror and an Italian flag decal on the right side of his hood. Today, the Italian flag somehow looks more prominent. Danny is so used to seeing it that he never really notices it anymore. But, today, it somehow seems different. Maybe things will change.

Danny unlocks the front door and spots the white cat at the top of the stairs. The cat looks at Danny, and so Danny feels obligated to look at the cat. They stare each other down until the cat flinches and ducks back into the house.

Danny drops onto the kitchen chair. Ma enters.

"I talked to Donny. Mimmo's in Italy . . . in his town. You have to go and find him," she says.

"Wouldn't it be easier to call?"

"*No.* You have to go."

Danny looks at the back of his mother's head. "You made more sense when you smoked."

"Danny, Donny says that it's the only way, and the good news is that Mimmo has four children. Each of them represents a chance."

"I have to think about this."

"There's nothing to think about. They're your only hope."

"I don't even speak Italian; I don't know how to . . ."

Ma interrupts Danny. "We're throwing a fundraiser at Larry's. You'll take PatG with you."

Danny's phone rings. He looks at the screen . . . "Marla." His heart feels happy about the call, but then his mind steps in and takes over.

Danny walks into the front room so that his mother doesn't hear his conversation. He answers in a low voice. "Marla, what's up?"

"Hi, Danny—I miss you. Can we see each other this evening?"

"Marla, I'm not feeling great, and I have a lot to sort out. Really, I'd have expected you to understand."

Marla sniffles.

"Please don't start," Danny says. "You know I hate when you cry."

He hesitates. For a moment he lets his heart drive and it overcomes his mind. "All right, be there in an hour," he tells her.

Danny walks into his room. Ma yells in from the kitchen. "Danny, you ought to stay home and leave that girl alone. You need to save your energy."

Danny ignores his mother.

"Danny! I'm making you some Lipton tea," she yells, as if she'd make any other kind of tea.

Danny ignores Ma and navigates his way down the stairs. He feels better than he's felt in a long time and enters his car. He winds down the hill and gets on Federal. He arrives at Marla's apartment at about eight p.m.

Danny has a key to her front door, but he knocks.

Marla's voice filters softly through the door. "Who is it?" she asks.

"Me."

Marla opens the door and immediately gains access to Danny's heart with her smile. It was the first thing that caught Danny.

"You forget your key, Danny?"

"No."

"Come on in. I'm so happy to see you."

Danny looks into the apartment, and his mind begins to scoot his heart to the side. "Where's everyone at?"

"They're out. We have the place to ourselves until we leave to go see PatG at the club," Marla says.

Marla's five inches taller than Danny. She puts her arms around him and rests her head on his head.

Danny's mind gets shoved hard by his buddy in the lower extremities. Marla doesn't need a lot of coaxing and they're soon lying diagonally.

"I love you, Danny. I always will," Marla whispers.

An hour later, Danny is leaning against the bureau in Marla's bedroom watching her dress. Now that the guy downstairs has been satisfied, Danny's mind again takes control. "Marla, I think you should get off the bus."

Marla stops combing her hair and turns to Danny. "What?"

"Honey, it's time to stop. We're not going anywhere. . . . Maybe we were *never going anywhere*. . . . And now . . . now . . ." Danny wavers.

Marla moves toward him. "Are you okay? We can stay home."

"Stop," Danny says.

Marla moves her right hand to his arm. "PatG's waiting; he'll be disappointed."

Danny looks into her eyes. "Marla, you're young and beautiful." He hesitates before continuing. "Honey, you've had your experience with an older guy. Are you sure you want to give it a go with a dying guy?"

Tears well up in Marla's eyes. "Danny . . ."

"Marla, honey, just get a new start," Danny says in a voice that's almost a whisper.

Tears are now flowing down Marla's cheeks. "A new start? With what, Danny? I'll never be able to get back what I gave you."

She reaches down for his hand. He softly pulls it away, walks out of her room, and leaves the apartment.

Danny gets into the car and drives to Nick's. He sits in the parking lot trying to sort things out. It strikes Danny that true love ended when people convinced themselves that they couldn't be in love or love others unless they loved themselves first. Boy, he thought, what he'd do to meet the person who said that idiotic phrase . . . a cream pie right in the face.

Danny walks into Nick's. The club seems dimmer than usual. PatG is at the microphone singing "Cherry Love." *"Hanging by the bus stop, waiting from dusk 'til dawn, dancing on moonlit steps selling yourself for a song! Cherry, Cherry, love, Cherry, my only love, Cherry, Cherry, love, what is it you're thinking of!"*

A few patrons clap their hands. PatG bows. "You're all too kind, I'll be back in a bit." He sets the microphone down, switches the mixer off, and walks over to Danny. "Where's the love of your life?"

"Don't call her that." Danny shakes his head. "She's young, with everything ahead of her. She doesn't need this. She'll only get hurt. It's better that she begins to get on with her life." Danny looks at his shoes. "Without me," he says to himself more than to PatG. "It's better if I let her be. Let's leave her out of this." Danny raises his head. "Please," he coaxes out.

"Danny, did I ever tell you the story about Paolo Tarsi?"

"No, and I fear that you might now."

PatG puts his arm around Danny. "Paolo Tarsi was an Italian artist. At sixty-five he began a relationship with a twenty-five-year-old woman. It was the scandal of the town. I mean, a man going with a woman forty years younger than him!"

Danny interrupts. "Mick Jagger's with a woman forty-three years younger."

PatG nods. "Can I continue?"

"Sorry," Danny says.

"After eight years together, *she* died of emphysema. Paolo, who was seventy-three at the time, fell into a depression. He began drinking heavily and prayed for his death. Every day was torture. He told his brother that he wanted to commit suicide but lacked the courage. He left art, sold everything he had, and eventually lived on the streets in his home city of Ferrara. Finally, one day, he got hit by a truck. When the truck driver kneeled over him to see how badly he was hurt, Paolo hugged and kissed him with tears of joy in his eyes. Paolo was happy that he was finally going to die."

PatG looks into Danny's eyes. "He was ninety-five."

Danny smirks and continues to stare at PatG. "You made that up."

"I did not; I swear." PatG puts his right hand to his heart.

Danny and PatG stand in silence until Nick, the owner, joins them. "Hey, Danny Boy, I'm closing next Saturday for your party," he says.

"Thanks, Nick," PatG answers.

Nick notices Marla walking in the front door. "Hey, Danny, your shoestrings just walked in."

Danny spots Marla, downs his drink, and rubs his head.

"Danny, don't be an idiot," PatG says. "She loves you. You should have married that dame a long time ago."

Nick's listening. The men watch as Marla stops to speak with friends.

"Maybe Danny doesn't want to break the rule the media made up," Nick says. "They put out the propaganda saying that you shouldn't date anyone who's less than half your age plus ten."

PatG interrupts. "You forgot to deduct a year for every million the older person's got."

Danny scratches his head and nods. "Nick, what's the 'shoestring' thing?" he asks.

"Shoestrings help you keep your shoes on, right?" Nick starts to explain, but Marla's arrival cuts him short.

"Hi, Nick," she says, then turns toward PatG. "You gonna sing 'It's Your Time' tonight, Bublé?"

"Please—Dean Martin, Boz Scaggs, Al Green, but don't compare me to Bublé. That guy sings 'Mack the Knife' like Mack's sister."

Marla moves to Danny's side. "You forgot this, Romeo." She hands Danny his belt. PatG bellows, "Woo!"

Nick's got a smile from ear to ear. He slaps PatG's hand. "Hey, Al Green, get out there. I wanna hear 'You Make Me Happy.'"

PatG picks up the microphone and turns the mixer on. Danny looks at Marla and makes a smile that she fears might break his face.

"Listen to PatG, Danny," Marla says.

"*Ooh how you made me happy when my skies were blue, and oooh how you destroyed me when you were untrue.*"

"Danny, whatever happens, I'll never be untrue."

Danny sips his beer. At the end of the song, Marla moves closer. He hugs her, and she rests her head on his shoulder.

It's almost 1:30 a.m. when PatG does his last song. Marla moves to the exit and winks at Danny. "I'll leave the door unlocked," she tells him.

PatG grabs his songbook, mixer, speakers, and microphones and heads out at about 2:30 a.m. He purposely passes Marla's on the way home and spots Danny's car. "Yes! That little lady's got your number. The gear will have no problem coming up for takeoff," he mumbles.

PatG stands outside his house and finishes a cigar. He only smokes for festive occasions or when he is nervous. Tonight, he seems to be wearing both hats. He is nervous about their trip but inexplicably happy at the same time.

Danny heads home at about seven a.m. and reads the sign in front of Larry's: He's Not Here. *"Saturday night Danny Hubble Smoker, $50 cover, All you can eat and free beer. –Larry, Chairman & Marla, Chairwoman"*

Danny walks into the kitchen on the way to the bedroom and Ma is already up making tea. "You shouldn't be hanging around with that girl. She's old enough to be your daughter."

"She's also old enough to be my sister."

Ma turns to face Danny but only sees his bedroom door closing.

"What do you think she'll do while you're in Italy?"

Danny opens up the door enough to fit his face in the gap. "She'll probably do what you'll do, have wild sex parties."

Ma looks around the counter and grabs a wet tea bag. It hits the door and falls to the ground.

Danny opens the door a slit. "Let's face it, there could be worse things!"

Danny pulls back the covers and lays his head on the pillow. He's sleepy, but at the same time bubbly, giddy. It feels like Christmas. Ma makes herself another cup of tea and adds to the list of names in her notebook. She works at it for an hour and then closes it. On the front of the notebook is written, "Danny's Party."

Ma also feels well. She can't recall feeling so motivated to do something in her entire life. She puts on her jacket and heads out.

A few minutes later Ma walks into Larry's bar.

"Ma! I never seen you in here before!" Larry yells, smiling.

"That's 'cause I've never been in here before."

"Well, welcome, Ma. Welcome."

"How are sales going Larry?"

"We got a problem, Ma."

Ma's face turns pale.

"We already sold almost 300 tickets and full occupancy is 120."

Ma smiles. "My Danny's loved."

"He certainly is, Ma. He's helped out every family on the Hill at one time or another. We don't have an insurance man. We have a friend, a family member who's always looking out for us." Larry smiles and then turns serious. "Ma, don't think the people don't know how many times Danny's put up his own money so families don't go uninsured. We also know he's backdated many a document. I can't tell you what he did for me to make sure that my hospital bills were covered when I had problems with my ulcers," Larry said.

Larry's voice raises with intent. "Ma, folks go to jail for what our Danny does to save our people." Larry looks Ma in the face. He wants to be sure that she understands how proud she should be of her boy.

Ma's eyes open wide. "He's a good boy."

In an effort to lighten things up, Larry slaps his hand against the bar. "Danny's one of Fineview's best, and we take care of our own, Ma. You know that. We take care of our own."

Ma's spirits are soaring. She smiles broadly, excitement is building inside of her, until she spots Marla walking into the bar.

"And, Ma, here's our chairwoman. We can thank her for half of those ticket sales."

Ma moves her head to look at Marla with a robotic jerk. "Thank you, Chairwoman."

"Oh, Ma, we all love Danny," Marla says.

"Our little chairwoman in particular." Larry smiles.

By the time Saturday arrives, 500 tickets have been sold. The liquor, food, and two hundred gifts to be raffled off were all donated.

Danny wanted to be at the door to greet the people as they came in, but PatG, Marla, and Larry talked him into not showing up until eight p.m.

At 7:45, a Pittsburgh police car pulls up in front of Danny's home. The officer silences the siren and bellows into the police megaphone, "Danny Hubble! Ma Hubble! Danny Hubble! Ma Hubble! You're being taken into custody and brought to Larry's: He's Not Here"! Come out with your dancing shoes on and your pockets empty!"

As they pull away, the siren blares and the dome lights cast shadows over the trees and houses. The squad makes its way down Belleau Street, heading up Rising Main and turns onto Meadville. Abruptly, the car comes to a stop. The crowd is flowing out of Larry's and the squad car can't move forward.

The policeman puts his arm on the seat and looks back at Ma and Danny, "Sorry folks, your ride ends here. I couldn't make it through that crowd with a missile."

Ma looks at Danny and puts her hand on his arm. "They're all here for you, son."

Danny smirks. "Ma, looking at all these people makes me want to change my mind about going to Italy."

"Don't talk like that, Danny. You go get the match and you come back to us." Ma starts to cry openly and places a handkerchief to her eyes.

Danny looks at her strangely. "I don't think I ever saw you cry."

Ma had seen much in her life and though this occasion was created from disaster, it was the pinnacle of her life. She would not live in vain, no matter the outcome.

"And I don't think you'll ever see me cry again."

"Okay, Ma. Let's go."

The policeman smiles, gets out of the car, and opens the backseat passenger door to let Danny and Ma Hubble out. His partner shines the squad car's spotlight on Ma and Danny as they make their way through the crowd, toward Larry's. PatG's music is blasting through the doors and windows of the bursting bar. As Ma and Danny approach, the crowd cheers and begins chanting, "Danny! Danny!"

As Danny and Ma make their way through the mob, the crowd breaks into several spontaneous rounds of applause.

Ma and Danny get to the door and the music stops. PatG is standing on the stoop with a microphone in his hand, the ever-dependable Irene standing next to him. She has worked for weeks, keeping track of donated gifts, food, and beverages, along with the tally of who was coming and who had paid. She has a look of satisfaction on her face. PatG begins, "Ladies and gentlemen, the moment that we've all been waiting for, Ma and Danny Hubble!"

Marla and Larry approach Ma and Danny. Marla grabs Danny's arm and Larry, Ma's. They escort them to the end of the bar. "Ma, Danny," Larry says, "me and Marla thought that the best place for you would be behind the bar, that way everyone can say hello or farewell without having to look for you."

Danny is already tired but promises himself that *no matter what*, he will remain standing and pay tribute to Fineview. . . . And in fact, he does.

At five past five on Sunday morning, Kevin, the final guest, stops at the door. "Hey, kid, I'm gonna miss you."

"I'm gonna miss you too, Kev." Danny smiles. "Hey, I heard you won a year's free cable."

"Who needs cable? They've already got me brainwashed with the regular networks. But maybe I can get some Eye-talian stations so I can see what kind of place you're in."

Danny moves out from behind the bar. He hugs Kevin. "I love you, Cal."

Kevin looks at Danny and nods. "I love you, too."

Marla and Larry emerge from the door to the back room. Irene is with them, smiling. "Danny," Larry says, "We tallied up $78,569 for you guys's trip and whatever else."

Danny releases Kevin, who starts to open the door and turns back. "You know, Italy is the home of the Catholic Church. I heard that they have even more statues than we have in our churches. As a kid I was in a lot of churches, a lot of times. I never heard one of those statues talk. Let me know if any of those Italian statues talk back to you out there."

Danny smiles. "I will, Cal."

Kevin waves and then he's gone.

It's Monday afternoon, and the airport clock reads five past three. An airline agent is watching Irene, Ma, Marla, and Danny. "Sir, you still need to get through security. You'll miss your flight."

"Coming . . ." Danny looks at the three of them.

"Come back soon," Ma says.

"Come back soon, Mr. Hubble," Irene echoes.

Marla doesn't utter a word. She hugs Danny. Tears begin to run quietly down her cheeks.

Danny hugs her back and, at the same time, speaks to everyone. "Okay. Stop it, all of you," he says.

He takes Marla's arm and accidentally knocks his own hat off. He breaks away from their embrace and picks up the hat, putting it back on his head. "Arrivederci," he says.

Danny smiles and begins to walk away, heading toward the men's washroom.

PatG walks out of the bathroom, dressed like John Travolta in *Saturday Night Fever*. "Let's go, goombah!" PatG yells.

"Remember, Ma, no more smoking," Danny calls out.

"Danny, Mr. Hubble, don't you have to remind me about something?" Irene asks.

Danny concentrates. "Yes, Irene, hold down the fort at the office."

Irene turns to Ma. "Mr. Hubble told me to hold down the fort . . . at the office."

"I heard," Ma says.

"And, Irene, remind her that she promised me she wouldn't smoke anymore," Danny adds.

"I have to remind you that you promised Danny you wouldn't smoke anymore."

"I don't need you to remind me," Ma says.

"But Danny, Mr. Hubble, told me to make sure I remind you," Irene pauses, "that you promised Mr. Hubble you wouldn't smoke anymore."

Ma shakes her head. Marla watches Danny and PatG until they disappear behind the security wall.

Suddenly, she rushes toward the checkpoint. "Love you, Danny!"

Danny hears her and peers around the wall and blows Marla a kiss. Marla turns and takes Ma and Irene both by the arm. "Let's go home, girls," she tells them.

Chapter 5

Welcome Home

The plane's full. Danny takes the window seat and gazes out at the Pittsburgh skyline. Pittsburgh has been his home his whole life. He can't help but wonder if he'll ever see the city again. He glances at PatG, who is sitting in the aisle seat going through an Italian vocabulary book.

"You know, everyone stared at you, boarding in your *Saturday Night Fever* costume," Danny says.

"Who cares? I'll fit right in. Mamma says that they're forty years behind us." PatG looks down proudly at his jacket and pants. "The whole outfit only cost 99 dollars, including the shoes," he says.

"I think you overpaid."

PatG ignores him. "The Hill's incredible. Rui and Floyd donated most of the food, Larry and Nick all the booze. Did you see all those gifts that they had for the raffle? All donated. People love you, Danny."

Danny nods as he continues to look out the window.

"Larry said he never worked harder in his life. I told him he did it 'cause he loves you. You know how Larry hates that word. He told me that he only did it 'cause you're too short to be Rod." PatG shrugs. "I had no idea what he was talking about. Of course, with Larry, that happens almost anytime I talk to him."

The plane landed in New York after almost two hours in the air. Since they didn't have a lot of time between flights, Danny and PatG had to rush to their next gate and board.

A half hour after takeoff, Danny is busy watching *Assassin's Creed* while PatG's watching *It's a Wonderful Life*.

"I got to go," Danny whispers. "You ever take a dump on a plane?"

"Yeah."

"Is there any trick to it?"

"No, but let me go first. I just got to leak."

Danny decides to wait in the aisle by the bathroom and looks relieved when PatG opens the door and leaves. Just as Danny is about to go in, he sniffs and looks strangely at PatG.

"What are you sniffing about? I told you I just had to piss."

A few minutes later, Danny is still sitting on the throne when someone knocks on the door. Danny looks up to make sure that the door is locked and ignores the knocking.

The knock continues.

"PatG, is that you?" he asks.

"Sir, open this door." Danny cringes—it's a woman's voice.

He starts to pull his pants up and squirts soap into one hand, waving the other to keep the water running. "What?" he calls out.

Danny hears more voices from outside. He breaks the perfume bottle off the plastic stand and splashes it all over.

"Sir, open this door immediately!" the voice yells.

The door caves inward. Danny's buttoning his pants as it opens.

The woman moves toward him. "Sir, you've been smoking," she says.

A male flight attendant sticks his nose in the cubicle and scrunches his eyes.

Danny looks at him. "What do you smell like, Jimmy Choo?" he asks.

A third flight attendant arrives, then a fourth.

Danny stares at the pack of them. "I don't smoke."

The first flight attendant is wearing a look on her face as if someone had just spread feces on her chin. "Sir, I want your name."

"Why? Don't you like your own?"

"As a flight crew member, I am an agent of the US government."

"Give me a break. Who isn't these days?"

"Sir, you're creating a disruption."

Danny looks up into her eyes. "Well, I guess you have no choice. . . . Throw me off the plane."

The flight attendants look indignantly at each other. Danny heads to his seat.

"Mark his seat down," he hears the woman say.

"He says he didn't smoke," the male flight attendant tells her.

"That's only what he says!" she insists.

"Will they arrest him in Italy?" another flight attendant asks.

"Not likely. As far as my experiences go, the Italians don't take these things seriously. When he returns to the United States, he'll be in for a big surprise." The flight attendant looks at her underlings. "American exceptionalism," she says.

Danny arrives at his seat. "I'm going to kill you," he whispers to PatG.

"I can't hear you." PatG points to his headphones.

Danny looks at him sternly and sits down. "You lit up a cigar in there. Why didn't you tell me?"

PatG smiles faintly. "Two drags."

Danny looks back at the flight attendants, who are still huddled together and carrying on like someone had been murdered. "*Now* I know why they search the passengers for weapons at the airport," Danny says.

PatG takes his headphones off momentarily? "What?"

"Now I know why they search passengers for weapons at the airport," Danny repeats.

"Oh yeah, why?"

"To protect the airline attendants."

PatG puts his headphones back on and continues to watch the film.

"Take them off," Danny says as he slaps at PatG's headphones. "Tell me about Italy."

"I've never been there."

"Okay, but tell me about Italians, what your mother says about Italy."

PatG hits the screen and turns off the film.

"Pause it, that way you can continue watching it where you left off."

"Danny, I know the film by heart. It ends, just like our trip is going to end," PatG says.

Danny stares and PatG begins lesson one. "Ma says Italy is a land of five hundred city-states. Often, towns five miles from each other have different languages, though today, the whole country speaks Italian except for some in Tyrol, near Austria."

Danny's favorite flight attendant holds out a tray with cups of water on it.

"Water?" she asks insolently.

Danny smiles broadly. "No, but how 'bout a cigarette?"

He turns back toward PatG.

"Ma was only back once. She says that they're forty years behind the United States."

"Yeah, I know—you said that, Tony Manero."

"She says that Italy has been conquered by dozens of invaders and that Italians are a mixed race. We have people as dark as Africans and as light as Scandinavians. She says that our love for our families is what binds us."

"Most Italians I know are dark," Danny says.

"That's because the last wave of immigrants came from Puglia, Campagna, Calabria, Basilicata, and Sicilia."

"Meaning?"

"They came from the south."

"Well, you just be careful there." Danny stares at him seriously. "No womanizing."

"I'm not a womanizer."

"You've been with a lot of women."

"No," PatG says, "I didn't force anyone. Today, the problem's not womanizers; it's the media assisting women to destroy men."

Danny nods, "Oh, all right, then be careful of the Italian men-destroyers."

"Thank you," PatG says crisply, "*I will.*"

The captain's voice breaks in over the loudspeaker, announcing that the plane will soon land in Rome. Danny's curious about what intentions the flight attendant might have. He isn't sure what the inside of an Italian jail looks like, and he isn't crazy about the idea of finding out.

They get off the plane, and Danny looks around, but surprisingly, he doesn't see his accuser anywhere. He and PatG walk through the airport to catch their flight to Bari. Everyone looks friendly except for the soldiers carrying machine guns, but even they smile as people pass.

The flight from Rome to Bari is over in less than an hour. Danny looks down at the thousands of acres of olive trees as the plane begins its descent. Even though they're flying close to the city of Bari, there are no tall buildings that he can see. The plane lands, and as Danny walks down the steps, he notices that the plane has a name painted on the front of it between the nose and the exit door. The plane is called "SAN FRANCESCO D'ASSISSI."

A brown dog is sleeping about five feet from the bottom of the airplane stairs. Obviously, the dog is a regular at the airport and has decided to nap. All of the passengers carefully step around the animal, so as not to wake him.

Danny removes his hat, wipes his brow, and looks at his watch: six forty-five. He puts his hat back on and looks around. The place looks like a desert with thousands of olive trees.

They arrive at the five hundred-foot-long terminal—most US airport terminals are at least five times the size—and Danny turns to PatG. "Kind of scary. What time is it?"

"Add six hours. It's forty-five minutes past noon here."

"Yeah, and like your mother said, take off forty years," Danny retorts.

"Hey," PatG says, "the airport is called Karol Wojtyla! What the hell kind of Italian name is that?"

"A Polish one, named after a dead pope."

In the terminal, two officers dressed in gray are speaking in Italian.

"The American authorities want us to arrest a passenger for smoking on the plane," one says. "They say it's a criminal act."

"On the plane from Rome?"

"No, on a plane from New York to Rome."

"Why didn't they arrest him in Rome?"

"They said that they couldn't find him."

"What is it that we're supposed to do with him?"

"I don't know—look it up in the book."

"They smoked on planes for seventy years. Tell them that we couldn't find him either. Let's get a coffee."

The police walk toward the bar.

"Americans still don't have healthcare and universities for all. Somebody ought to be arrested for that."

At the entrance to the terminal, Danny watches as a cart tied to a forklift pulls up. A man jumps off and throws a box marked FRAGILE onto the conveyor belt.

"Fragile," Danny says to himself.

PatG and Danny grab their suitcases and head for the exit. One of the police who refused to look for the American who smoked on the plane points to Danny and PatG's suitcases and then to a steel table. Danny lifts his suitcase. Simultaneously, a dark-skinned man who looks to be in his sixties arrives and whispers into the ear of the agent. The police wave Danny on without the slightest change of expression.

The man takes Danny's arm and in a heavy Italian accent says, "I am Vito."

Danny pulls back his arm. "PatG, what's going on?"

"Is he with you?" Vito asks, pointing to PatG.

Danny nods. Vito nods to the official, who waves PatG through as well.

Vito takes Danny's bag. "Who are you?" Danny asks.

"I'ma Vito. You're Massimo coosin. You are Danny from Transylvania."

"Who's Maximo?" Danny asks.

"He'sa my coosin. He send me your picture on my phone. He say, I got to take care of you."

They struggle toward the exit. People are trying to edge their way inside, and women are waving handkerchiefs and yelling.

"Let'sa go," Vito says.

"Where are we going?" Danny asks.

"We gonna go to-a your town."

"I'm from Pittsburgh."

"I know Pittsburgh. . . . Transylvania."

Danny rubs his head. PatG follows Danny and Vito to a tiny Fiat. Vito opens the trunk.

"I got family in Chicago. They got family in Pittasburgh. We say in Italy, family of my family, so even if we are not directly blood-related, we are related through our families. And you are a-coosin of my coosin. . . . Transylvania's a beautiful place."

Vito starts to sing John Denver, in his own words. "*Take my home to the place I belong, Transylvania, Rocky Mamma, take me home to the country rose!* John Seattle—I cry when he die."

Vito smiles at Danny and PatG.

"So you say 'family of my family'??" Danny asks.

"Family relations," PatG tells him.

"You say family of my family," Vito corrects PatG. "Or, *mezza parenti.*"

"Where are we going?" Danny asks.

"Altamura, your family's town."

"Are you from there?" Danny asks.

"I was from there but *mia moglie,* my wife, she's from Santeramo. My father-in-law, he gave-a me a job. He sells a-furniture. So when I got married forty years ago I move-a to Santeramo. My family lives in Santeramo."

"How do you speak English?"

"I donna speak English. I wasa never inna England. I speak American. I lived inna Norta Carolina. Dey make-a furniture dere. I was dere for six years. I teacha dem how you make-a furniture. Den I come home."

"It must have been tough on your wife," Danny says.

"But tougher on my mudder. I go to de statesa for six years but I go home. My mudder, the poor woman. I never move back to Altamura."

"Too bad. How far's Santeramo from Altamura?" Danny asks earnestly.

"About 10 kilometers."

Danny's riding in front while PatG's crammed in the back with the luggage. The car arrives at a "T" in the road. Danny sees several blue signs outlined in white.

Five signs with the names of various towns are stacked on top of one another, with an arrow pointing to the right. Next to them are five identical signs with identical town names pointing to the left.

Danny turns to speak to PatG, but his head is blocked by a suitcase. "Hey, look at that."

Vito nods his head in approval. "Italia, a country of-a choice."

The car sharply turns to the right. PatG grabs the ceiling.

"Whew, it's hot," PatG says.

"Hot? It's-a May. This is a-nothing," Vito says.

53

They are now about twenty minutes outside the airport. The streets are empty. They pass a white sign with "Altamura" written in black letters.

"Does anyone live here?" Danny asks.

"About 9,000 peoples but they a-eatin'. *Mangia.*"

Vito parks next to a building made of rock on an ancient stone street.

"These roads, this building, are ancient, incredible," Danny says. "Is this a hotel?"

"Da stones-a are about-a twelve hundred years old. Da building is-a about nine hundred years-a old. This is home; you-a gonna sleep here."

"Who lives here?" Danny asks.

"My mudder. She take-a good care of you."

Vito looks at PatG. PatG smiles.

"I don't want to put her out," Danny says.

"No problem. She like-a company. She by herself. My sister, she livesa wit her husband and children."

"Where's their home?" Danny asks.

"Across da street."

Danny is peering across the ten-foot-wide road when a smiling, old woman, dressed in black with a bandanna on her head opens the door. Danny and PatG smile back at her.

"How old is your mother?" Danny asks.

"She's *ottanta-sei. . . . Scusa.* I mean eighty-six."

"And your father?"

"Oh, he die-a young."

"Oh? I'm sorry."

"Yeah he was eighty-two. My mudder, she still weara black. She's a-mourning."

"When did he die?"

"Two thousand and seven October 17. Seventeen a bad number. Every seventeenth, I donna drive-a da car."

"Did your father die in a car crash?"

"No, he was-a too ol' to-a drive."

"How did your father die?"

"He falla froma de tree. He was collecting de olives."

Danny hesitates, then asks, "Why don't you drive on the seventeenth?"

"Seventeen's an unlucky number. Don't you remember? I tole you."

Chapter 6

Italian Wish

Danny and PatG move their luggage into the house with Vito's help. Inside, the kitchen table is set with wine, cheeses, bread, and olives. The ceilings, walls, and surfaces are decorated with hanging peppers and garlic, pictures of saints, and religious statues.

Vito's mother leads them across the kitchen and opens a door. Inside the room are two small beds and a closet.

"I sleepa here when I wasa boy."

"Come si chiama tua madre?" PatG asks slowly.

"Oh, she'sa Carmela, but calla her Mamma. That's what I call her."

Without missing a beat, Vito turns to Danny. "You gotta de name who you gonna see?"

"Yeah, I got it here."

"I need to use the john," PatG says.

"John?" Vito asks.

"Banyo," PatG says meekly.

"You calla *de bagno* 'John'?" Vito asks perplexedly.

"Yeah, what do you call it?" PatG asks.

"Bagno."

Mamma takes PatG's hand. She opens a door and PatG steps in.

Danny hands a piece of paper with a name written on it to Vito. In the background, the sound of PatG peeing is heard through a small window in the kitchen wall.

"Domenico Ciancia. Dey gotta a de bakery. How you know him?"

"He made bread with my mother," Danny says.

"Your mudder, she's bake-a de bread?"

"She was the oven."

55

Vito pauses and looks at Danny curiously. He looks up in thought and then focuses back on Danny. "I finda dis man. He know you here?"

"No."

"Oh, it's a surprise? Italians love surprises."

"Oh," Danny says, "then he's really going to love this."

"Dat's great," Vito says.

PatG is studying the tiny bathroom. Every niche is being used. Soap, toilet paper, towels—they all have their custom-made place. The shower looks barely large enough for a normal person to fit into. Next to the toilet is a short strange-looking urinal.

PatG washes his hands and walks out. The three men begin eating as Mamma serves more olives, more cheese and more pasta.

"Vito, what's with the urinal next to the toilet?" PatG asks.

"That's a da bidet, it's not da urinal."

"What do you use it for?"

"To wash yourself."

"But you have a shower. Why do you need a bidet?"

"You can't shower every time-a you go to da batroom."

PatG, and now Danny, look at Vito.

"What are you gonna do? You go to dump, and you smasha what's left into your skin wit paper? Ickk."

PatG and Danny cringe.

"Here, da man he come home at one to eat. After he eat, he maybe want to give da wife a shot. After, he has no time to shower. He go to da bidet, wash his tool, and leave. He happy, and de wife, she double happy."

"Why's that?" Danny asks.

"She got to play and she don' got to clean up da shower."

PatG and Danny are unmoved.

"It saves a-lots of soap and water too. We no got all dat clean, fresh water you have."

The three men finish. The table is full of plates, olive pits, lupini shells, and wineglasses. It's a sight. PatG smiles; Danny shakes his head. "I'm beat," he says.

"Mamma, she make-a you bed," Vito says.

"No, no," Danny gets up and grabs a plate. He intends to help Mamma clean up.

Vito puts his hands on Danny's shoulders. "Sit down, my friend. You in Italy. Mia madre pleasure to serve you." Vito cuts a strawberry and looks at PatG. "What do you do?"

"I'm a performer."

Vito looks confused.

"I sing."

Vito is impressed. "Tonight, you sing for us."

"I don't have a band."

"Don' worry. I find it."

PatG shrugs. "Okay."

Vito's mother exits the bedroom. "The bed, itsa ready."

"What will you do?" Danny asks Vito.

Vito places his hands together, puts them against his right ear, and closes his eyes. "Neenah nana. We take-a de sack."

PatG and Danny are standing in the eight-by-eight-foot room. Vito's mother walks in, lowers the shutters, and leaves. PatG and Danny close the door and lie down in the beds. The room is pitch black.

"Hey, Danny."

"Yeah?"

"What do you think?"

"I think that I like being Italian."

A few hours later, PatG walks into the kitchen from outside the house. Danny is in the kitchen. Mamma's making coffee.

"Where did you go? I can't *communicate*. She tried to put my shoes on when I got out of bed."

"Danny, this place is great . . . and the women. Oh, the women."

PatG goes into the bedroom and begins organizing his clothes, then returns to the kitchen. "Get ready. We're going out."

"What time is it?" Danny asks.

"It's almost five thirty in the evening."

Within half an hour, PatG and Danny are stepping out of the house and walking down the ancient street, which is made of mammoth-sized stones. Clothes are hanging on all the balconies and a slight desert breeze softens the air. The homes are all made of rock and the town looks like something out of a film depicting medieval times.

"This way, Danny," PatG says as they reach the end of the street.

The street opens into a large piazza about half the size of a football field. In the middle of it is a fountain made of a smooth, beige marble engraved with dozens of plants and fish. The fountain is the size of a helicopter pad and reaches twenty feet into the sky. Several kids are playing soccer in the middle of the square, which is lined with bars on both sides.

To the right stands Piano B, and Danny can't help but watch the men who are sitting at the small tables in front of it. Some of the men are playing cards; others are drinking coffee. Caffè Ronchi Striccoli occupies the left side of the square. There, the tables are mostly occupied by couples enjoying beverages and/or ice cream.

Danny and PatG walk into Caffè Ronchi and join Vito, who is standing and sipping grappa. Danny listens to the music echoing over the loudspeakers and looks at PatG.

"Hey, that's you."

"I gave them a CD."

"*G, il caffè no fa lo raffredare,*" (G, don't let the coffee get cold) the bartender says.

"*Si, si,*" PatG responds.

Danny looks at the bartender and his scrumptious young assistant, Francesca. Danny then looks back at PatG. "Hey, don't get too comfortable."

Vito looks at PatG and shakes his head. "Friend, in Italy, watcha you step."

"What do you mean?"

Vito pulls down the skin under his right eye. "That's-a de bartender granddaughter. Open your eyes." He turns, slaps his hands together, and looks to the door. "Tommaso!"

Danny looks at Tommaso, the man entering the bar. Tommaso is carrying an accordion and looks to be about fifty—he has a full head of black hair, a pearly-white smile, and is dressed in a sharp button-down shirt and a pair of dress jeans. Everyone turns as Tommaso begins to play his accordion.

"New York, New York, New York, New York, New York . . ."

Tommaso stops playing and walks over to Vito. In Italian, he asks, "Who are our new friends?"

Vito puts his arm on Danny's shoulder. "Dis is Danny; his people are from Altamura."

"Yes," Tommaso responds. "He has a face I've seen before. Is he related to the baker?"

Vito does not answer and puts his hand on PatG's shoulder. "And dis PatG. He is American singer."

"Welcome," Tommaso says, looking from one to the other. "PatG, do you know any songs from Baglione o Battista, Raf, or Antonacci?"

"I know 'Caruso' and a few Zarrillo songs, one or two Celentano, and lots of Sinatra."

Tommaso smiles widely. "I like your repertoire."

PatG and Danny drink their *caffè* while Vito finishes his grappa. As they prepare to leave, the occupants of the bar wish the trio farewell in loud voices. The three walk into the piazza and head toward the Centro Storico, the center of town, strolling along winding streets that appear to be a part of an ancient maze. After about three minutes, they find themselves in the Piazza Del Municipio. The city hall is a ravishing building, and the Italian flag towers above the edifice. Red and white are the town's colors. Below the flag, a red and white cloth banner gently floats on the breeze.

On both ends of the piazza are churches. Danny and PatG stare at the buildings. "This is incredible," Danny says.

PatG is awestruck as he looks at a crowd of people standing in front of an ancient church. He shifts his gaze to the clock above the cathedral. "Amazing, when was the clock?"

"1859," Vito answers.

"And the church?" PatG points to a church facing the clock tower.

"San Michele Church—she's built around 1600." Vito then points to the church on the opposite side of the square. "La chiesa di Santa Maria Assunta completed about 1250."

A soccer ball lands near PatG. He carefully passes it back to a boy, who looks to be about five.

"This place is magical," Danny says. "Why would anyone leave this town for anywhere?"

"After war, da people were very poor. You can't eat ancient buildings. American soldiers came-a here inna about 1945, and-a Torritesi were tankful—dey dream of going to da U-S-of-A, but most go to Brazil, Venezuela, e Argentina."

A little boy runs up to PatG, Danny, and Vito. "Signori, Tommaso wants the American singer to come and entertain," the boy says in Italian.

The trio saunter back through the old streets to Caffè Ronchi.

Tommaso smiles widely. "Americano, sing!"

He plays, and PatG accompanies him.

"Femmina, tu sei una mala femmina . . ."

Danny looks over at the bartender's granddaughter. She is staring at PatG. There is a morsel of intention in her eye.

Although they play well together, it's clear that the accordion player is not sure what the song, "Love That Girl," is. When PatG gets to the last, "*And someday, you'll be mine*," Danny looks over at the bartender's granddaughter. She smiles. PatG returns the smile and nods.

It's now dark, and PatG, Vito, and Danny leave the bar and walk back into the piazza.

A heavyset man with one eye closed approaches and Vito stands and kisses him on both cheeks. "Don Antonio," he says.

After the kisses, Don Antonio nods and walks on.

"Who's that?" Danny asks.

"A boss," Vito responds. "It's time to eat."

Danny, PatG, and Vito pile into Vito's car and drive the four kilometers to Vito's home in Santeramo. Vito winds through the town's tiny streets and parks in front of Via Napoli 8. He hits the horn, and a woman accompanied by two young daughters come out onto the balcony.

The three men get out of the car. "Doze are my women," Vito says. "My wife is Luisa and my daughters are Carmela, like my mudder, and Elisabetta, like my mudder-in-law."

The women rush back into the house. Vito, Danny, and PatG make it up the marble stairs.

"It's got to be 20 degrees cooler in the staircase than it is outside," Danny says.

"Da marble and da shade," Vito quips.

He walks through the front door of the apartment. His wife and two daughters, who are in their early teens, are waiting in the vestibule. Each of his daughters kisses Vito on the cheek.

"Vito, are these the Americans?" his wife asks in Italian.

Vito nods and his wife pushes the hanging beads that cover the kitchen doorway to the side. "Sit down," he says to his guests.

PatG and Danny each take a chair at the table. Vito's wife and daughters put olives, wine, bruschetta, cut salamis, artichokes, hot peppers, and mushrooms soaked in oil on the table.

The men are seated on one side of the table and the women on the other. Carmela, the oldest sister, makes the sign of the cross and prays. Danny and PatG also make the sign of the cross. Carmela stops praying and everyone says amen. Luisa gestures for Danny and PatG to eat.

PatG takes an olive pit out of his mouth. "I've never had olives like these, and the artichokes and tomatoes on the bruschetta—the flavors are unbelievable. Food just doesn't taste like this back home."

"De olive should be eaten under de tree," Vito says, smiling.

After an hour, the plates are empty, and the girls begin to clear the table. Danny stands and takes a plate; Vito's wife smiles and takes it out of his hand. The women put clean dishes and a basket of oranges and strawberries.

PatG opens an orange and begins to eat it. "My mother was right, the oranges in the spring are sweet like sugar."

Danny seems to be having a tough time opening his orange. Vito's wife takes it from him, expertly peels it, and places it on Danny's plate.

Vito looks at Danny. "I founda Mimmo Ciancia."

Danny and PatG focus on Vito's face, which begins to disfigure itself, giving both the impression that Vito is not happy about his communication and that they might also not be elated.

"He's a funny guy with four kids, a young wife, and a bakery."

"Wow, Danny, four kids," PatG says.

Vito squeezes an orange peel together and rubs it on his neck. "My wife-a, she go-a crazy for citrus."

His wife seems to know that Vito is talking about her. She comes close and Vito slaps her on the rump. "Dey saya dat Mimmo go to America young and come back old."

Vito then raises a strawberry. "Everyting in its season." He hands the strawberry to Danny and concentrates on his next words. "Dey say he was in America for not a longa time. I tink maybe de food, all dose chemicals. I don' know. Some saya dat maybe he was dere witout papers, proper *permissione*. I tink he want to stay and couldn't take-a the food or was trown away."

"Ma says that he ran away from immigration, right Danny?" PatG asks.

Danny nods.

"Whata do you wanna from him?" Vito asks.

"I need to ask him a favor."

"A man like dat, a favor?" Vito puts his hand at eye level and twists it.

"Great," says Danny.

"Don' worry, my friend," Vito pats Danny's hand. "I gonna help you."

Danny looks at the carafe of wine. "I don't know if you can help me."

PatG stands up. "I'll see you back in Altamura."

"My son Gino, he drive-a you, G," Vito says.

Vito pulls down the skin under his eye. PatG smiles and leaves. Vito turns to Danny. "Don' worry . . . I help a lot of person. I gotta my nephew he was a goin' to jail for four years."

"I don't understand. You helped out your nephew who was going to jail for four years?"

Vito sets a bottle of liquor on the table. "He sell-a the cigarettes to a police. De police yell. My nephew he droppa de price. But de police, he-a tired dat everyone sella de cigarettes and no-a follow the law. My nephew, he in a world of shit."

"How did you help him?"

"I gave his boose-a fifty cartons of cigarettes."

"Boss . . . That's bribery."

"No, no. It was a gift."

"What happened to the policeman?"

"No one like-a him. He make-a too much noise. They take away his sticker."

"Badge. My problem's medical."

"I can help. My coosin's the president of our hospital."

Danny nods.

"One time, my anudder coosin, he get in trouble. He no work. De truth is he like-a too much de women. He go and go. You see de African girls on the road from the airport?"

"Yes," Danny says, nodding slightly.

"Ita help you keepa your appetite."

Vito's wife walks in. Vito winks at her, she blushes.

"Luisa, I gonna eatta you."

Danny's face becomes red and he turns away from Luisa. "Kiss you," he mumbles.

"No eat her. Don'a worry she no speak de English."

Vito looks at his wife and yells, *Tu sei bellissima, ti mangerò!*

His wife blushes again and smiles.

"What did you say?" Danny asks.

"I tell her in Italian. . . . Anyway, my coosin who like-a de *femmine*. He missa de work. He gotta pay de bills. He gotta wife anda kids. He go to de *dottore* and he say he no-o see. Dat way he can geta de pension. He go one time and he bringa de doctor de fruit. He go anudder time and he bringa de doctor de vegetables. He go anudder time and he bringa de wine. But dis doctor he no wanna do noting. He make-a my coosin poor."

"Wait, wait. Your coosin—your cousin wanted disability so he could be with prostitutes?"

Vito nonchalantly nods his head. "I guess you could say dat, but no exactly."

"It sounds like he wanted disability pay because he was blind. But he was not blind?" Danny presses.

"Aspetta, that'sa right. My coosin, he bringa wine, he bringa de vegetables, he bringa the frutta."

Danny's patience is wearing thin. "*To the doctor who was going to say that he was blind.*"

Vito nods and winks.

"I understand," Danny says.

"Well, inna de end, dis doctor say he gonna sign, che my coosin hea blind. My coosin, h-ea happy. He gonna getta de pension and dey gonna pay him back pay. Dis way he pay alla de bills."

Danny rubs his jaw. "Okay, okay. What happened?"

"I tell you, my coosin, he bringa all de wine and all de vegetables. But before de doctor sign de papers . . ." Vito makes a sign of the cross and kisses two fingers on his right hand. He then makes a small circle with them.

Danny watches Vito's fingers and then looks back at him. "What?"

Vito looks at Danny indignantly and raises his voice. "He-a die! After my coosin empty his house. He-a die. After my coosin bringa de wine, fruit, and de vegetables, he-a die!"

Danny rubs his eyes and looks to the side. "And so . . .?"

"And So! After my coosin he-a bringa de wine and he bringa de vegetables and he bringa de fruit? He-a cleana his house for dat doctor! He-a cleana de house!"

"I got that," Danny says irritably. "So what *did* our hero do?"

"Hero? My coosin? No, he's no hero. He likes the *femmine* too much dat's all."

"Yeah, I got that too. What did our protagonist do?"

"Protagonist?" Vito asks suspiciously.

"*What did your cousin do?*" Danny screams.

"My coosin he go to da doctor's son. De son take-a de place of-a de *papà*. He say my coosin go to de specialist a San Giovanni. But my coosin he explain dat he notta blind and de son he say he no sign. My coosin he-a mad. I mean de son he ate-a de frutta and he ate-a the vegetables and he drinka de wine too!"

"Logical," Danny says softly.

Vito nods satisfactorily. "It is logic, logic de bastardo! My coosin he tell de doctor he gonna kill him. Because it's his fault dat de family of my coosin no eat. I mean my coosin he gave de fadder de wine and . . ."

Danny interrupts. "Okay!"

"I go and talk to him."

"Did it help?"

"I get my coosin a pension mentale, depression."

"Oh, he was depressed?"

Vito looks confused and indignant. "No. Why do you ask?"

Danny stares at Vito, not knowing what to say.

Vito looks indignant. "No one in my family getta depress ever. We-a happy people. De father was a bastard. *Signore benedica.*" Vito crosses himself. "The law is if you blind you gotta go to San Giovanni."

"What's San Giovanni?" Danny asks.

"It is de town of Padre Pio's hospital."

"*I want to see their fruit,*" Danny says sarcastically.

"Me too," Vito says, nodding his head in agreement.

"So what did they do?"

"I tol you. I talk to de son. He feel bad dat his fadder take all de fruit, all of de vegetables . . ."

"*Yeah, I got it,*" Danny says.

"He feel responsabilla. He call a coosin dottor and we get my coosin de pension for being mentally depress."

Danny seems to be having a hard time following.

Vito raises his right hand and squeezes his thumb against his index finger. "He wrote on the documents dat my coosin he'sa crazy. . . . I tell you he is crazy. Dose African girls, he know dem all by name. If I tell dem I his coosin, dey make-a a discount. You wanna go tomorrow?"

Danny smiles sourly. "No. I'll pass. Thanks, though."

"I gotta lotta coosins. What do you need?"

Danny sighs. "I need Mimmo Cha Cha to take an HLA compatibility test for me."

"You canna find someone in America a take-a de test? Youa smart man. You can'ta pass a de test yourself?"

Danny looks away and then back at Vito.

Vito stares at Danny, senses trouble, and realizes that the favor is important.

Danny's eyes take the form of that of a sad puppy's. "I'm sick. I need a bone marrow transplant. Because we're related, he may be able to help me."

Chapter 7

Blood Pulls

(*Sangue Tira*)

Later in the evening, Vito, PatG and Danny are walking in the piazza.

"I heard of dat, de test. I gotta de coosin in Milano. All of de famiglia dey go to see if dey could help him. But dey don't give no test. They checka de blood."

"That's what I need Mimmo to do. I need him to check his blood," Danny says.

"I tink he do it. Are you hees coosin?"

"No."

"His nephew?"

"No."

"His brudder? . . . No, you notta his brudder, aah." Vito nods his head. "I getta de photo. . . . Your mudder she make-a de bread wit Mimmo." Vito rubs his chin. "Dis is no gonna be simple. He gotta four kids. Dey can help you too?"

"Maybe."

"Hisa wife-a, Franca—she-a young. He-a sixty-six. She-a forty-three or forty-five or someting. Itsa not easy witta de young wife. You know. Someting like dis can give her to make-a de . . ."

Vito raises his right hand and folds back all of his fingers, except for his baby finger and the finger next to his thumb.

Danny looks at Vito's hand. "What's that?"

"I mean, maybe she go-a crazy and . . ." Vito makes the sign again.

"What's this?" Danny makes the sign.

"Datsa de corna."

Danny squints his eyes.

"Qua in Eetaly, we no kill. I mean people rarely get violent. It's not dat people don' have guns or dat dey can' get dem. Dey can, like anywhere else. But, I mean Roma, she's-a 3 million people—dey kill maybe sixty people a year. Napoli—dere dey are

65

hotter tempered. Dey have 1 million and dey kill-a eighty. Dere dey gotta lotta . . ." Vito makes the sign with his hand again. "Half of all da murders in Italia, dey are from de corna. De resta, dey de Mafia. But de Mafia, dey don' wanna kill nobody."

"Oh?" Danny questions.

"No. Killing, eets-a bad for beesiness. I mean if General Motors starta kill its workers?"

"Of course . . . But what is the corna?"

Vito balls his right hand into a fist, grabs his upper right arm with his left hand, and begins to pump his fist up and down. Danny watches closely.

"And den . . ." Vito makes his right hand flat and moves it across his neck.

Danny scratches his head. Vito sees Danny's confusion and whispers, "Your *papà*."

"He's not my *papà*," Danny says looking over at PatG.

PatG smiles tightly and raises his eyebrows.

"But he's not your coosin," Vito says.

Danny nods.

"He's not your uncle or your brother?"

Danny nods again and then catches himself. "*Please continue explaining,*" he says.

"Your *papà*, he maybe twenty-five years older den his wife-a. Maybe he no like-a before." Vito makes the up-and-down motion with his right fist. "Maybe she looka for reason to do le corne. He never tell her dat he got udder children; she make-a de corna. He find out and he keel her. Everyone know dat he keel her, but he no go to jail cause everyone know dat she," Vito makes the sign with his fingers, "she make de corne."

Vito hesitates, looks at PatG and then at Danny. "We fix it. I talk to Don Antonio. Dere's more den one way to drink a cat."

The three arrive at the bar, and PatG walks ahead of them to sit by the stool closest to Francesca.

"Buona sera, Francesca," PatG says.

Francesca smiles.

Danny and Vito watch PatG watching Francesca.

Danny shrugs. "What's her story?"

"She a nice a girl, but she gotta *sfiga*."

"What's *sfiga*?" Danny asks.

"It means she's unlucky," PatG responds.

Vito nods in agreement. "She unlucky. Her *fidanzato*—fiancé—he die in a car accident."

"How old is she?" Danny asks.

"Francesca? Twenty-three, twenty-five."

"PatG's forty-eight."

"*If* he's a gentleman, no problem," Vito says.

Danny shrugs and rolls his eyes. "Who's Don Antonio?"

"He's a boss."

"Why would he want to help me?"

"He's a good boss. Good bosses help de people."

PatG stays at the bar and Vito leaves to look for Don Antonio. Danny walks to the Piazza Del Municipio and heads to the San Nicola church. He enters and takes his hat off—he feels that he has no choice but to walk slowly. Each and every centimeter of the edifice is adorned with painting, mosaics, and sculptures. The radiance and feeling coming from each work send Danny reeling mentally. *Some of this artwork must have taken years to complete. How and why were people so driven to make these artistic endeavors?*

Danny starts to think that maybe there is more to being a Catholic than he realized.

The following morning, Vito's mother walks into the bedroom where PatG and Danny sleep. They're up but half nude. Mamma picks up a pile of clothes and walks out.

"What's she doing?" Danny asks.

"Probably going to wash clothes," Patg says.

A few minutes later, Danny and PatG walk into the kitchen. Vito's seated at the table. "Good morning, good morning. We go to Mass, and then you gonna see."

"Mass?" PatG questions.

"Today's a June 13. It's de feast of Saint Antonio. Everyone dey-a go to Mass."

PatG and Danny follow Vito to the cattedrale. People pass and exchange greetings with him as he finishes his cigarette. He takes his last puff and the three enter the crowded church.

PatG struggles to understand the service; Danny doesn't get a word. When the time for communion arrives, Vito has to coax them into the aisle.

As they wait in line, Danny whispers to PatG, "This place is beautiful."

"I ain't been to Mass in ten years," PatG whispers back. "Hate to see it crumble."

After the service Danny, Vito and PatG walk together in the piazza. People nod and wave to them as they make their way through the square.

"I wish I could talk to them," Danny says.

"Just smile and nod or wave," Vito says. "Dey can understand your heart."

Danny looks at PatG. "You know what you said about the church crumbling, PatG?"

"Yeah." PatG looks at him curiously.

"I don't believe in miracles or curses or anything but my symptoms—tiredness, blackouts, dizziness—they're almost nonexistent. Strange."

PatG looks at the ground. "É un *posto strano*."

"What does that mean?" Danny asks.

"Italy is a mysterious place," PatG says.

Vito looks at PatG. "I see-a your Italiano is much better."

"Yeah, it's funny how I've become more and more comfortable."

"It's Francesca—there's-a nutting like a young, beautiful woman to help one learn . . . and feel more comfortable."

PatG nods and smiles.

"Don' be too relax. Remember that sometimes the wrong-a action can get one kill," Vito nods and says seriously.

They walk into a small bar in the piazza that PatG and Danny have never been to.

"*Tre caffè per favore!*" PatG yells.

"*Pago io,*" says one of the patrons.

"*Grazie,*" says PatG.

Vito and Danny smile at the generous man.

"What's goin' on?" Danny mumbles in PatG's direction.

"The guy paid for our coffee."

Vito is listening to the two Americans.

"Should we accept?" Danny asks.

"In Italy, dey say, *Se non accetti, non meriti*." Vito says.

Danny turns to PatG. "What does that mean, Professor?"

"If you don't accept kindness, you don't deserve it."

The three of them finish their coffee and then watch kids play soccer in the square. At 12:45 p.m., Vito leaves for Santeramo while PatG and Danny head to Mamma's for lunch.

That evening, at about five o'clock, PatG and Danny are walking. They hear Vito yelling at them and they turn. "Danny, G.!" Vito screams again.

Danny and PatG walk toward Vito, who is accompanied by a twenty-year-old man, who Vito introduces as Nicola. Nicola looks Danny up and down, then hugs and kisses him.

Vito takes a handkerchief out and wipes tears from his eyes.

"What's this?" Danny asks.

"Danny, dis-a you brother, Nicola."

Back in Danny's office, Ma's sitting in a chair in front of Irene's desk. The clock shows 11:00 a.m.

"I wonder what Mr. Hubble's doing?" Irene asks.

"It's five in the afternoon. He's probably reading the paper."

"In Italian?" Irene asks.

"Do you want tea?" Ma answers.

Next door, Rui's sitting at his own counter. Three customers are sitting with him.

"Well, Danny Hubble's helped more people than anyone I know," Rui says.

"Before you canonize him, get me some coffee," a patron rips.

Rui stands and gets the coffee pot. "I know he's gonna be all right."

Ma and Irene walk in.

"Maybe Danny was Mother Teresa of the Hill, but his ol' man was no prize," one of the patrons says.

Ma and Irene look at each other.

"Good morning, Ma Hubble, Irene," Rui says in a loud voice. "We were just talking about how we're all pulling for Danny."

"I heard," Ma says as she looks over at the patron, who gets up and leaves.

"I'll bet PatG's showing Danny a good time in Italy," Rui says.

"I certainly hope so," Irene answers.

Nicola enters the family bakery in Altamura. His father, Domenico, is short, bald, and muscular. The two converse in Italian.

"Pà, Vito, the guy who married the daughter of the furniture maker of Santeramo, wants to introduce you to a man from Pittsburgh."

"I don't know any man from Pittsburgh," says Mimmo.

"Vito is a nice man, and he says that this man is related to us."

69

"We have no relations in Pittsburgh."

"Are you sure, *Papà*?"

"What kind of question is that? Do you think that I'd lie to you?"

"Vito says that maybe you didn't know about this relative."

"Nicola, I have things to do. I wish you were as good at helping me as you are at aggravating me."

"Vito says that the man says he's your son."

Mimmo looks sternly at Nicola. "Have you lost your mind?" he says. "Don't ever say anything like that again."

"Pà, he looks like you, like your—like our—family. Vito says this man needs our help."

Mimmo rushes toward Nicola, and the discussion heats up. Nicola stands still, not cowering in the least bit; Mimmo looks in his son's eyes. "I am your father and I will always be your father! You will respect me or risk the consequences."

The two men seem to be two statues etched in stone.

"Do you understand me, or are you man enough to take the repercussions?"

Tears form in Nicola's eyes as he contemplates his next move. His decision will be critical.

Irene and Ma leave Rui's and sit on each side of Irene's desk.

"Are all of these people late?" Ma asks Irene.

"No, some have paid."

"Did Schmidt pay?" Ma asks.

"He'll never pay."

"He damn well better pay," Ma says sternly.

"He can't," Irene says solemnly.

"He can, and he better, and he will."

"It's impossible."

Ma looks harshly at Irene. "What do you mean by that? Why is it impossible?"

"He died," Irene says softly.

"But he owed us money. What do we do about the money?"

"It goes into the Out Bucket," Irene says.

"What?"

Irene points to the wastepaper basket. "We're out it, it's lost."

"But it's so sloppy. Why wasn't Schmidt current with his bills?"

"No money."

"That's not our problem!" Ma yells.

"Mr. Hubble saw it differently."

Ma stares out of the window.

"Mrs. Hubble," Irene says softly.

"Mrs. Hubble," she repeats.

Ma turns toward Irene. "Call me Bridget, for heaven's sake."

"Do you think Italy will help?" Irene asks.

"He's searching for a donor."

"I know."

"And how do you know?"

"I added, Bridget. I added."

Ma looks hard at Irene. "What are you saying?"

"I know that Mr. Hubble could not sire children," Irene says mildly.

"Just what else did you know about my husband?"

Irene touches her hand to her mouth.

Back in Altamura, Nicola is staring at his father. "*Papà,* I love you, but I learned from you how to be a man. We may be able to help this American, and he may be family." Nicola stands a bit taller as he continues to speak. "As men and as Catholics, it is our duty to help others. Can't you at least hear him out?"

Mimmo looks down and then suddenly flings his arm into the air without even glancing at his son. "Nicola, please leave."

"But father, we must talk." Nicola insists.

Mimmo silently stares at his youngest son, who wisely decides to exit.

Danny, PatG, Vito, and Nicola are at a tiny table having coffee. In the background, several men are arguing.

"How is it that you speak English?" Danny asks Nicola.

"We take a foreign language from the second grade . . . I like U2, so I translate. They're Irish, but they speak English."

"You speak well," Danny says.

Vito looks toward Nicola and raps his knuckles on his forehead as he would on a door. "Your father, he is a hard head."

"I think my mother can help," Nicola says.

"I don't want to create problems," Danny mutters.

Vito looks at Danny. "Your fadder say he no remember nottin'. You know." Vito makes his right hand into a fist and pumps it.

"My mother says that I'm his son," Danny says as he chews a wooden coffee mixer.

"You are," Vito says emphatically.

Danny and Pat stare at Vito.

"How do you know?" Danny asks.

"Nicola say dat you de twin, not only by your looks, but by your ways," Vito says.

Danny scrunches his eyes and smirks.

"Don't you see?!" Nicola instinctively yells in happiness. "My mother will see too. She's wise," he declares.

"I should just go home," Danny says to no one in particular.

"Bull. These hardheaded DPs . . ." PatG gripes.

"Are you sure it's your only chance?" Vito asks.

"Faded genes," Danny mumbles.

"What?" Vito asks.

Danny regains composure. "I have a rare genetic makeup. The best chance I have is another sibling. The second-best possibility would be one of my parents, and my mother is not a match. Finally, the sons and daughters of my parents offer less of a chance, though it's still possible that they will be a match. With my unique genetic makeup, the chances of one of them being able to donate bone marrow are far better than the chance of finding a matched donor in a bone marrow or stem cell bank."

Nicola takes Danny's hand. "Listen . . . We gonna help you."

Danny stares at Nicola. "It's crazy. Why should he care?"

"You're family . . . *Sangue tira.*"

Danny looks at PatG. "Maestro, what's that?"

"It means that the blood in your veins pulls the blood in his veins."

Chapter 8

Turning Back

The following morning, PatG wakes to noise and stands up and opens the *tapparelle* (shutters). The light shines in on Danny packing his bags. PatG looks at him, but Danny continues packing as if PatG is not there.

"You'll go home to die."

"The olive does not curse the tree as it falls. Nicola taught me that."

PatG smiles tightly and nods. "'Passion dies; love is.' Francesca taught me that."

"Romeo, don't get yourself killed over it."

"Love's the only thing worth getting yourself killed for," PatG solemnly fires back.

Danny stares at the wall and then at PatG. "That's not you talking; you're not right."

The room is covered in silence.

"PatG, I'm quickly heading toward death, but you're acting like a madman, and you may beat me there."

"Maybe I lived like a madman before, but I'm talking sense now. This place does something to you. I can't explain it," PatG says.

"You don't need to," Danny answers.

Danny stares at the crucifix above the doorway. He then takes a folded shirt in his hands. "I feel at home here. I know that I belong. I love this place. That's why I've got to leave."

"You're not making sense, Danny."

Danny stares back at PatG. "Aren't I?"

PatG takes Danny by the arms. "Give it a chance. That kid Nicola would do anything for you."

"I know—that's another reason why I'm going to leave."

Danny finishes packing his suitcase and opens the bedroom door. Vito is sitting at the kitchen table. Danny walks out, followed by PatG, who's still in his underwear.

"Vito, what are you doing?" PatG begs.

"I promise Danny dat I will take him to da airport."

"But you can't. These people need to take the exam to see if they can help him, give him a bone marrow transplant."

Vito looks to the ceiling. "I try to talk him out of it. What can I do?"

Danny brushes past Vito. Mamma is standing in the kitchen by the stove. She sees Danny in the doorway and picks up his suitcase, then heads back into the bedroom with it.

Danny looks at Vito. "Vito, you promised. Stop her. This is hard enough."

"Mamma, Mamma! Porta la valigia fuore."

The tiny woman moves back into the kitchen. Vito grabs the suitcase. "We're going to miss da plane."

PatG runs into the bedroom and grabs his shirt. He rushes to put his pants on. "Hey! Wait! Hey!"

He gets one shoe on and, with the other in his hand, runs out the door. Vito and Danny are already driving away and are a block down the old stone road.

PatG returns to Mamma's kitchen. She has a handkerchief to her nose and is sniffling. PatG takes her in his arms. *"Non piangere, Mamma. Non piangere* (Don't cry, Mamma. Don't cry ")*.

Vito and Danny drive in silence all the way to the Karol Wojtyla airport named after the peace-loving Pope John Paul II. Danny looks out of the car at the endless rows of olive trees. He notices that a tear is rolling down his left cheek. He touches it with his finger. Vito continues to concentrate on the road.

After twenty minutes, Vito pulls in front of the airport. He looks at Danny. "Danny, please don' leave. You have to give hope, some time."

Danny quietly opens the door and reaches into the back seat for his suitcase. He feels a bit dizzy and steadies himself by grabbing the top of the car.

"Vito, do we have a few minutes? I'd like to take this all in." Danny looks up to the green palm trees and the orange sun. He breathes in through his nose, attempting to smell the air. He closes his eyes. He's watching the kids play back in the piazza in Altamura. He's watching the old men play cards in the bar. He moves into the aisle at the cattedrale. Then he hears someone yelling his name.

"Danny! Danny!"

He looks in the direction of the sound. A Vespa scooter is speeding toward them. Nicola is driving. PatG has his arms around him and is holding on for dear life. Vito smiles silently.

"Danny!" Nicola screams as he and PatG get off the scooter.

"What are you guys doing here?"

Vito moves to the other side of the car to be next to the trio.

"Danny, Danny! You can't go," says Nicola. "We will help you—I will help you. You are my brother."

Danny is mesmerized by the material substance of Nicola's words. Since he has arrived, his thoughts have been mounting inside of him like a volcano. He has met plenty of Italians and people he thought were Italians in his life, but never understood Italy. Now, with each passing day and each experience, his life is changing. He feels that he has changed.

"Nicola, you are my brother and so, I *must* leave. It's not fair for your family," Danny hesitates and looks at the three men, "our family to be ripped apart for me."

Nicola is visibly crying. Danny continues, "I've only brought discord. I swear, this was not my intention, but family and love sometimes mean sacrificing one's happiness so that the others can be happy, one's life so that others can live."

Nicola speaks through his tears. "We will be happy; we will live. *Papà*, he is a hard head but he will come around. We will all be happy. Please, Danny, you must give hope, give time."

Danny stares at Nicola.

Vito smiles. "Yes, let's-a give-a hope a chance."

Danny contemplates the words, "Give hope a chance."

"What is a week?" Nicola asks.

Danny's no longer sure of what he should do.

"If I cannot make progress, then you can leave next week," Nicola says.

Danny is still holding the top of the car. He seriously feels faint. It's the first time since he's arrived in Italy that he feels weak. "I don't know if I'll be here next week, the way I feel at this moment."

Nicola, PatG, and Vito move to Danny's side, then guide him and his suitcase back into the car. PatG gets into the back seat, and Nicola follows them back to Altamura.

Vito opens the door to Mamma's house. She sees Danny's suitcase and smiles. She takes it from her son's hand and carries it into the bedroom.

PatG and Nicola help Danny sit down in a kitchen chair. Danny gazes into the bedroom. Mamma is almost finished unpacking.

PatG smiles and looks at his friend. "'Woman doesn't need to act like a man . . . She's a woman.' That's what Francesca says."

Danny smiles and begins to laugh. "'A woman could pull a bus with one of her pubic hairs.' That's what Vito says." They all laugh.

Vito's mother finishes unpacking and exits.

Vito stands, "Danny, you need-a some rest. I be back in few hours. We go get *ricci*. *Ricci* will set you back straight."

Danny looks at PatG. "Ricci?"

"Sea urchins. Many believe that they-a have magical power," he says.

"And what do you do with them?" Danny asks.

"You eat them!" Nicola interrupts. "You eat lots of them."

Danny balances himself—first on the chair, then on the wall, then on the door frame—until he reaches his bed. Mamma closes the *tapparelle* and exits. PatG closes the door behind her.

At noon Vito returns. Danny is awake on his bed. The *tapparelle* are slightly opened, and his eyes are fixed on the ceiling. Vito walks in.

"Danny, you feel all right? You wanna to get-ta de *ricci*?"

"Sure," Danny says. He sits up and slides his feet to the floor.

Nicola, PatG, Vito, and Danny travel 40 kilometers to Santo Spirito, a small seaside town. As they make their way up the tiny main street, an old woman stands and puts her chair in her house to make room for the car.

They park near the shore. Danny looks out the window at the scuba blue sea.

The men get out of the car and begin walking down the jammed walkway. Vito approaches a guy next to a cart filled with plates of *ricci* and *vongole,* which Danny gathers are clams. Vito bargains with the vendor and nods for Nicola to take a tray of *ricci.* Vito takes another tray of ricci, as well as a tray of *vongole.* The four of them sit on a breaker wall to eat the sea urchins and clams with bread.

Danny smells the *riccio,* then he sticks his tongue inside of it. Nicola snaps a picture.

"Don Antonio speak to your father," Vito says.

"Is Don Antonio a mafioso?" asks Danny.

"Dere's Don Antonios in all towns. Some are good, some are not." Vito nods his head. "Italy is-a free because de government, corruptorations, de church, and de Mafia coexist. We not aworry about getting beat up by de police. Our government cannot become too powerful . . . de church, de Mafia. . . . It's de greatest form of government on de planet and da proof is dat we live almost four years longer than de Americans and we have less murders in all of Italia, a nation of 60 million, den da United States has in small city.

Danny stares, his mind racing.

"And," continues Vito, "de Italian is de greatest lover."

"Okay, how in the world do you prove that?" Danny asks.

Vito smiles. "Who was de greatest queen of all times?" Vito asks.

"Cleopatra?" Danny asks in response.

"Precise-aly," Vito states. "And Cleopatra could have had da best lovers from de Africa or anywhere in da world."

"Okay. Where are we going with this?" Danny continues.

"She marry Egyptians because she was-a forced to, but-a her two lovers were Caesar and Mark Antonio. She could have had lovers from de entire world-a, anywhere but she chose Italians."

Danny smirks.

Vito continues. "That's why-a de Italian is part of de greatest race on da planet. We are Latins."

"But you're Europeans," Danny retorts.

"Precisely. We are Latin Europeans, like our brudders, de Latin Americans, da greatest race on de earth. And our society is de best on de planet."

"That's why we always complain."

"That's why you always complain?" Danny asks hesitantly.

"Dat's-a right," Vito says. "We always-a complain so dat we cannna stay on top." He looks at Danny and sees that Danny's perplexed.

"We complain to de European heads in Brussels, we cry-a to de Church, da Americans . . . anyone who will-a listen."

"Why?"

"*Lamenta rende.* If we complain enough, maybe dey get tired of listening to us and give us someting. It's like da king and da old woman in-a da Bible. Da king, he got so-a tired of listening to de ol' woman ask-a for justice dat he tol' his people to give her whatever she ask for because he didn' wanna to hear her no more."

Danny smirks. "What does 'Don' refer to?" he asks.

"We call priest and big men 'Don.' If Donald Trump live-a here, many would call him "Don Donato. To us, Don is more important den presidente."

"So does Don Antonio run the town?" PatG asks.

"He's a like de king. A just king is da best-a form of government. You don' read-a philosophy in da United States? Today, capitalism wears-a da face of democracy-a. But it is no longer democracy-a. Couple people run da show, da masses have-a no idea what is-a going on. Da wealt is owned-a by da corruptorations."

"Why do you say corruptorations?" asks PatG.

"You like it; it's-a my word. You can use it witout pay me. I say corruptorations because dey changed. Da CEO an' his minions take a da lion's share of da profit. Dey give da shareowners crumbs to-a be quiet an' de employee, dey profit from. Dey take away dere healt'care, childcare, right of-a happiness and feed it to de CEO an' da real Mafiosi."

Danny laughs. "Are you sure you've never lived in the United States?"

PatG is irritated. "Europeans always say that, but your system does not work either." he says.

"My frien', I am not aliterate. I read, I have my-a favorite nephew. He work-a in Brussels. He is an economist. In da United States dey say a family makes $60,000. But dis is-a before taxes and healthcare. . . . It's-a really about twenty-five or tirty tousand, depending on de employer. Wit' da healthcare, da childcare, da schools—including university—and-a no real estate taxes on-a dere primary residenza, Europeans make dat much wit'out working a day."

"And how do they do it? Someone has to pay!" Danny says.

"We have-a your old system. Until Ronald Reagan, da top tax bracket in da United States was 70 percent Until 1954, it was-a 94 percent. When Reagan kill de unions, and lowered da taxes on dose who could afford to pay-a them, he killa de middle class. We don' have da European system. We have de old US system."

Nicola stands and winks at Danny. "U.S.A. The best."

Danny smiles tightly and tilts his head.

Vito continues enjoying the role of sage. "Americans no longer tink. If guy who made-a 10,000,000 dollars a year paid 90 percent income tax-a, he still get-a 5,000 dollars cash five days a week-a. But your system give-a him tax credits e deductions, while da family making $60,000 gets da . . ." Vito makes a fist and pumps it. "Dey get the shaft."

"I don't want to talk politics. I want to eat *ricci* and look at the beautiful women," PatG says.

"This is not-a politics; it is-a common sense." Vito says.

"So you would rather have a monarchy?" Danny asks.

"It depends-a. If de king is benevolent, dere is no better form of government. But da world is-a round, and eventually, in a monarchy, de people are eaten by-a da lion. In a democracy, dey're eaten by a pack of rats."

PatG is surprised by the conversation. He feels like he would be betraying his country if he didn't defend the system. Then he re-thinks. A country is a people, not a system.

"My friend, Obama, Bush, Trump . . ." Vito looks into PatG's eyes. "Dey're the rats."

PatG has never liked any of the people that Vito's mentioned and is happy enough to let the discourse drop. Now, if Vito had said that Abraham Lincoln, Martin Luther King, Jr., or John F. Kennedy were rats, there would have been a conflict.

Danny looks at the clam in his hand. "Hey, this thing is still moving."

"Of course it is. It's-a fresh," Vito replies.

"What should I do with it?"

"Eat it. Itsa fresh. No one should ever eat fish if-a it isn't fresh." Vito takes one and sucks it off the shell.

Back at Larry's: He's Not Here, Kevin's drinking with Larry, Paulie, and Markie.

Paulie is a short, wiry electrician who could pass for a thirty-year-old, but he's almost forty-five. He's on his third marriage and has seven kids, if you count his step-kids—and he counts them because he says he pays for them. Paulie has an Italian last name and refers to himself as an Italian American. He's been known to argue that Italians are not white. He says that, as a kid, he was called wop, greaseball, and spic—he's not going to allow the media and the government dictate what he is, and he also has no problem being referred to as wop, greaseball, or spic. He says that sticks and stones may break his bones, but names will never hurt him.

Markie's forty-five years old, and he drives a truck for Universal Alloy. He's married to his third wife but has no children of his own. He considers himself a philosopher and likes to quote Voltaire. His father, Jackie, worked for Universal until he died a few years ago. His father hung out at Larry's like Markie does today.

"Ol' Danny may come home in a box," Larry says.

"Have you heard from him?" Markie asks.

"Nah, but I hope he's getting to some of those churches. Italy ought to be a nice place to see the Lord," Larry says.

"Yeah, and all those paintings and statues," Paulie adds.

"Let me ask you Catholics something. You're always talking to statues. Any of them ever talk back?" Kevin asks. He looks at them one by one. "I saw the Lord clearer in a bar than in a hundred churches." He downs the rest of his beer and heads for the door.

Everyone watches Kevin leave. Once he's gone, Paulie says, "If he talks about the Lord like that again I'll sock him."

"That probably wouldn't make the Lord happy," Larry says. "Remember when Hulk Hurley threatened to sock Kevin last year?"

"Yeah," Markie inserts. "Kevin jumped out of his second-floor window on top of the Hulk and almost bit his nose off."

Vito, Nicola, PatG, and Danny are in the car on the way back to Altamura.

"I hope *Papà* listens to Don Antonio," Nicola says.

"Doesn't he have to listen?" PatG asks.

"Not even Don Antonio can interfere with a man'sa family," Vito replies.

"It used to be like that in the United States." Danny adds.

Ma and Irene are looking at pictures in Ma's kitchen.

"This is Danny when he was seven," Ma says.

"I wish we could have been closer," Irene blurts.

"You were close enough," Ma refutes.

"Mr. Hubble was a fine man," Irene says.

"Drink your rum," Ma responds.

It's late in the evening in Altamura, and Francesca is washing glasses and cups. Tommaso is playing the accordion, and PatG is singing "Al di là," a song about a man who is singing to his deceased wife.

"*Ci sei tu, ci sei tu per me . . . La la la la... La la la la. La la la laaa . . .* (You are there waiting for me . . .)"

Francesca is drying a glass. She turns and stares at PatG and watches as the crowd cheers and applauds. PatG bows and walks over to Danny, who is sitting by the door.

"It's a Wednesday evening. What a crowd," PatG says.

"Yeah," Danny says. "It's quite a place. They don't get it, though."

"They don't get what?"

"They don't understand how lucky they are. Nicola speaks about America as if we live like kings. I think they watch too much television."

"Yeah," PatG says. "They love to complain, and their poor live like our upper-middle class. Healthcare, childcare, schools, universities, no taxes on your first home . . . What else does anyone need?"

"The grass is always greener," Danny says.

"I'm going outside to smoke a cigar for a while. Want to come?"

"No," Danny says. "I don't feel so hot."

PatG's standing under a streetlamp. He blows out cigar smoke, and Francesca arrives and kisses his cheek.

Early Thursday morning, Vito, PatG, and Danny are in the bar. Francesca brings them coffee and rolls. Vito notices a tiny envelope in between PatG's cup and saucer.

PatG gazes and then walks outside with the envelope. Vito shakes his head. Danny smiles.

"Yahoo!" PatG yells. He walks back into the bar and tucks the envelope into his back pocket. PatG looks at Vito. Vito looks back at him sternly, then smiles.

"Italy's the most beautiful place on Earth," PatG says.

Vito shakes his head, looks at Francesca, and raises his cup. "To the beauty of Italy."

Francesca smiles from behind the bar.

Back at Ma's house, it's late at night. She is snoring on the couch, and Irene is sleeping on the chair.

The doorbell rings. Irene stirs, walks to Ma, and shakes her. "Ma, there's someone at the door."

"It's PatG. He's here for Danny," Ma says without opening her eyes.

Irene puts her hand on the doorknob, then she looks up. "Bridget, PatG's in Italy for Danny." She turns to Ma, but Ma has already begun snoring again.

A few minutes later, Marla's sipping tea with Irene in Ma's kitchen.

"I'm sorry about your parents," Irene says.

"People say I'm with him trying to replace my father. These are the box-head people."

"Box-head people?"

"Yes. They try to put everything in a box and tell everyone else how they should live, what is right and what is wrong."

"Honey, people put things in boxes because it's easier than trying to understand them."

"I love that half-pint to death. I don't know what I'd do if something happened to him," Marla says.

"I know, honey."

"I don't think that Danny really gets it. Sometimes he's so childish."

"All men are, honey," Irene smiles. "I mean most men are childish—actually, all I've ever met."

Irene startles as Ma gets up off the couch and walks toward the kitchen.

"I said to stay away from my son! Danny! I want this girl out of here!" Ma heads into the bathroom, slamming the door behind her.

Things are even less peaceful at the Ciancia household.

Nicola and his father are screaming. Mimmo with his hardened, wood-like hand slaps Nicola in the face. His wife, Franca, runs in. *"Basta! Basta!"* she shouts.

Nicola leaves the house and walks directly to the bar. He doesn't know it, but he has his father's handprint bruise on his cheek.

"Any news wit *Papà*?" Vito asks.

"Not yet, but we're talking about things." Nicola peeps meekly.

Vito laughs. "Is that the result of your conversations?"

Nicola smiles. Danny leaves.

After about fifteen minutes of discussion, PatG, Nicola, and Vito walk to the bakery. When they arrive, Mimmo's serving customers.

"They're twins," PatG whispers.

The last customer leaves, and Mimmo picks up a bread knife and stares at Vito. "*Non sono fatti tuoi!* (This is none of your business!)"

PatG moves behind Vito and in a hushed voice says, "Little guy's a bit emotional."

"*Signor Ciancia, ti prego di ragionare.* (Mr. Ciancia, I beg you to be rational)," Vito says.

"*Ti prego di andarsene o morire!* (And I beg you to leave or die!)" Mimmo responds.

"*Papà! Papà!*" Nicola screams.

"*A casa! A casa!* (Go home now!)" Mimmo tells him.

"*Ma, Papà!* (But Papà!)"

"*Adesso!* (Now!)"

Nicola runs out the door.

"*E voi due, via!* (And you two, leave!)" Mimmo shouts. He comes around the counter with the knife in his hand.

PatG smiles. "I don't stay where I'm not welcome."

He and Vito leave.

Danny and PatG are feeding pigeons in the piazza when Nicola approaches. "Danny, my mamma wants to know you."

Danny looks at him. "To know me?"

"If she means the biblical sense, this could become interesting," PatG says.

"Cut it out," Danny swipes.

"She says that she must see you," Nicola adds.

Chapter 9

A Brother's Courage

Danny, Nicola, and Vito walk to the corner house. An olive tree takes up the whole front of the building.

"This tree is a thousand years old," Nicola says.

Danny stares at it. "A thousand years old?"

"We have a de olive trees dat are two tousand years old all over Puglia," Vito says.

The trio walks up the steps. Nicola enters.

"Mamma . . . Mamma."

Nicola's mother arrives at the door. "*Entra. Entra.* (Come in, come in)," she says.

They follow her inside. Nicola's mother looks at Danny, hugs him, smiles, and nods as she pulls away. "*Sangue del mio sangue.*"

Danny feels awkward. His arms remain glued to his side. By now, he has begun to understand some Italian but he doesn't want to blunder. "What is she sayin'?" he asks.

"Blood of my blood. You gotta de same blood as her children," Vito replies.

Nicola takes Danny's arm and pulls him toward the door.

Vito smiles. "Let's a-go. She'll talk a-to her husband for you. No one hasa de power over a man dat hisa wife has. Even Don Antonio has a to pay attention to his wife," he says and winks at Danny.

Danny holds his chest as he makes his way down the stairs of the Ciancia family home. Nicola and Vito notice. They each take an arm.

"Take it easy, Danny. Take it easy," Vito says.

"*Tutto apposta*—everything's fine," Danny says, but as he tries to lower his foot onto the next step, he begins to cough and hold his chest.

Tears come to Nicola's eyes. "Let's go to the hospital."

Danny continues to hold his chest as they move him into the car. Vito presses the pedal to the floor and the tires emit a small puff of smoke as they depart. After a few minutes, they pull in front of a squalid three-story building with a large statue of the Madonna over the entrance.

Escorting Danny, they meet a cigarette-smoking nurse dressed in white. There are butts all over the entrance floor. Inside, the hall walls are dingy and peppered with spots where the paint has peeled off.

The nurse takes the last puff from his cigarette and throws it on the floor. Vito, Nicola, and Danny sit in tiny chairs. The nurse disappears through a doorway in front of them.

Back at the bar, the phone rings, and Francesca answers. She listens to the voice on the other end of the line for a few seconds and her face quickly turns to fear. *"Bene . . . Bene . . ."* She turns to her grandfather. *"Devo trovare l'Americano.* (I must find the American.)"

Her grandfather looks at her sternly.

"Nonno, Nonno, per piacere. (Grandfather, grandfather, please.)"

He nods. Francesca kisses him, removes her apron, and exits.

PatG is in a small park next to the piazza. A group of men are gathered around a table playing Italian cards.

"Scopa! (My point!)" says a man wearing a pink bandanna. *"Ti piace, ne?* (You like that, hah?)"

The man he's speaking to has a tiny crucifix dangling from his ear. *"É troppo presto a ridere."* (It's too soon to laugh.)"

The man in the pink bandanna throws down a card. The guy with the earring matches it. *"Scopa!"*

The man in the pink bandanna is discouraged. He throws down another two cards. The man in the earring matches them both. *"Scopa! Scopa!"*

PatG grins.

"Che cazzo ridi, Americano?! (What are you laughing at, American?!)"

"Non sto ridendo. Stavo pensando di un angelo, mio angelo. (I was not laughing. I was smiling, thinking of an angel—my angel.)"

Francesca runs up behind him. "*Patrizio, Danny sta all'ospedale.* (Patrick, Danny's in the hospital.)"

The man in the earring looks at Francesca and then at PatG. He nods to the other card player, who nods back and says, "*Suo angelo.* (His angel.)"

In the hospital, the nurse returns with a doctor who is wearing a white smock and a stethoscope and has a cigarette hanging from his mouth.

"It's a de doctor, Loreto," Vito says.

At that moment, a young sobbing girl, with a bloodied towel wrapped around her hand, rushes in. Accompanying her are a crying man and a hysterical woman, her parents, and four other family members. The doctor takes Danny's arm, and they follow the screamers down the hall.

He seats Danny in the emergency room. The family continues yelling and crying as Dr. Loreto unwraps the girl's hand, exposing a gashed finger. *"Metti trepunti.* (Put in three stitches)" he tells the nurse.

The nurse nods and then coaxes everyone but the parents into leaving. He then prepares a steel platter with thread and a needle. As he does, the door bursts open, and Francesca and PatG rush in.

"Danny, Danny, are you all right?" PatG asks.

"Still kickin'," Danny replies as the three concentrate on one another, trying to consider what else to say.

The nurse is making fast work of the little girl's finger and is just putting a mesh ring over it.

The doctor still has a cigarette in his mouth. He approaches Danny.

"No good-a de smoking," he says. He grins and walks over to the girl. Once he's examined her finger, he takes her arm and waves her and her parents out with his right hand.

"Grazie, Dottore . . . Grazie," the father says. The doctor nods kindly, puts his cigarette out on the floor, and returns to Danny.

"Take-a offa your clothes."

Danny stares at him.

"Take-a offa your pants."

Danny is still speechless.

"Take-a offa your shirt."

"Now we're getting somewhere," Danny says.

Danny removes his shirt; Dr. Loreto places his hand on Danny's back and thumps it with a knuckle, repeating the motion on Danny's chest. He then shines a light into Danny's eyes, puts on his stethoscope, and listens to Danny's breath.

The doctor nods. "Leukemia. Maybe you gotta leukemia."

"Yeah, I know," Danny says sarcastically.

"Dat's no good."

"That's what they say," Danny returns.

"Why you come-a to Italy witta leukemia?"

Danny looks at Vito. Vito addresses the doctor in Italian. "*Lui é figlio di Ciancia u fornaio. É qua per vedere se il padre può aiutare.* (He's Ciancia the Altamura baker's son. He's here to ask his father for help.)"

The doctor knocks his head with his knuckles.

"Well?" Danny asks.

"He say you fadder is a hard head," Vito responds.

The doctor looks at Vito, Nicola, PatG, Francesca and, finally, at Danny. "You musta go home . . . If you getta bad here . . . Dat'sa not good. The doctor speaks directly to Vito. "*Un uomo deve moriire con la sua famiglia nel suo paese.* (A man must die with his family and in his own town.)"

Danny looks down and opens and closes his left hand.

"I have to die somewhere."

"Me and your father are *fra cugini*?"

"*Fra cugini?*"

"Dey're not coosins, but dere coosins are coosins. Dey're . . ." Vito makes a ball of each hand and then reopens them. ". . . dey're between coosins."

"Are you related?" Danny wonders.

"To who?" Vito asks.

"To my father's people."

Vito shrugs. "Altamura is only a town and, Gesù, he say we all brothers. Some say the closer de blood, da stronger de rope." Vito makes one hand into the form of a rope and tugs. "Odders say, blood is blood."

"You go home *a domani*, tomorrow," the doctor says sternly.

"My ticket's for Tuesday," Danny says.

"You come wit ITA Airlines?"

Danny nods. "Part of the way."

The doctor raises his finger, gets out his cell phone and begins to tap out a number. "*Cugi . . . Come stai? E la signora, i bambini? Bene, bene, bene. Senti ho un problema.* (Cousin, how are you? And the missus, the kids? Listen I have a problem.)"

The doctor looks at Danny. "What'sa your name?"

"Doc, without a transplant I'm dead and in no rush to go home."

"Don' worry. What'sa your name? My coosin, he do it all. Donna worry." The doctor speaks into the phone. "É per *cambiare il biglietto per un parente di Ciancia, quel testardo fornaio.* (It's for changing the ticket of someone who belongs to the family of that hardheaded baker, Ciancia.)"

The doctor turns to Danny again. "What'sa you name?"

"Danny Hubble."

As Danny speaks, the doctor notices the weakness in Danny's voice. This time, when he returns his attention to his cousin, his voice is more urgent. "*Cugi . . . ti chiamo dopo. Volevo sapere se potevi cambiare il suo biglietto. Puoi?* (Cousin, I'll call back—I wanted to make sure you could change his ticket date if needed. Can you help?)"

"*Grazie cugino, ti voglio bene anch'io.* (Thank you, Cousin. I love you too.)"

Vito looks at the doctor and winks. "*Grazie, Dottore. Ci siamo facendo quel che possiamo. Lui serve un donatore per un trapianto midolosseo.* (Thanks, Doctor. We're doing what we can, but he needs a matched donor for bone marrow transplant.)"

The doctor nods. "*Infermiere, ossigena.* (Nurse, oxygen)."

The nurse wheels a green tank of oxygen over to Danny.

"Take-a dis wit you. If you feel pain or trouble breathing, take it."

The doctor breathes loudly in and out. He puts a plastic mask on. He attaches a tube. He turns a handle and oxygen exits.

"You take dis and you be okay. I will talka to Signor Ciancia." The doctor winks.

"Thank you. What do I owe you?"

The doctor looks puzzled. "Owe?"

Danny looks at Vito. Pat is concentrating on the doctor's words.

"Don't worry about it."

"But what about the oxygen tank?"

"Bring it back when you done. Are things different in America?"

Danny, Nicola, Vito, PatG, and Francesca leave the hospital. Francesca walks back to the bar; the others get into Vito's car and go to Mamma's home.

As soon as Danny gets into his room he grabs for the bed. Vito, PatG, and Nicola sit him down. Nicola and PatG remove his socks and shoes.

"*Mamma, porta un po d'acqua fresca.* (Mamma, bring some fresh water)," Vito says.

Doctor Loreto makes his way up the steps to Mimmo Ciancia's home. It's late in the evening and he is sure that the baker will no longer be at work. He knocks at the door.

Franca, Mimmo's wife, answers. *"Dottor Loreto, che piacere.* (Doctor Loreto, what a pleasure.)"

The doctor walks in.

"Mimmo, Mimmo. Dottor Loreto é qua." Franca moves to the stove. *"Dottore, caffè, liquore?"*

"Si, si, dammi un limoncello."

Franca pours limoncello into a small crystal glass. Mimmo is dressed in a red, long-sleeved collared shirt, which is tucked into his brown pants. He has slippers on his feet.

"Mimmo, limoncello?" Franca asks.

Mimmo nods and sits down across from Dottor Loreto.

The doctor smiles and begins speaking rapidly in Italian. Mimmo's fidgeting nervously. Every so often, he shakes his head. *"Non é vero, Dottore. Non é vero.* (It's not true, Doctor. It's not true)," he tells Loreto.

But the doctor ignores him and continues for what, to Mimmo, seems like hours. Finally, Loreto pauses; he raises his glass to his lips and finishes the limoncello. *"E se é veramente fig?* (And if he is your son?)" he asks.

Mimmo has had enough. He slams his hand on the table. *"No! Non é!* (He's not!)"

Doctor Loreto puts his cup down and raises his hands. *"Bene."*

The following day, Nicola and Danny are sitting in Danny's room. Danny has the oxygen mask on. "They serve McDonald's in American children's hospitals . . . Who can prove what kills you faster? Italians live almost four years longer. That probably has something to do with it," Danny muses.

"Someday, I want to go to America," Nicola says.

"Why?"

"Everyone's rich. The women are beautiful. The streets are safe. Here, everyone does as they please."

Danny gazes.

"Want to get a *caffè?"* Nicola asks.

Danny does not answer.

"Are you okay, Danny?"

"I'm fine." Danny takes the mask off. "Let's go."

Danny and Nicola make their way over to the bar. Patrons greet them when they arrive.

"Ciao, Danny."

"Salute, Danny!"

"Danny, vuoi un caffè?"

PatG's sitting at a side table. He gets up and hugs Danny. "My friend, come and sit down."

The two sit and Francesca brings them coffee. Nicola is speaking to friends at the bar.

"He doesn't leave your side," PatG says.

Nicola walks over to their table as PatG finishes speaking. Danny doesn't notice Nicola's arrival.

"He's a good kid. I'll miss him," Danny says.

Nicola stares at Danny. "You are not going anywhere."

Danny smiles, but all eyes turn to Mimmo as he enters. *"Fuori Nicola!"* (Nicola, get out!)

Nicola looks from his coffee to his father. His eyes tear.

"Fuori!" (I said to get out!) Mimmo screams. Nicola slowly stands and, with his face down, follows his father out.

"Who was that?" Danny asks.

"Your father," PatG says. He watches Nicola leave.

"I've caused enough trouble," Danny says.

"You, my friend, didn't cause anything. The guy's an ass," PatG says.

"Still," Danny says, "when the show's over, you gotta leave."

Back in Danny's Pittsburgh office, Ma's sitting at Irene's desk. Irene is standing over her with a paper in her hand. Ma's banging the buttons on the telephone. "It's useless!" she says.

"Calm, Bridget . . . Calm."

"Easy for you, to say; he's *not* your son." Ma throws the phone on the floor and rests her head on her arm and sobs.

90

After a few minutes, Nicola walks back into the bar and up to Danny and PatG's table. "I will take the exam."

Danny smirks. He's jumping for joy inside, but he does not want to betray his feelings. "I'd rather it be me dead than you," Danny says.

"*Mia madre* says that we're brothers. I must help you." Nicola smiles. His eyes are glassy. He then hesitates and leans down and hugs Danny. Danny purposely remains numb, but after a few seconds, he can no longer stop himself. He returns his brother's embrace, squeezing him in a long hug.

PatG stands. "I'll let you settle family matters," he says, and leaves.

Nicola looks at Danny. "The fox jumps one hundred times for the grape. But he can't reach it, so he convinces himself that the grape's sour. This way he can go on living. Papà is that fox, but he does not forget. The sour lives inside him. His grape was America."

Danny looks on admiringly.

Nicola continues. "Mamma has made her decision. It would have been impossible to go against both of them, but now, my mother, she's on our side. My father will never change, but me and my brother and sisters may be willing to help. I for sure."

Chapter 10

Mothers' Universal Love

Danny didn't think much about death as much as he thought about leaving. His desire to not be a burden was much stronger than his desire to live.

The morning after his talk with Nicola, the two of them are walking together, arm in arm. It isn't easy for Danny to get used to having his arm through the arm of another man, but Nicola is his brother, and he is getting used to it. While they are out, they run into PatG and Francesca.

"I'm leaving," says Nicola.

"Where are you going?" asks PatG.

"Home. I have an exam."

PatG leaves his girl's side and wraps his arm around Danny. The three of them continue on to the park, where they watch the kids play soccer.

"I'm going to go home and lie down," Danny says.

"I'll walk with you. We need to talk," PatG tells him.

Nicola waves. PatG looks at Danny. "I want to marry Francesca."

"I know."

"How do you know?"

"You say you want to marry every girl after a week."

"Stop clowning around, Danny. I'm serious."

"You always say that too."

"This time I mean it."

"PatG, she lives in Italy; you live in Pittsburgh. She lives in a stable environment; you live with your mother, who is the sole source of your stability. What could you offer her?"

"Danny, I'm serious. This is not like buying a car. It's about emotions and feelings."

Danny stares at PatG. "Take two aspirins and call me in the morning."

Danny goes into Mamma's house to rest, and PatG returns to the bar. Shortly after PatG arrives, one of the town police walks in.

"*Caffe!*" the policeman shouts.

Another patron enters. "Un'affogato." (a dessert with seven liquors, and whipped and ice cream).

Francesca's grandfather looks at the patron. "At this hour?"

The patron nods.

The policeman sits down and sips coffee. Francesca's grandfather finishes making the *affogato* and hands it to the patron, who moves next to the policeman, removes his hat and pours the *affogato* over the policeman's head.

"Give your parking tickets to the people who can afford to pay them, not to people like my aunt," the man yells in Italian.

He exits, and the policeman pushes the ice cream off his head and onto the floor. Francesca's grandfather gives him a rag and the policeman tidies himself up.

"*Acqua,*" the policeman says.

Francesca comes from the back room and brings him a glass of water. The policeman drinks the water, puts his hat on, and leaves. Francesca's grandfather starts cleaning the fruit juice machine.

"I'm moving here," PatG says, to no one in particular. "Can I see you tonight?" he asks Francesca.

"PatG, whatta are you intentions?" She quickly walks to the back of the bar, purposely giving PatG time to think about his answer.

When PatG arrives at Mamma's house, he finds Vito and Danny talking out front.

"I feel comfortable here," Danny says.

"Dat's normal. Italy's where de souls of your people are . . . It's your home," Vito says.

"It's a strange place," Danny replies.

"Italy's de home of the family, de renaissance, de Mafia, and freedom." Vito smiles. "We find order in disorder. Da government, church, corruptorations, and de Mafia fight for power, and de people breathe da freedom left by-a da holes dat dey make in da fabric of our nation."

"But your young people listen to English music and dream of the American way of life," Danny responds.

"Yes, our-a youth is-a spoiled by quick richness. But dey *are* Italian." Vito raises his finger to make a point. "Southern Italians are-a Arabic Europeans who have more in common wit de Tunisia den wit Milano."

PatG watches, as if Vito has the winning numbers for tonight's lotto that PatG has tickets for.

"Italy speaks hundreds of a dialects. We have a different foods. It's a quilted fabric made of five hundred pieces. Dere's no other place like it in de world."

Nicola walks up to the trio. He looks at each—PatG, Vito, and then Danny. "My mother invited you to eat with us today."

Danny's shocked. "What about your father?"

Nicola shrugs his shoulders.

"Ma tuo padre può uccidere questo. (But your father will kill him)," PatG says.

Nicola ignores him and waves to Danny. "Come on."

"Where are we going?" Danny asks.

"To pay respect to your family."

Danny, Vito, PatG, and Nicola drive through the town's tiny streets and arrive at a long, grayish-white wall that looks to be about ten feet tall. They get out of the car and walk to the cemetery's entrance. A fifteen-foot-tall crucifix stands just past the gates in the center of a walkway. They enter.

Danny and PatG look over the grounds. Nicola leads the way. Each of the tombs are enshrined in walls that are ten feet tall. Pictures of the deceased are on the front of each tomb, along with their dates of birth and death. Some also feature poems or phrases.

PatG stops. "Danny, listen to this. This is the end of the poem from the great Totò, Antonio De Curtis."

A king, a magistrate, a great man,
on entering this gate comes to the conclusion
that he has lost everything, life and even title:
haven't you yet reached this reckoning?

So, listen to me . . . don't be obstinate,
put up with my proximity . . . what do you care?
only the living indulge in these buffooneries:
we are serious here . . . we belong to Death!

PatG laughs. "My mother loves this poem—'*A Livella,*' 'We're All the Same When We Die.' It's about a wealthy man objecting that a garbage man is buried next to him."

Vito nods. They walk another twenty feet and Nicola points to a tomb; it reads "CIANCIA LEONARDO, 1913-2014." There is a bouquet of flowers laying on the tomb's ledge. Nicola kisses the photo.

"This is Grandfather and his parents."

Danny looks up at the tombs beside Leonardo's.

"Come this way," Nicola says.

They walk about twenty yards further and Nicola points to a tombstone on the wall.

"That's Zio Michele. He was crazy. One day, his donkey kicked him. He punched it in the head. It died."

Nicola keeps walking and points to the next stone. "This is his wife. She hit him over the head with a pot and told him to go with his donkey, but he did not die—he lived another thirty years."

Nicola continues to walk, then stops and points at another photo. "This is our cousin Giovanni. He died when he was seven." Nicola rubs his hand over the laminated photo of the boy and then kisses the picture.

He points to a picture of a woman next to the tomb of Giovanni. "This is his mother. She killed herself over the pain."

"She's beautiful," Danny says.

The office rings at Danny's office in Pittsburgh.

Ma jumps. "I'll get it, it's Danny."

She picks up the phone and Irene gets as close as she can to the earpiece without rubbing against Ma's head.

"Danny! Danny!"

"Hello, ma'am. Is this Hubble Insurance? I need a quote."

Ma passes the phone to Irene without looking at her and walks out the door. A few minutes later, Irene sits next to Ma in a booth at Rui's.

"He called a few days ago, Bridget."

"Yes, but he didn't say anything."

"That's not true. You told me that he said not to worry and to tell Marla that he would write to her."

"Does that seem like anything?"

"Well . . ." Rui arrives with a pot of coffee.

"Chili, girls?"

Ma and Irene are sharing the pain of loss and have found some solace in each other's company. That's not to say that Ma doesn't want to strangle Irene from time to time.

Irene and Ma are at Mass in Saint Alcuin Church. The pews are sparsely littered with other faithful of the hill.

Irene whispers, "I always feel good after Mass."

Ma whispers back, "Nothing can make me feel good except my Danny coming home."

The priest, Father Kurt, descends from the altar, genuflects, and heads down the aisle. He stops at Ma and Irene's pew. "Girls, do we have any news from our Danny? We're all praying for him."

Ma is silent. Irene looks at Ma. "He says not to worry, Father, and to tell Marla—"

Ma interrupts Irene. "Father, he's fine. He says not to worry and that he'll be home soon."

"Great news, Ma." Father Kurt squeezes Ma's arm. "Hang in there." He smiles and then looks at Irene. "Both of you," he adds.

PatG and Danny are in their tiny bedroom. PatG's tying Danny's tie.

"I feel like I'm going to my first communion . . ." Danny takes a long pause and then looks at PatG. ". . . to be assassinated."

"It'll be okay."

"Where will you eat?" Danny asks PatG. "Mamma's by Vito's today."

"Yeah, I know. He wanted me to come too, but I'd rather stay here. Don't worry though—enjoy yourself."

"Enjoy my own hanging?" Danny says.

They hear a horn.

"Vito's here. . . . How do you feel?" PatG asks.

"I feel okay."

"Bring the oxygen just in case?"

"No. I don't want them to pity me."

Mamma, PatG, and Danny are all piled into Vito's car. After a short drive, they pull up in front of the Ciancia home. Danny, Vito, and PatG get out.

Vito kisses Danny and wipes under Danny's left eye with his handkerchief. Danny turns to walk toward the house.

"Wait a minute, Danny." PatG runs to Danny, kisses him on both cheeks, and then hugs him. "Be calm—everything will be all right—and, remember, if you get run out of town, make it look like you're leading a parade," he whispers in Danny's ear.

Danny squeezes PatG.

"*Ti voglio bene, PatG.* (I love you, PatG.)"

"*Ti voglio bene anch'io, Danny.* (I love you too, Danny.)"

PatG and Vito get back into the car. They drive to Vito's home in Santeramo. Mamma gets out of the back seat and walks up the stairs. Vito hands PatG the car keys.

"You sure you-a wanna to do deese?"

PatG smiles and nods.

"Dere could be trouble."

PatG rolls his eyes.

"You know de street?"

PatG nods and smiles again.

"Don'a smile. It's not funny."

PatG nods.

"You eat al L'Aragosta; dey wait."

PatG remains quiet.

"You no gonna say not'ing?"

"*Grazie.*"

Irene and Ma are walking out of St. Alcuin's church when Irene turns to Ma. "Bridget, do you feel better?"

"I feel . . ." Ma does not finish her sentence.

"There's Kevin," Irene points up the street. "Kevin's looking a bit wobbly."

"Kevin!" Ma yells.

Kevin turns and walks to meet them.

"Going out for the day, Kevin?" Ma asks.

"No, I'm coming home from the night." Kevin reverently takes his hat off and presses it against his chest. "Ladies."

"We went to church," Irene says.

"Oh, and what did you do there?"

Irene hesitates. "Why, *we prayed.*"

"For who?" Kevin asks.

"Why, we prayed for everyone. Didn't we, Bridget?"

"Did you pray for me?"

Irene looks at Bridget. "We prayed for all of Danny's friends."

"Well stop it! Last time someone prayed for me, I broke a leg." Kevin tilts his hat and smiles. "Top o' the morning to yous."

PatG drives back toward Altamura. He arrives at the outskirts of town, parks, and after ten minutes, he sees Francesca walking toward the car.

Danny knocks on the Ciancias' door. It opens almost immediately. Nicola smiles and hugs Danny. "Come in," he says.

Franca and her two daughters respectfully nod to Danny. Nicola sits him at the table. Danny's happy about that—he doesn't feel so hot. The women continue preparing the meal.

Nicola pats Danny's hand. "He'll be home soon."

Danny nervously rolls his watchband.

Francesca rests her head on PatG's shoulder. PatG is singing, "*And I love that girl, yes I love that girl and someday she'll be mine!*"

Francesca looks at him and smiles. They are cruising along the Adriatic coast. The scuba blue of the sea is as deep as the brown in Francesca's eyes.

After another fifteen minutes, they pull off the road and into the parking lot of L'Aragosta Ristorante. The valet and the owner are expecting them. The valet takes the car, and the owner escorts PatG and Francesca into the restaurant.

"This is *PatG* de American singer," the owner announces as they enter. Everyone in the restaurant looks as they walk to the veranda.

"The best people eat here, Mr. G." The owner pulls out a chair for Francesca and then another for PatG. "Mr. G, you must sing for us. We gotta de accordion player."

PatG smiles and nods. Their host walks away quickly.

"*Io sono nervoso per Danny* (I am nervous for Danny)," PatG says.

Francesca pats his hand and smiles. "*Non ti preocuparti.* (Don't worry.)"

A waiter arrives. "Mr. G, you wanna de wine?"

"Si."

The waiter hands PatG a wine menu.

"*Patrizio, prendi bianco per il pesce.* (Patrick, get white for the fish.)" Francesca says.

"*Va bene, e per noi?* (Okay, and for us?)"

The waiter smiles; Francesca laughs.

"I'll bring you a nice Locorotondo," the waiter says.

PatG nods and winks.

Ma and Irene are walking. "Without a transplant, Danny dies," Ma says.

"I know," Irene answers.

"It's a lost cause," Ma adds.

"They're the only ones worth fighting for, Bridget."

Danny is fidgeting. The women are still preparing the meal, and Mimmo is still not home.

The accordion player's a serious, chubby boy. He steps onto the veranda. PatG begins singing, "*Penso che un sogno così non ritorni mai più. Mi dipingevo le mani e la faccia di blu . . . Volare ooh oooh cantare oh, oh . . .*"

PatG stops and walks over to Francesca. "*Fammi mangiare con quella che amo.* (Let me eat with the one I love.)"

The patrons clap. A man stands and toasts. "*All'Americano.* (To the American.)"

Franca and her daughters begin putting the food on the table. Nicola stands and introduces his sisters. "This is Maria; she's almost thirty." Maria bows her head. Nicola continues, "This is Anna; she's twenty-four years old." Danny smiles, and Anna bows her head as well. Neither of the sisters are wearing makeup. They have their mother's natural beauty and the confidence that inner splendor brings to its host.

Noise from an opening door filters into the room, and the house falls into a frightening silence. Antonio, the oldest Ciancia brother, walks in. He looks into the dining room and yells at his mother.

"That's Antonio. He's the rooster." Nicola makes like a rooster with his arms. His sisters laugh.

Antonio walks in and notices that he's being mocked. "*Non sarà da ridere per Papà!* (It will not be funny to Father!)" He looks at Danny. They both smile tightly then turn. The kitchen opens again. Everyone runs to their seats.

Back at L'Aragosta, PatG looks in Francesca's eyes. "I'd like to move here. *Stare qua.*"

"*America é grande e ricco. Italia é piccolo e povero.* (America is big and rich. Italy is small and poor)," Francesca says.

"*Vuoi stare cumme?* (Would you like to be with me?)"

"*Ho rischiato grande venendo con te oggi. Certo, certo mi piacerebbe stare con te.* (I took a big risk coming with you today. Of course, I would like to be with you)."

Mimmo walks into the dining room, looks at the unwanted visitor, and yells and screams at his wife. Mimmo's communication, though in a language that Danny does not understand, is clear. This man does not want Danny at his dinner table or in his house.

Everyone remains still as Mimmo and Franca converse toe-to-toe, nose-to-nose. Danny's stomach is doing cartwheels. He doesn't want to be here, or even live any longer. He doesn't have the courage to leave, and he certainly wouldn't have the courage to end his life.

Danny stares at the table cloth. He fosters the nerve and attempts to rise.

Nicola grabs his hand under the table, holding him down. "She will take care of him, don't worry," he whispers to Danny.

Mimmo begins ranting. He is not speaking in Italian but in an incomprehensible dialect, a language as hard as the days of ancient times. Danny can feel the harshness and the fury in his biological father's voice and words. No one but Franca has the courage to look at Mimmo's face.

"*Questi sono i miei figli! Questa e la mia famiglia!* (These are my children! This is my family!)" Mimmo passes his open hand in front of his kids, bringing it down quickly and slamming it on the table.

His hardened palm hits the wood like a sledgehammer. Plates move; glasses spill; the girls jump and cry in terror. It was his final maneuver. The eye of the storm had passed. Then, just as suddenly, a silent calm is escorted in by Franca. Her voice has all the impact of a cure for a child's fatal disease. "*Mangiamo,*" she gently says.

Without looking for storm damage, Franca eloquently sits down at the table—the queen of the universe, the empress of herself, and the sovereign of her family.

Mimmo looks at the wall and down at his wife sternly. She soothingly turns to him and takes his hand. Softly she says, "*Mangiamo?*"

Her husband stares forward at the space between him and eternity. He is not in control. The tips of his maiden's fingers push ever so lightly against his skin, and his body obeys. He sits.

Nicola begins the prayer. Everyone bows their heads. "*Caro Gesù, benedici questo cibo . . . e aiuta tutti malati della nostra famiglia. Amen.* (Dear Jesus, bless this food . . . and help the sick and all our family. Amen.)"

Mimmo raises his head slightly. His eyes look, but they do not see as he focuses on Anna, Maria, Antonio, Nicola, and, finally, Danny. His mouth begins to make sounds but they are unintelligible. His mind does not accompany his movements.

Danny is beginning to feel weak. He would gladly give his soul to not be here. "I don't want to make problems," he says softly.

"Shh." Nicola nods his head in deference to and in the direction of his mother.

Franca looks at the oval table. She is addressing the most important gathering of her life.

"*Questo uomo potrebbe essere il sangue dei miei figli, il sangue del mio sangue.* (This man may be the blood of my children and the blood of my blood.)" She pauses and a yellow butterfly lands on the bread. Everyone looks at its majesty. The stark silence amplifies the sound of its beating wings.

"*Siamo Cattolici,*" she continues, "*Non mandiamo via stranieri che servono aiuto, figurati un uomo che potrebbe essere uno dei nostri.* (We are a family of Catholics. We do not turn away strangers, let alone turn away a man who could be one of our very own)."

Mimmo is drowning in confusion. Shame morphs into feelings of incompetence. His eyes are focused on the yellow butterfly as it takes flight. *"Mangiamo,"* he says softly, *"mangiamo."*

Nicola whispers to Danny, "My father wants to eat, not talk."

Franca rises to serve the pasta. She fills Mimmo's plate and then Danny's.

Nicola continues to whisper into Danny's ear. "My mother served you after my father; this says that you're not a guest. She served you before the rooster. This says that you're the oldest brother."

Nicola looks around the table. The family starts to eat.

"Why do you have the electric chair and capital punishment in America?" Maria asks in excellent English.

Danny hesitates and glances at everyone before responding. "To stop the killing."

"You kill people to stop killing?" Nicola asks.

Danny shrugs. "I think that's the reasoning behind it."

"Like Iraq and Vietnam," the Rooster adds.

"Do you like Rihanna?" asks Anna.

Danny's face twists. "I could take her or leave her, I guess."

Franca speaks to Nicola who turns to Danny. "My mother wants to know when you go home."

"*Martedì*—Tuesday," Danny says and smiles. Franca smiles back.

Mimmo's head is buried in his plate of pasta.

Franca again speaks to Nicola. "My mother wants to know when you come back?"

"Tell your mother that I hope to live long enough to come back."

Nicola turns to her and explains a bit about Danny's life. Everyone begins jabbering. The conversation swells, sounding like a beehive.

"Danny, tell us about your sickness, your disease," Anna says.

"I have leukemia."

Anna concentrates on Danny's face but it's all that she can do to focus on the incredible words that flowed from his mouth. "But you have to do something so you live."

"I need a bone marrow transplant."

"My mother says that you are our brother. Is this true?"

Danny cautiously observes Mimmo's expression; his biological father's gaze assaults him like an intense, overshadowing cloud.

"I don't know. I don't know." Danny is confused and feels as if he will pass out. "Nicola, can you take me home?"

"It will be okay, Danny. Try to eat something."

"I don't feel well. I'm going to collapse."

"*Danny deve andare.* (Danny must leave)," Nicola says.

Mimmo's face betrays his concern for the stranger. He reaches for strength and finds an obvious stance. "*Nessuno parte fin quando non avremo finito.* (No one leaves until we're finished)," he blurts out.

Franca will not overplay her hand. The gains have been too significant to jeopardize them by throwing them to the wind. She lifts her gaze to her husband's face and then she looks away submissively, communicating to Nicola with her eyes.

"Danny, it's offensive to leave before we're finished eating."

"Tell your father that I will leave when I please."

Danny stands; so does Mimmo. The room bursts into a flaming, uncontrollable opera as the whole family begins to sing out.

Mimmo moves toward the door, and Danny stares into his eyes. The weakness that he felt moments ago has disappeared, along with any fear that he's ever felt of living or dying.

Danny opens the door and leaves.

Chapter 11

It's a Family Affair

PatG and Francesca drive Vito's car down the winding, ageless roads from Santo Spirito to Altamura. It's easily 95 degrees in the car. The balmy breeze drifts in from outside and the warmth is invigorating to the lovers and their love.

"*Amiamo, ma abbiamo paura di perdere.* (We love, but we're afraid to lose)." PatG says. He looks at Francesca. "*Dimmi qualcosa d'amore.* (Tell me something about love)."

"*Sei meriti amore, ti fa trovare la strada.* (If love finds you worthy, it will direct its own course)," Francesca replies.

PatG slows the car. "*La benzina é finite.* (We're out of gas)."

Francesca looks mischievously at her driver, who has drops of sweat beading down his chest.

"No, Patrizio, non é possibile."

PatG veers off the empty road and the car rolls to a stop under the shade of an olive tree. He turns to Francesca.

"*Dov'é la stazione di servizio più vicino?* (Where is the nearest gas station?)"

Francesca cups her hands and places them to her mouth. "*Oh mio Dio.* (Oh my God)."

"*Forse ha lui un po' di colpo.* (Maybe God is a bit to blame)," PatG says smiling. "*Ha messa donne belle e semplice come te sulla terra per stregarci.* (He put women, pretty and good like you, on the earth to cast spells on us.)"

PatG starts the car. Francesca is confused.

"*Benzina?* (I thought we were out of gas?)"

"*Abbiamo tanto.* (We have plenty.)"

"*Triste, perché ti amo.* (That's sad because I love you.)"

PatG smiles and moves the car back off the road.

Danny's walking slowly in the direction of home.

Back in the Ciancia household, Nicola tries to leave, but his father grabs him. Nicola breaks his father's hold and exits. When Mimmo attempts to follow, he is blocked by Franca and his daughters.

Mimmo looks at them and spits on the floor. "*Sulla tomba della mia madre avrò niente da fare con quel uomo!* (On my mother's grave, I will have nothing to do with that man!)"

Across town in a large villa, Vito's sitting with Don Antonio.

"*Don Antonio,*" Vito says, "*É una situazione pazzo. Ciancia é stato diportato. C'é l'odio per la vita che voleva fare.* (It's a crazy situation. Ciancia was deported. He is angry about the life he wanted in America.)"

Don Antonio's wife arrives with *caffé* and cookies on a silver tray. "*Ha una famiglia e una bella vita.* (He has a good life and family)," he says.

"*Don Antonio, amico, l'uomo é insaziabile.* (Don Antonio, my friend, men are never satisfied.)"

Don Antonio nods in agreement.

"*Don Antonio, puoi provare un'altra volta?* (Can you try to help again?)"

"*Si. Provo.* (Yes. I will try.)"

Vito stands up, takes Don Antonio's hand in his own, and bows his head. "*Grazie, Don Antonio.*"

Vito's almost to the door when Don Antonio calls out to him.

"*Amico! Il mio potere é limitato quando l'uomo non é ragionevole.* (Friend! My power is limited when a man is irrational)," Don Antonio says. He smiles, and Vito nods. "*Ci sono pochi scelti con un testardo. E poi si distrugge la speranza.* (The way to deal with a hard head would destroy all hope.)"

"*Grazie, Don Antonio,*" Vito says, pretending not to understand the Don's inference.

Vito quietly shuts the door and Don Antonio tells his wife to get dinner on the table.

His wife nods from the kitchen. "*Si, capo.* (Yes, boss)," she says satirically.

Nicola races down the stairs and heads down the road toward Vito's home; at the same time, PatG's heading up the street in Vito's car. Nicola and PatG see Danny's body lying on the street simultaneously. Nicola hurries toward him, and PatG swerves to a stop by Danny's body.

"Danny!" PatG screams.

"Danny!" Nicola cries.

Danny's body remains lifeless. His skin is white and chalky.

PatG puts his ear next to Danny's nose. "He's breathing, slightly," he says.

They put Danny into the car, and Nicola calls Doctor Loreto and Vito. Doctor Loreto arrives at the hospital at almost the same time as they do. A male nurse rushes out to meet them with a rolling cot. With not the most efficient demonstration of technique, they get Danny out of the car and onto the bed. They dash into the emergency room, and Doctor Loreto gives Danny oxygen.

Danny's eyes open slightly. Nicola and PatG both smile. Vito pats his hand.

"My son. You're not in good shape. This is a small-town hospital," Doctor Loreto says.

Danny's eyes open a little more.

"I have a coosin; he's a doctor in Rome," Loreto continues.

"How did I know he was going to say that?" Danny asks slowly.

Doctor Loreto looks at Vito. "Did you talk to Don Antonio?"

"Yes, I spoke with him."

"What did he say?"

"Well, he said that he cannot force a man in family affairs. But he will try again."

Doctor Loreto looks at Nicola. "Nicola, and you, can you convince your papà?"

Nicola frowns. "My brother and sisters and I will take the exam."

"And your father?"

Nicola makes a pistol of his right hand and twists it.

"Will Papà even allow you to take the exam?"

"No one can stop us."

The door to the emergency room bursts open. Maria and Anna enter. Anna kneels next to Danny. She cries and kisses his hand.

"You take de plane Tues-a-day. I call my coosin *a Roma*, see what he says and I come later . . . You're in good hands," Doctor Loreto says.

"Doc," Danny says.

The doctor does not hear him.

"Doc!" Danny screams.

Loreto returns to Danny's bed.

Danny stares at the doctor. He knows that all eyes are on him. He pauses and then grasps the last bit of courage from within. "What if I don't make it until Tuesday; what will happen then?"

The doctor looks slowly to the side and one by one, studies the faces of the crowd. Each of them is looking at him lovingly, hoping that he has the power to say the secret words that will make Danny heal. They continue to stare at the doctor. Loreto's face transforms into a mask of harsh truth.

Slowly, one by one, they return his judgment with contempt and scorn. It was in moments like these that he hated the decision he had made, not to become a stone worker as his father and his father's father had been.

"You must die at home," he says.

Danny waves to the doctor, beckoning him closer. The doctor puts his ear next to Danny's mouth and listens. He has heard Danny's words and understands them. The doctor stands straight up, looking all around Danny's face, everywhere but into his eyes. Danny takes Loreto's hand and tugs. Loreto is forced to return Danny's gaze. Loreto nods.

"Promise?" Danny asks. His voice has regained strength, the strength that comes with conviction.

The doctor looks at him, purses his lips, and nods again.

The crowd jumps as Loreto booms, "I call my coosin at Bari so you all can takea de test Monday morning."

"America is the land of the dollar. Italy is the land of the coosin," Danny says.

Loreto smiles. "No one can eat the night before or the morning of the exams." Anna and Maria nod their heads as a sign of their grave endorsement. The doctor walks out.

Danny looks at Nicola. "I'm so sorry," he says.

"For what? We are sorry. If we had known, we would have found you." Nicola hesitates and rubs Danny's head. "It is right that our family is together."

There's a soft yet firm knock. Maria opens the door. Francesca walks in holding a tray.

"My Nonno say-a drinka dis, Danny. It-a help you *respirare*," Francesca says.

Danny removes the mask and sips. "What is it?"

"*La menta calda.* (Hot mint.)"

Danny nods, takes another sip, and smiles.

It's Friday morning in Hubble Insurance's office in Pittsburgh. Ma's reading a magazine. Irene's filing papers, envelopes, and folders when Marla enters unannounced.

"Hi Marla," Irene says.

"News?" Marla asks.

"He called and talked for a moment." Irene looks in Ma's direction.

"Hello, Mrs. Hubble," Marla says.

Ma ignores her.

"Do you have a number for him?" Marla asks.

"The number we have doesn't work," Irene says.

"Where is it?"

Irene hands Marla the paper.

Danny is sleeping in a hospital room. Nicola is sleeping under Danny's bed, while PatG is sleeping next to Danny in a very uncomfortable-looking chair. Traces of light sneak between the light-green wooden shutters and fall onto Danny's zebra-striped face. A tear rolls down past his temple and falls gently under his earlobe, never to return.

Seemingly, the sound of the pattering tears wakes PatG, who gazes at the man he loves more than he has ever loved anyone. He notices the shiny wet streaks and remains still, but not unmoved. How will he face life without Danny?

PatG has never amounted to much—of a mechanic, singer, son, or friend. But Danny was always there to solemnly listen to the voice that made others cringe and heed the stories that made others laugh snidely. He waited patiently when PatG didn't show up for appointments, watched in silent comprehension when PatG brooded. And Danny was right. PatG did fall in love every week, but Danny never spoke a cross word or made even one uncharitable gesture.

Out of respect for his buddy, PatG remains quiet. Tears do not come from eternal wells and respect should be paid to tears that pass uncloaked.

Some wise men try to impart that we can judge by not judging, cry by not crying, and love by not loving, but complexity in all of its simplicity reigns in the soul of PatG tonight. He sees how Danny's breaths express a solemn, measureless worth and each of Danny's tears embodies a sea in a drop of holy water.

PatG doesn't sleep much the rest of the night, and at seven a.m., he is shaken from his half-state of unconsciousness. Two women in white smocks roll a portable kitchen into the room, prompting Nicola to stick his head out from under the bed. The workers offer everyone coffee and milk, cookies, and bread.

The three men pick and sip at the food and drink, but three sparrows would have eaten more. At about seven fifteen a.m., Maria and Anna walk in with fresh homemade rolls, pears and apples, and a short stout of *caffè*. The aroma of the brown-black potion could have entranced a god.

Maria puts a large cloth napkin around Danny's neck. He feigns resistance and happily loses.

"Today, we will bring you back home, to Vito's mother's house. No one should be in a hospital if they don't need to be," Maria says.

And, sure enough, they brought Danny back to Mamma's.

That evening, Mamma's kitchen is full of the laughter of Maria, Anna, and Vito's mother. Anna's leaning with her hand on Danny's head. He's looking up at her from the corner of his eyes.

PatG walks in and smiles upon seeing Anna's position. "How we doing, partner?"

"Good . . . Better," Danny responds.

"Wanna take a walk? It's beautiful out," PatG says.

Maria looks sternly at PatG. "No, he's a not well."

"No, look, I wanna get some air," Danny says.

"Danny," Maria says, her facial expression reminding Danny of her mother.

"Please. I'll be right back; I promise," Danny says.

"What, are you guys his sisters or something?" PatG chides.

Maria and Anna kiss everyone goodbye and are off on their way. Mamma begins to wash cups and dishes.

"PatG, PatG. Hurry," Danny says.

"Feeling bad again?"

"Horrible. I gotta take a leak"

PatG smiles. "That would've been curious."

"If I'd have taken a leak while Anna and Maria were here, I wouldn't have to worry about my leukemia anymore."

"Why's that?"

"They'd have heard it all through that little window and I'd have died of embarrassment."

Danny gets out of the bathroom and he and PatG walk to the piazza. It's one thirty a.m. Families and their children are chattering, playing, and walking about as if it was noon in Central Park and as if they were living in paradise.

PatG and Danny sit near the bar.

"I'm gonna go home with you Tuesday, fix some things, and return," PatG says.

"You're what?"

"I'm going to come back here, just like you'll come back when one of your relatives is a match," PatG says.

"PatG, that's highly unlikely and if it happens, they can ship it. The way I feel . . . don't bank on me making any flights."

PatG stares.

"If you leave, PatG, do you really think you'll return?"

They're interrupted as Anna runs up to PatG and Danny. She's breathless. "Danny, I go back to look for you at Vito's Mamma. The phone rings. The woman speaks in English. Vito's Mamma cannot understand. I spoke to her. It's your lover on the phone."

Two elderly men stare.

"Danny, hurry, your lover from America."

The elderly men turn to each other. "*E la sua amante a telefono.* (His lover is on the phone)."

One of the patrons looks at Danny. "*Bravo, Danny. Bravo.*"

The other patron smiles and says, "*Forza, Ciancia.* (Go get her, Ciancia)."

The patrons make kissing sounds and the others standing and sitting around them laugh. A few men pat Danny's back and clap as he leaves.

Anna walks with Danny to Vito's mother's house. Danny enters and takes the antique gray phone in his hand.

Danny listens momentarily. "Ma, what's going on? Why did you say you were my lover?"

Ma's voice comes through the phone loudly, filling the room. "*I said no such thing. I said I was your mother.*"

Danny rubs his head, "Okay, I get it. Lover, mother."

"*Danny, come home. Irene says 'hello.' . . . And someone wants to talk to you. I'll put them on.*"

"Danny, it's Marla."

"Hi," Danny says.

"Danny, you never called. How are you? What are you doing?"

"Dying. What are you doing there?"

Marla looks at Bridget and Irene. They both turn away as Marla continues talking softly into the phone. "Danny, I miss you. I want you to come home. Whatever happens, we'll get through this together."

"Don't *do this*. Marla, *wake up*."

"But Danny, I need . . ."

Danny cuts her off. "Marla, give it up honey. I can't fill your needs." He hangs up the phone and hits the wall.

Marla runs out of Danny's house crying. Ma goes into the refrigerator and moves some jars and comes out with a pack of cigarettes.

"You promised Danny you wouldn't smoke, Bridget," Irene says.

"Yes, and he promised that everything would be fine. We're even."

"It's not his fault, Bridget."

Bridget looks sternly at Irene. "Okay, then whose fault is it?" She inhales and blows smoke in Irene's direction. "You and my husband both thought that I was so stupid."

"That's not true," Irene says emphatically.

"Well, what is true?"

"Bridget, we're family."

"I'm not Moo-slem."

Irene gazes at Ma. "I'm not a Moo-slem either but the two most important people in my life are the most important people in your life."

Danny's in his bed sleeping with oxygen. He doesn't know it, but Anna's sitting in the chair next to him. Facing the other way, he throws off the blankets and stands up in his bare chest and underwear. He puts his slippers on and turns right into Anna's smiling face.

"Oh, jeez," Danny says as he grabs his blanket and covers himself. "Oh, sorry. *Scusa, scusa, scusa.*"

Anna stands and then walks out of the room laughing.

Not long after, Doctor Loreto arrives and tests Danny's blood pressure. A cigarette is hanging from his mouth. "Danny, will you do me a favor?"

"Sure. I don't know what a bald, short, fat forty-seven-year-old dying of leukemia could do for anyone but, shoot."

Tears come to Doctor Loreto's eyes. "Calla your own doctor in America. I'm a family doctor. I'm *not* qualified."

Danny stares and takes a deep breath. His facial expression demonstrates his profound discomfort.

Loreto leans close to Danny's ear. "This could get ugly. I'm not the one to best handle this situation." He pulls away from Danny and smiles tightly.

"Doc, Americans die four years earlier than you Italians. The only thing they can offer a man like me is expensive brainwashing propaganda."

Loreto, somewhat confused, nods and purposely speaking loudly, says, "I'll leave you in the good care of your sister, Anna."

Anna smiles and enters the bedroom holding a tray of *caffé* and homemade cookies. "*Mangia,* Danny," she says.

Danny's voice is faint. "You know, a guy could get used to this." He smiles warmly at Anna, but his face is that of a man dying of leukemia and, seemingly, close to the end.

PatG and Vito are seated on a bench close to the house.

"Americans always bring change. Be careful witta that girl. Dose you leave behind pay for your sins," Vito says.

"What do you mean?"

"Francesca's family trusts me." Vito looks away briefly and then returns and stares into PatG's eyes. "What are your intentions?"

PatG looks at Vito earnestly. "Intentions? What if I told you that my intentions were serious?"

"Hopefully dat is the case. You must understand, if you leave-a de mess here, I'm responsible also. You use-a my car, my house. My family could pay dearly."

PatG is absorbing the weight of Vito's words. "Why did you help me?"

"I love Americans."

"It seems that all Italians do," PatG quips.

"You saved us in da war. Now I hope we can save ourselves from you—de television, de music, the junky food anda de fast life. Half of you don' even know what a man or woman is. De tings," Vito hesitates, "de tings dat have broken de American family and have made American people sick-a with diabetes, depression, bipolar, and all de otter diseases dat biological and social experimenting for dollars brings-a."

PatG focusses on Vito's words.

Vito continues, "Italians live longer and better den Americans. Our people complain because dey are spoiled and dey do not know da trut . . . dey do not want to know da trut because knowing de trut would eliminate da convenient alibis for dere failures."

"Don't worry about Italy becoming like America. It will never happen."

Vito nods. "I'm not soa sure. I hope dat you learn the trut before itsa too late—I am-a sorry and I hope dat I do not offend you. I do love-a Americans, but I do not love-a many American tings, de way your corruptorations control de government and make bully wars for greed, claiming virtue, all over the plant."

"Planet," PatG says.

Vito smiles thinly and continues. "Your Kardashian tv and 10,000 Starbuck-a bars owned by one-a company, your-a invasions, assassinations, torturing, backing of apartheid, overtrowing governments . . ."

PatG tries to smile. "But your youth, they're Italian."

Vito looks relieved. "Tell me, PatG American, what do you see in Italy?"

"I see culture, love, and commitment."

"And Danny. What does he see?"

"I don't know what Danny sees."

"The doctor wants him to leave."

"I don't know if Danny wants to leave." PatG looks into Vito's eyes. "Maria's taking him to school today."

"What is the life that Danny has to go home to?"

PatG gazes far away, seeing nothing in front of him. Vito stares at him and, after a few seconds, PatG snaps out of his stupor. His face wears a look of discomfort.

Chapter 12

The Roots of Italian Culture

Maria and Danny are walking toward Maria's school.

"I'm a bit nervous. What can I tell these kids?"

"Just tell them about your work; maybe they will ask questions about America. It will be fun. You will like it."

"Will they understand me?"

"Danny, they take a language from second grade on; they are now in fifth. Many listen to English music and watch English films. You speak some Italian, and I'm sure you can make them understand."

Maria opens the classroom door and stands in front of twenty-five ten- and eleven-year-old children. Danny is waiting outside, scanning the school hall; there is a Padre Pio statue at the end of it. He looks inside of Maria's classroom. A crucifix is at the center of the room above her desk. In the corner, close to the window, is a statue of the Blessed Mother with flowers laid at her feet.

Danny is lost in thoughts about church, state, morals, and laws. *In Saudi Arabia, the government cuts off heads to punish drug dealers and murderers; in the United States, the government murders convicted people in an electric chair or by poisoning. It seems strange that groups of individuals might war over the presence of a crucifix.*

He's utterly confused and woken from his stupor when he hears his name. "Danny! Come on in, *venne ca,*" Maria says.

The students laugh. Danny moseys in with his hat in his hand, looking more at his shoes than at anything else.

"*Danny é un agente del' assicurazione.* (Danny is an insurance man)."

Danny nods and bows nervously.

A student blurts out, "Be a good boy."

"Gennaro!" Maria scolds.

Danny raises his hand. "That's okay; that's okay."

Danny smiles at Gennaro and the rest of the class, and then begins speaking. "My name is Danny. I am from Fineview, part of Pittsburgh, Pennsylvania in the United States."

A girl raises her hand. Danny points to her and nods. She stands. "Is it cold in Pittsburgh?"

Danny rubs his palms together. "It can be very cold in the winter. We get lots of snow and temperatures hit minus 30, *meno trenta.*"

The class laughs.

"*Minus trenta . . .* My balls would freeze!"

"*Gennaro, continui e ti butto fuori.* (If you do not stop, I will throw you out of the class), Maria says."

"Yes, it is cold. *Freddo* in the winter, *ma inverno, primavera, estate ed autunno*— Danny says the seasons in Italian—all are beautiful. We have lots of forests, mountains, and skiing."

Another girl raises her hand. Danny nods, giving her permission to speak.

"How is the food?" she asks.

Danny thinks about Rui's chili and smiles.

"The food is interesting. Some of it is very good."

"What is your favorite food?" the same girl asks.

Danny is stumped. He has never thought about his favorite food or even if he had a favorite food. Ma is no gourmet, and in Pittsburgh, he ate fast food and take-out 50 percent of the time. "I don't have a favorite food; I like most everything."

He nods at the next student. "Why did America invade Iraq and Afghanistan?"

Danny is stumped again. "That is a tough question. I personally was not in favor." He realizes that the class is staring at him and thirsting for some sort of explanation. He clears his throat. "I'm not sure why we invaded Iraq and Afghanistan, and today, more than ever, the American people are against the decision to do so."

Gennaro raises his hand. Danny gestures for him to speak. "Why don't American presidents go to jail for invading their neighbor's country?"

Maria looks on intently. She is proud of her students' line of questioning.

"It is very difficult for the president of the United States to go to prison," Danny responds.

Gennaro and the rest of the class continue to stare at Danny, waiting for a better answer.

Danny realizes that he will not get off the hook so easily. "We have the strongest military in the world. The president is in charge of the military. Who would throw him in jail?" he asks.

Gennaro, who is still standing, raises his hand. Danny nods at him again.

"You are saying, Mr. Danny, that the United States is above the law."

Danny tugs his finger into the collar of his shirt. "I would not say that."

A girl raises her hand and Danny is only too happy to change the line of questioning. The girl stands. Maria points at Gennaro and lowers her hand. He sits down.

"Why is America so dangerous? You have a five times better chance of getting murdered there than in Italy, and a three times better chance of committing suicide, per capita."

"The United States is larger than Italy," Danny replies.

The girl smiles. "Per capita," she repeats.

"Yes, I don't know," Danny admits.

"Can I ask another question?"

Danny nods.

"In 1998, a U.S. Marine pilot, flying one hundred miles over the speed limit and six hundred feet below the minimum height for flying, cut a cable car line in Cavalese, Italy. Twenty skiers died. The pilot was shipped out of Italy and never came back. He was acquitted of any wrongdoing in the U.S."

Danny's pale face begins to color. Maria realizes that he's in over his head and has likely never heard of the Cavalese tragedy.

"Okay, okay, can we change the subject? Mr. Danny is not an expert in international law. He is an insurance man. Ask him about things that he would be more familiar with."

Another girl raises her hand and stands. "Mr. Danny, do you like Rihanna?"

Danny smiles; this is more like it. "She's all right. My favorite American performers are Boz Skaggs and Al Green." Danny catches himself and continues, "and PatG."

None of the students have ever heard Al Green or Boz Skaggs. A few have heard of PatG, who has been singing in the bars of Altamura with Tommaso, the accordion player.

A boy raises his hand. Danny recognizes him but doesn't know from where. Danny nods, and the boy stands. "I'm Francesca's cousin. I have heard PatG sing. I like it. I like it when he sings in Italian—his accent is funny. Do you think he loves my cousin?"

Maria covers her smile. Danny looks toward her, but she refuses to throw him a rescue line. Danny clears his throat. "Your cousin is a very nice woman. I think that PatG likes her very much."

The boy interrupts Danny. "My father says that if PatG's not respectful, he will break his leg caps."

"Massimo!" Maria yells.

Massimo turns red. "*Scusa.* I mean kneecaps."

Danny smiles and wants to liberate Massimo from Maria's wrath. "That's all right, Massimo," he reassures him. "PatG has heard similar things many times in his life."

Massimo stares at Maria with a "how do you like them apples?" expression. Maria signals for him to be seated by lowering her hand.

Danny is starting to feel a bit odd, and he winks at Maria and points to the door. "*Con permesso?* (With your permission, I will leave).

Maria nods. *"Bravo, Danny, bravo,"* she says and looks at the class. *"É vero, classe?"*

The class yells, *"Bravo!"* and they applaud as Danny bows slightly and walks out. Maria follows him. They stop in the hallway.

"Do you like the school, Danny?"

"Very much. I was surprised by their questions."

"Yes, times have changed. . . . To my generation, the United States was the nation of big shoulders. But these kids have the internet and can get news online. They see the poverty in the United States, the healthcare situation, and the crime. . . ."

"Where will you go now, Danny?"

"I'm going to find PatG."

Maria kisses him on the cheek and takes his hands in hers. *"Grazie fratello.* (Thanks, brother.)"

Danny smiles and turns away. He exits the school and heads to the bar. On the way, Danny sees a group of guys in their late teens, maybe early twenties, kicking a soccer ball around. Francesca spots Danny as he enters the bar. She smiles and points to the piazza.

Danny walks back out of the bar and takes a closer look at his surroundings—one of the guys playing soccer is PatG. Danny remembers that PatG played soccer when they were younger—Danny always thought it was a boring sport, but now he's amazed and impressed. Not only does PatG fit right in, but he looks to be a valid recruit.

Danny walks closer to the group and PatG spots him.

"Where have you been?" PatG asks.

"You know where I have been. I told you that I was talking to Maria's class."

"Vito is coming."

"Why?"

"We're going to eat by the sea."

"Okay," Danny says, "but I want to bring my oxygen."

"Let's head to Mamma's. Vito will pick us up there," PatG responds.

Danny and PatG walk into Mamma's always-unlocked house. Mamma smiles.

"Mangiamo fuore con Vito, Mamma. (We will eat out with Vito today)," PatG says.

Mamma smiles again and nods. Danny grabs his oxygen and PatG changes his shirt. Vito walks in, smiling as usual. The three get into the car and travel through the towns of San Giorgio, Mola di Bari, and Cozze. Finally, they enter the town of Polignano Al Mare. Vito pulls into the road that hugs the ancient town and the surrounding sea.

A man waves to the car, and Vito parks. They exit the car and Vito puts a two-Euro coin into the man's hand. The valet nods, Vito nods, and the world is at peace.

They walk into Hotel Ristorante Grotta Palazzese. Vito seems to know his way— they pass two men at the reception desk and walk through two white swinging doors.

On the other side is the most beautiful site that PatG and Danny have ever seen. They are suspended in air, on a floor that is inside of a grotto. The sea is in front and rushing under them to kiss the walls of the grotto seventy feet below.

Marco, the owner is dressed in a blue suit. He greets Vito and nods to PatG and Danny. "Vito, your table is right this way."

They follow Marco to a table overlooking the sea. Danny, PatG, and Vito go to the rail and look down. The water is clear and tinted emerald, along with that same scuba-blue. Below, they see the sea floor, crowded with coral and fish.

"There are no words," Danny says.

Vito nods.

"Hey, they're bringing food," PatG says. "I'm starved."

The trio walk eloquently to their table, where they discover an assortment of raw and cooked fish. They sit down as their waiter arrives.

"Vino?"

"La Verdeca di Gravina," Vito says.

"Bene," nods the waiter.

PatG picks up a spongy, brown shellfish. "What are these called?"

"Tartufi," Vito responds.

PatG dips bread into the *tartufo's* soft shell. He bites into it and looks at Vito. "Interesting. I don't know if I like it, but it's definitely interesting."

Danny dips bread into a *tartufo*. He raises it to his lips and then pushes it into his mouth, chewing slowly. "I like it. I've never tasted anything like it, but I like it. "

"Vito, why do you think the food tastes so different here? We import Italian oil and wines and stuff," PatG says.

"Da apple is best eaten under da tree. Shipped 5,000 kilometers, it can never taste-a de same."

"That's another reason for me to move here." PatG remarks, smirking.

"I suppose that the biggest motivation is a certain girl named Francesca," Danny adds.

"That, and I don't want Vito's life on my conscience." PatG quips.

"How honorable," Danny says. He takes a long swallow of the Verdeca. "Oh my God, this is incredible—fruity and sweet, yet light."

They refill their glasses.

"Follow your heart; I take care of myself." Vito pauses. "It is also hard for me to believe that you would ever leave America."

PatG stares out at the sea. "Sometimes I feel like America's left me."

After fifteen minutes of silence and light conversation, Vito waves for the waiter to bring another bottle of wine.

"Vito, are Italians patriotic?" Danny asks.

Vito shrugs his shoulders.

"Vito, what's patriotism mean to you?" PatG asks.

"Disliking all countries except-a your own," Vito responds.

The restaurant begins to fill up. Danny, PatG, and Vito are feeling the effects of the Verdeca.

Marco approaches the table. "Vito, the guitar and accordion player are here. You promised that PatG would sing," he says.

PatG looks at Vito. Vito nods and smiles at PatG. "If you do move-a here, I'll be your agent," Vito says.

The men laugh, Marco waves the musicians over, and PatG stands.

"My life, I'd give for you, anema e core
I only live for you, anema e core
I have but one desire, and it's to love you
With all my heart, with all my soul, my whole life through

From stars, I'll make your crown and kneel before you
I pray you'll take my hand, for I adore you
Open up the doors leading to heaven
A heaven mine and yours, anema e core"

The tables erupt in applause as PatG continues to sing. The patrons are spellbound by his voice. Vito looks over at Danny in his oxygen mask, but Danny is staring at and listening to his friend, the only real partner he has ever had. PatG's voice gently echoes from the walls of the magic cavern over the sea. It's the most beautiful voice that Danny has ever heard.

PatG finishes and walks to his table. Many are trying to coax him into singing another song. "I don't want to ruin your dinners," PatG says as he smiles and sits down.

"The acoustics in this place are incredible. I've never sung like that before," PatG says to Danny and Vito.

Danny is still in a stupor. PatG looks at Vito. Vito nods and speaks. "We are different people in-a different places. You cannot-a compare how you sound-a or who you are-a here to any udder place."

Danny's oxygen tank does not go unnoticed, nor does PatG's affection for him and Vito's admiration for them. The three arrived as strangers and left with intimate respect, as treasured family members in the heart of each patron.

"This isn't the way to the car," Danny says.

Vito nods and points. "We're not going to the car."

PatG and Danny look at each other. PatG winks. Danny has little choice or will to do anything but shadow their host.

Dusk turns to dark and the trio are sitting with drinks in an apartment 200 meters from the place of their feast.

A beautiful woman in her forties enters. She rubs Vito's face.

"There'sa nottin' like an Italian woman. . . . Nottin'," Vito says.

"What are we doing here?" Danny asks. As soon as the question exits his mouth, he realizes why they are there and is confused as to why he asked.

"I'm come once a month for ten years," Vito says.

As he speaks, two dark skinned girls enter. They nod to the madam and walk nearer to the men.

"Questa é Antonella," the madam says.

Antonella leans forward gently and smiles.

"Chi lo vuole? (Who wants her?)" the madam asks.

Danny smiles at PatG and Vito.

"Danny, she's your woman. Love her wit all your heart," Vito says.

"Questa é Fillippa." Filippa kisses the three men on each cheek.

"Chi lo vuole?" the madam asks again.

"*Ci sono tutte e due per Danny.* (They're both for Danny)," PatG says.

Danny looks momentarily panicked.

"Danny, pretend you're back home," PatG says, "pretend you're in Las Vegas."

"I hate Las Vegas," Danny says.

Vito intervenes. "There is an old Italian saying, 'No man is a scoundrel, yet all men are scoundrels.' I believe that this also refers to women. Danny, tomorrow is not guaranteed for anyone. We are here now. Love them for all you are today, Danny,"

The woman prods the girls to Danny. Each of them takes an arm and pulls him through a dark oak door. Other women follow.

After more than an hour, PatG and Vito are back on the leather couch. A beautiful long-nosed vixen is sitting on Vito's lap with her arm around him. PatG and Vito are conversing calmly.

"Jesus's best friend was a prostituta. I know what de Church say, but its'a more important the actions of Cristo," Vito says.

"Yeah . . . but she repented," PatG says.

Vito pushes the woman off his lap, giving her his empty glass.

He turns to PatG. "For four million, nine hundred, and seventy-five tousand years, man was warrior and hunter. He was killed offa like de flies. He die very young and dere were many, many widows. Da woman, she outnumbered da man ten-a to one. He had two, three, four wives. Da stronger he was, de more wives he had."

PatG smiles. "Really . . . No. I mean I'm really enjoying the history lesson."

"Man was lion and da woman a lioness protecting her cubs, often from-a him. It isa true—life was-a preserved by da woman." Vito sails his pointed finger toward PatG.

"Twenty-five tousand years ago, woman learn agriculture."

"Why woman?"

"She was-a at home. She see sprout or something. Man selfish; man worry about fighting anda eating," Vito says.

PatG nods, "Okay, gotcha." He refocuses on Vito, the professor.

"About fifteen thousand years, she teacha de man how to grow tings. She domesticated da dog and da cat. Now she try to domesticate de man.

"This is good," PatG says.

"Good but not-a easy. He a wannna more women and he wanna young woman. It's-a his nature to sex an procreate and younger women do dat much more efficiently. It's-a natural for dem. Dis is all in man's DNA for five-a million years. In Italia, we say a lion always wanna fresh meat. Dat's why older lions still crave-a younger women."

PatG stares at him and then starts laughing. The madam walks in with fresh drinks.

"In America, you take-a three wives like a de Arab. You divorce and protect da individual. Or so you tink," Vito says.

PatG continues to laugh.

"In Italy, we try to protect-a da family. So de man, he gotta one wife. But he have-a de adventure. But he no breaka de family."

"You think that's right?"

"Look at de suicides of American children and de shooting in-a schools. Do you tink dat's right?"

"We're a strong, religious country," PatG says.

"You were macho chauvinists in de 1990s. Twenty years later, you're de country of de feminine male. You teach-a your children dat they have-a no sex. Priests molesting children is a sign dat your society is-a not well. You spread a de disease over da planet with-a your marketing and TV shows."

PatG raises his drink to his lips. "Unfortunately, you may have a point, Maestro, but fortunately, not all Americans are the same. The conservative movement will eventually change things to the way they should be."

Danny walks out of the dark oak door, arm in arm with the two ewes. Everyone gives the traditional kisses. PatG, Danny, and Vito exit.

The ride back to Altamura is quiet. Each man is in deep thought, maybe trying to sort reality, morality, and truth.

Danny, Vito, and PatG enter the bar. A few people greet them.

Francesca looks at PatG. He speaks to the others in a low voice. "Something's wrong. Did you see how she looked at me?"

"She knows," Vito says.

"What do you mean? It's impossible."

"Not for the Italian woman."

Danny laughs, slaps PatG on the back, and whispers in his ear, "Go get her, Valentino."

Vito hears the name Valentino and arrives bullet fast. "Did a you boys know dat Rudolfo Valentino came-a from Puglia?"

Chapter 13

The Test

Danny doesn't feel so hot, but it's Sunday morning and he promised Nicola that he would go with him to the eleven o'clock Mass. Danny looks at his cell phone: it's almost nine a.m. PatG is already gone, and Danny didn't hear him leave or come in, for that matter.

He wonders how things went with PatG and Francesca but he truly was not feeling good and he does not want to waste thoughts on things he has no control over. He puts on his shirt, pants, and slippers and goes into the kitchen, leaving his oxygen at his bedside. Mamma is psychic. She has the coffee brewing and Danny's plate set. Breakfast is the scrumptious, hard, thick-crusted wheat bread she makes, with berry preserves and fruit.

"PatG?" Danny asks.

"*Calcio* (soccer)," she replies.

Danny wants to get out to the piazza. He eats and then shaves. He is surprised that Nicola has not yet arrived. Danny walks out into the warm, golden sunshine. It is the first day of which he hopes, will be many that he will leave the oxygen tank at home.

Inside the church, Nicola, Maria, Anna, Franca, Danny, PatG, and Francesca are seated in the same pew. The priest raises the Eucharist; the family rises and holds hands during the "Our Father." Shortly after, they file down the aisle for communion.

"You leave the day after tomorrow," Nicola whispers.

"Yes, but I'll never leave here."

Later that afternoon, PatG's in the bar singing "Volare." As always, Danny's sitting near him, and is now wearing an oxygen mask. Francesca brings a cup of tea to his table and touches Danny's face.

"Hey, hey!" PatG waves a finger at Francesca. A few people laugh. PatG spots Francesca's grandfather looking and turns away. "Oops."

Back in Fineview, Irene is heading up the street, pushing a squeaky cart filled with clothes. Kevin is walking toward her.

"Hello Irene! Goin' to the laundromat?" Kevin asks.

"No."

"Oh . . . Honeymoon's over?"

"Danny comes home Tuesday."

"I see . . . Irene, do you know the two best words I never said?"

Irene's confused. This is her normal state when speaking to Kevin.

"No, Kevin, what are the two best words you never said?"

"I do."

Irene stares, trying to understand the riddle. Kevin has always been one big riddle to her—and to everyone on the Hill, except PatG and Danny.

Kevin bows. "And top of the mornin' to ya."

Irene continues on her way and Kevin heads up the street. No one notices the kick is missing out of Kevin's step, but he just hasn't been quite the same since his bosom buddies left. He has no one to speak to about it; Danny and PatG are the only two people on the Hill or in the world who understand him.

Danny walks out of the bar at ten p.m. He feels life's grasp loosening and knows that the end is near. Italy has shaken many of Danny's most concrete convictions, and death seems less traumatic now that he has experienced Altamura. He certainly doesn't want to die and hopes that a match will be found, but leaving will somehow be easier now that he knows the truth about what life is.

The following morning, Maria wakes up on the chair next to Danny's bed. She gently pushes his arm. "Danny, Danny."

Danny turns and smiles. "Today's the day."

"Yes, Danny, today is the day," Maria repeats.

Danny puts his hands together and shoos Maria away. "*Devo vestire.* (I must dress.)"

Maria looks at him with a soft, gentle face and speaks to him in the same voice. "You don't want help?"

"If you help, I would die."

Maria smiles and walks out.

Shortly after, Maria, Danny, and Vito's mother are seated silently in the kitchen. They hear a car horn. Danny looks at the old woman. She smiles and nods. Vito rises. Tears begin to roll down Mamma's cheeks. She rises too and grabs Danny. Maria stands and hugs the two of them.

"Go on, you two get out of-a here before we all start crying like a de babies," Vito says.

Maria and Danny get into the car. Mamma walks out of the house and watches the crammed vehicle pull away. She instinctively pulls out a handkerchief and begins following the car and waving the white cloth. "*Dio ti benedica!*" she cries, "*Dio ti benedica.*"

Antonio's driving and wearing a suit; Danny's in the passenger seat. Nicola—also wearing a suit—Franca, Anna, and Maria are cramped behind them in the tiny Fiat Uno. The car enters Bari and stops at a red light. A man cleans their car window. Antonio hands him some change. On Danny's side, a boy's selling packs of tissues. Danny gives him some change. Antonio looks over at Danny and smiles. "*Mangia e fa mangiare.* (Eat and help others eat)," he says. Danny nods and smiles back.

The car pulls up to the Policlinico di Bari: the hospital is dingy and unclean. They stop at the main gate, where Dottor Loreto is waiting in his vehicle. He winks at the guard and the guard raises the barrier.

The car slowly follows the doctor for about three hundred feet. Doctor Loreto points and Antonio maneuvers into a vacant parking space. The growing crowd walks up the stairs. At the door, is a tall sign that reads: *Primario, Professore Troccoli Giuseppe.* A man in a white smock opens the door, smiles and waves the Altamurani in.

They follow the white-smocked man up the inner stairs. The walls are beige and peeling. The word *"Genetica"* is written in blue on a large white sign next to two large doors at the landing.

The white-smocked man rings a bell. After less than five seconds, a female nurse opens the door and accompanies the pack into the hall. They walk several feet to Professor Troccoli's private office; Dottor Loreto enters alone and shakes Professor Troccoli's hand. The two colleagues briefly exchange greetings and Loreto exits. "Danny, you first," he says on his way out.

Danny enters. "Mr. Hubble, I am Giuseppe Troccoli." The doctor reaches his hand to Danny; Danny embraces it.

"Time is of the essence. We will ship the blood samples to Bologna. Excuse me if I do not explain, but I believe that you understand."

"Si, si, certo, Dottore," Danny says.

Danny leaves the room and, one by one, his four siblings enter. Five vials of blood are taken from each of them; Antonio is the last person to give samples. The nurse then puts the twenty-five vials into a refrigerated package.

Franca smiles broadly at her children and at Danny. Professore Troccoli and Doctor Loreto come into the hall. Professore Troccoli gazes at the group with a broad smile.

Chapter 14

Whispered Secrets and Demands

Doctor Loreto clears his throat and then chokes up with tears. He turns, fearing that his crying will become infectious.

Nicola notices Loreto's tears and hugs him. "I hope it's me," Nicola says. The festivities are interrupted by a knock on the hall door. A nurse opens the door slightly and after about twenty seconds, she quietly re-shuts the door and walks to the group.

"Professore c'e un altro Ciancia. Lo faccio entrare? (Professor, there's another Ciancia outside. Should I let him enter?)"

The doctor nods curiously. The nurse opens the door and Mimmo Ciancia, dressed in a suit, hat in hand, steps into the hall. The world stands still.

Mimmo is staring at his shoes and has the face of an ashamed ten-year-old as he walks toward the group. *"Professore Troccoli?"* he says without looking up.

"Si?" Dottor Troccoli says in the voice of a principal confronting a mischievous boy.

"Sono qua per fare l'esam per aiutare il mio figlio. (I'm here to take the test to help my son.)" Mimmo raises his head slightly and bows reverently.

"Bene, bene." The doctor shakes Mimmo's hand. *"Accomodati.* (Make yourself comfortable.)" He points Mimmo to the chair in his office, next to the table where the nurse had drawn the rest of the family's blood.

Mimmo moves toward the table and tries to sit, but he is tackled by his wife, Franca, then Maria, Anna, Nicola, and Antonio. *"Papà, amore, ti voglio bene. Grazie Gesù!* (Papa, dear, I love you. Thank you, Jesus!)" were some of the phrases Danny could make out. Translating the words of five blubbering Italians is difficult, but . . .

"Okay, we need to hurry to get this out. Everyone out, except the nurse, La Signora e Signor Ciancia," Professore Troccoli says.

The professor smiles tightly at Danny and then hugs him. *"Buona fortuna."*

"Grazie Professore," Danny says.

The professor looks at Danny and releases him. "Thanks is appreciated but unnecessary. If anything can be done, it'll be His doing." Doctor Troccoli points up to the wall behind Danny's head to an oil painting of Christ on the crucifix.

Doctor Loreto opens the door to the hall. Don Antonio's sitting on a bench outside.

"*Don Antonio, Don Antonio; bacio tua mano, Don Antonio.* (Don Antonio, I kiss your hand)," Dottor Loreto says. The two embrace.

It's Monday afternoon at the Ciancia residence. The dining room is packed, the table laden with various fruits. PatG, Francesca, Vito, and Dottor Loreto are present, as well as Danny and his family. Danny has oxygen tubes in his nose.

The doctor stands up with a glass of dark, almost black wine in his hands. "*Alla famiglia Ciancia.* (To the Ciancia family)." He hands the glass to Danny and, one by one, everyone at the table stands up with their wineglasses in hand. A tear runs down Danny's face. Soon, he is crying. His head falls to the table and he buries it in his arms.

"A toast to my dear friend, Danny. *Alla tua salute,*" PatG says.

The family touches each other's glasses and they all take turns touching Danny's glass, held out on the table by his extended arm.

Danny lifts his head. "Dottor Loreto, I think that I should get back. I'm not feeling great."

"Yes, Danny, and you have to be at the airport tomorrow morning so you not miss your flight."

Danny smiles at the doctor and embraces his family as each member rises to kiss and hug him, until only Mimmo is left. He bows his head and, with great effort, says, "Good-a bye, Danny. I gonna missa you."

The family applauds Mimmo's English and, slowly, Danny and Loreto make their way to the door.

In the car and halfway to Vito's house, Danny turns to Loreto. "I'm not leaving tomorrow."

"Danny, this is different; you're not making a choice to live here. You makea de choice to die here. This is not America."

"I'll wait on the results. If there's no compatibility, there's nothing for me in America."

"And your friend?" Danny smiles.

"PatG will do as he pleases. He always has," Danny says weakly. He reaches out to shake the doctor's hand. *"Grazie, Dottore."*

Their hands clasp.

A Month Later

Antonio is gripping Danny's hands and helping him out of a wheelchair. Danny's lips are closed tight in a smile. *"Vieni, ti porto a letto.* (Come, I'll bring you to bed),"* Antonio says.

Danny is now living in the Ciancia residence. PatG walks into Danny's bedroom and looks at the plastic-covered oxygen tent. On the tent is a sticker, "CIANCIA DANNY CAC DNL 76 S 24 Z 404 H."

PatG smiles. "What the hell is this?"

Danny's speech is weak and barely audible. "The ol' man raised hell at the hospital." He fights off laughter and continues almost in a whisper. "Antonio and Mimmo almost threw a guy out the window to get me government coverage. 'It's for my son!' he yelled. 'My son's entitled!'"

Danny tries to suppress another bout of laughter. "First the guy don't want to know me, then he wants to throw someone out of a window to help me."

"Italians are mysterious people," PatG says.

Danny nods. "We sure are."

"We should've asked Don Antonio to find you a donor."

"It's okay like this, PatG. It's okay." Danny hesitates and looks out of the window at the children playing on a balcony across the street. "It's a dream to check out this way."

Danny coughs. Almost immediately, the door opens. Maria and Anna enter. Danny raises his hand. *"Sto bene. Sto bene.* (I'm okay. I'm okay.)"

The two sisters leave.

"Your Italian's getting good."

Danny points to an Italian language book on his desk. "I'm studying. I write letters to my brothers and sisters and study Italian." Danny points to another book lying next to it. "Mimmo gave me a Bible, but I can't make heads or tails out of it."

PatG smiles.

"Live like you'll die tomorrow. Learn like you'll live forever," Danny says.

PatG takes his friend's hand. Danny nods and winks.

Chapter 15

Danny's Wish

It's Monday morning on the Hill and Irene's at her desk speaking with a young man, Mr. Sparks. "Sir, we have no bills, and our clients are very loyal. They love Mr. Hubble. He was good to them."

"I'm sure . . . I'm sure."

"I must talk to Mrs. Hubble and her son before I can decide."

"But of course."

There's a noise behind them. They turn and Bridget enters. She has an envelope in her hand and a crazy, blank look on her face.

"He's not coming back! Not tomorrow or next week or ever!" Ma screams.

"I'll come back later," Spark says. He stands and leaves.

Ma opens the envelope containing Danny's letter. She's staring at it, as if pretending to read from the page, but has it memorized. "Ma, life's about dying. It's beautiful. I'll write you soon."

Irene stares at Ma.

"Bridget." Irene mentions Ma's name but is not even sure why.

Ma's eyes are still staring. "He's delirious. He sleeps with a Bible that he can't read. What are those Eyetalians doing to him?"

Irene looks and smiles. "A Bible can't be bad, Bridget, even an Eyetalian bible."

"He's still waiting on the results," Ma says. "What are those Eyetalians doing? You know they kidnap people!" she yells.

"Why would they kidnap Danny?" Irene asks meekly.

"Why were you talking to Mr. Sparks?" Ma prods.

"Nothing important," Irene responds.

"PatG's mother's going crazy. There's a rumor that he's going to marry one of those Eyetalians!"

"Impossible. Why, I heard that many of them don't shave their armpits," Irene states categorically.

PatG, Dottor Loreto, Mimmo, and Franca are in Danny's room. Danny's skin and bone, pale, and asleep under the tent.

"Shouldn't he be in the hospital?" PatG asks.

The doctor shakes his head and waves everyone out of the room. They leave, including Dottor Loreto, who gently shuts the door. The women continue walking, leaving PatG and Dottor Loreto alone outside of Danny's room.

Dottor Loreto looks at PatG. "I sent his X-rays to Bari and my cousin in Pavia. There's nothing left to do."

"But in America?" PatG implores.

"Do you remember when Danny whisper to me? When he eat by his father and he come back here by himself?"

PatG stares, trying to focus on the past. "The day we found him on the street?"

"Yes." The doctor purses his lips and nods slightly. "He say dat if dere is-a no match, he wanna die here. He tell me dat day. I promise him dat I respect his wish."

They hear coughing and run back into the room.

Danny feebly raises his arm and waves PatG over. PatG lifts the tent and puts his ear next to Danny's mouth. "Spark's going to buy my business. Rui and Larry will take care of the transaction. They will divide it between Irene and Ma. There'll be something for your mother as well."

PatG stares blankly.

"I also told them to pay your tab at Larry's and at Nicks," Danny adds.

"Danny," PatG sighs.

"I don't have time for drama." Danny's voice begins to falter. He grabs PatG and pulls him closer. "There's a present for you in my drawer and my last letter to my mother and Marla. It explains many things. I want to sleep."

Danny's hand brushes PatG's fingers. "Please go."

PatG turns to leave but hears a whisper. "And, PatG, *figli maschi*. (May your children be male.)"

PatG looks back at Danny, turns, and quietly closes the door.

The following morning, PatG approaches the Ciancia residence.

Deranged yelling and screaming are coming from the house. He opens the door and runs to Danny's room. It's crowded, with every family member in it.

Mimmo and Antonio are struggling with Danny's half-naked, white body, trying to put his shirt on.

PatG grabs Nicola, who is sobbing.

"What are they doing?"

"They musta dress him before he gets a stiff."

PatG lurches forward, shoving Nicola away. He breaks through Mimmo and Antonio to hug his dead friend's body.

"Oh no. Danny! Danny! Ahhhhhhhhh!"

Epilogue

Five years later, PatG is working behind the bar with Francesca's grandfather. Francesca walks in, holding the hand of a four-year-old boy.

"*Patrizio, il cimitero chiude a l'una.* (Patrick, the cemetery closes at one)."

PatG takes his apron off and hands it to Francesca's grandfather. "*U Nonno, me ne vado.* (Grandfather I'm going)." Her old grandfather nods.

Inside the cemetery, the little boy runs ahead of Francesca and PatG.

"*Qua, Danny,*" PatG says.

The boy turns back and is face-to-face with the picture on the tomb of Michele Ciancia. "Mi-che-le Cian-cia," he says.

"*Bravo, Danny,*" Francesca says.

PatG picks Danny up. "Here's Uncle Danny. Give him a kiss."

Francesca rearranges the flowers beside Danny's picture. The picture is the one that they took with Vito at the restaurant by the sea. Little Danny kisses his namesake's picture. Above it is written, "DANNY HUBBLE CIANCIA." Francesca kisses her fingertips and then touches it.

"*Papà, mi avevi detto che mi insegna baseball come lo zio. Possiamo oggi dopo che mangiamo?* (Papà, you told me that you'd teach me to throw a baseball like Uncle Danny. Can you teach me today after we eat?)"

"*Devi mangiare tutto.* (You must eat everything)," Francesca says.

"*Si, Mamma,*" Danny responds.

Back on the Hill, in Danny's home in Fineview, Irene is knitting. Ma's watching wrestling when she suddenly turns to Irene.

"Danny just came to me."

Irene stops knitting. She raises her finger to her mouth. "It's five years Bridget. It's five years today."

She holds the sweater she is knitting up. "This will fit you fine, Bridget."

Ma ignores Irene and continues to stare at the wrestlers on the television set. She doesn't see any of them.

Irene stands up. "Bridget, can I put on PatG? The CD Danny always liked?"

Ma nods softly and switches off the television. PatG's jazzy music begins to flow.

Teflon Heart (patrick girondi)

What do you say about a guy?
Attitude and worn, white shoes.
Who gets up in the morning,
rushing round to pay his dues?

What can I do to convince you?
What we knew from the start?
And now I cannot forget you,
me you called the Teflon heart.

We search and search a lifetime
to possess that smile,
dream about that tingle
walking mile after mile.

In old worn out gym shoes,
not a lot of hope to spend,
little boys voyage,
to the very end.

Where's hope for the dreamer?
Bill collectors, sweat and cents.
Wading loss for a steamer,
fine flats and boy pup tents.

What can you do for a man?
Or an empty shopping cart?
Lost in some foreign land,
with his no-stick Teflon heart?

We search and search a lifetime,
to possess that smile,
dream about that tingle,
walking mile after mile.

In old worn-out gym shoes,
not a lot of hope to spend.
Little boys voyage,
to the very end.

The beginning
Patrick Girondi

Duomo di Altamura, Cattedrale di Santa Maria Assunta—the Cathedral of Altamura.

Cathedral of Altamura.

Mass in the Cathedral of Altamura.

Nativity scene, Cathedral of Altamura. The cathedral was completed in 1200 A.D.

Federicus guards outside the cathedral, Altamura. Federicus is a three-day annual festival in Altamura.

Reenactment of plague during annual Federicus Festival, Altamura.

Altamurani dressed as knights during Federicus Festival, Altamura.

Piazza at night during the Festival of the Madonna del Buoncammino, Altamura. This is an annual four-day festival.

Piazza during religious festival, Altamura.

Piazza during religious festival, Altamura.

Piazza during religious festival, Altamura.

Festival of the Madonna del Buoncammino with Caffé Ronchi in the background.

Some of the clan at the bar, Altamura.

Wood-fired focaccia from Altamura.

Faded Genes: Searching for a Cure and Finding Home in Altamura, Italy: Screenplay
by Patrick Girondi

EXT STREET IN BLUE COLLAR AREA FINEVIEW, PITTSBURGH DRIZZLING

Jazz playing in background.
A short middle-aged man gets out of a cab. An old woman holding a cat is gazing out of a second-floor window at him. He walks up the stairs overloaded with documents, opens the screen, and inserts key into inner door. A calico cat races out.

He drops everything and kneels to gather files.

A FALLEN DVD OF *ALL-STAR WRESTLING*
He picks the DVD up and hides it between the papers.

INT HOME MODEST MIDDLE-CLASS APARTMENT, SHORTLY AFTER

Danny's sitting in a cluttered kitchen. An elderly smoking woman (Danny's mother) is doing dishes.

                    DANNY
     I'm going to get rid of them cats.

                    MA
     Do you want tea?

Ma turns. An ash falls onto a plate. Danny rolls his eyes.

                    DANNY
     (mumbled) The little rats pop up
     everywhere. I'll give Kenny Hess a
     few bucks to fix 'em.

She turns.

138.

                    MA
          I think he nailed Mrs. Hegel's dog
          to the tree.

                    DANNY
          So do I.

Danny turns around.

                    DANNY (CONT'D)
          Look, the old man's dead and no
          one buys insurance from someone
          that smells like cigarettes
          and has cat hairs all over his
          clothes.

                    MA
          Your father never had
          problems . . . of course he didn't
          spend all of his time listening to
          broken-down singers.

                    DANNY
          Well, times have changed. Music
          takes me away from insurance
          policies and sick people . . .
          PatG's not broken down . . . he
          can be a jerk from time to time
          but . . .

                    MA
          You've been saying that all
          your life. It never stopped you
          from saving him . . . and you
          two still hang around like a
          couple of thirteen-year olds. And
          Kevin . . . I don't even want to
          get started on Kevin.

                    DANNY
          I'm relieved.

                    MA
          Drink your tea.

Danny's removing cat hairs from his suit.

                  MA (CONT'D)
          You look pale.

                  DANNY
          I feel weird.

                    MA
          Go and get a checkup.

Ma wipes her hands. Danny turns and looks at her.

                  DANNY
          They'll tell me that I shouldn't
          be living with someone who smokes.

Danny waves smoke away. His mother lights another
cigarette.

> MA
> Did you bring home my DVD?

Danny points to the stack of papers. She picks up the DVD.

Ma's FACE GLOWS AS SHE LOOKS AT IT

> MA
> Dr. X and the Crusher. You're my best.

> DANNY
> I'm your only.

MA'S CIGARETTE ASH IS AN INCH LONG

> MA
> Why are you taking the cab?

> DANNY
> PatG's working on the car.

> MA
> Oh, he's a mechanic again?

> DANNY
> No. He's a singer who fools around with cars.

MA puts DVD in the player. Danny sits, puts head-phones on. Ma is jumping and swinging at the wres-tling on the television set. Jazz is audible coming from the headphones.

E/I RUI'S CHILI PARLOR EARLY MORNING NEXT DAY

Rui's occupies a thin slice of a dilapidated build-ing at the bottom of the "Hill" on a busy street.

Danny is sitting on a chrome stool drinking coffee. A dark fifty-ish Nicaraguan (Rui) cleans sugar from

the counter with his hand and pours it into a large
deep pot.

DANNY LOOKS AT HIM AND RAISES HIS EYEBROWS.

> DANNY
> They're going to close you.

> RUI
> (Nicaraguan Spanish accent) Why
> would they close me?

> DANNY
> Cause you throw anything in there.
> Someone said you put lighter fluid
> in it the other night.

> RUI
> Rumors. Lighter fluid spilled. I
> cleaned the bar before I scoop the
> crumbs. . . . I think.

> DANNY
> Why do I do this to myself?

Danny shrugs and gently shakes his head.

> RUI
> My chili's more nutritious than
> Heinz ketchup.

Rui picks up a bottle of Heinz ketchup.

> RUI (CONT'D)
> Monosodium sorbate, I put in
> coffee. Sulfate assimborbate 3, I
> put in donut crumbs. Glucuronic
> acid, I put in . . .

                    DANNY
          Okay. Okay.

                    RUI
          Besides, I'm Number 1.

RUI POINTS TO NEWSPAPER ARTICLE HANGING IN GLASS
ON THE WALL

                    RUI
          The college kids line up on Friday
          and Saturday night to eat my
          chili.

                    DANNY
          I don't know why, it never tastes
          the same way twice.

                    RUI
          Bingo. I give America what it
          wants.

                    DANNY
          What might that be?

                    RUI
          Diversity.

                    DANNY
          I've never seen you eat it.

Rui lines up his right index finger with his nose.

                    RUI
          I'm not American.

Danny puts two dollars on the counter. Danny exits.
Rui pours the contents of Danny's coffee cup into
the chili pot.

INT. DANNY'S SMALL OFFICE NINE O'CLOCK FRIDAY MORNING.
LINOLEUM FLOORS AND BROWN STEEL FURNITURE

Danny reading newspaper with glasses on. A 60ish
woman (Irene, Danny's secretary) enters.

> IRENE
> Good morning, Mr. Hubble.

> DANNY
> Morning.

Without looking.

> DANNY (CONT'D)
> Who paid Old Man Schmidt's policy?

> IRENE
> I did.

> DANNY
> I told you not to pay policies
> with our money unless you tell me
> first.

> IRENE
> I told you.

> DANNY
> When did you tell me?

> IRENE
> Wednesday.

> DANNY
> Wednesday . . . What was I doing?

> IRENE
> You were talking to Marsha.

> DANNY
> Marla . . . Don't talk to me when
> she's here.

                    IRENE
          Yes Mr. Hubble.

                    DANNY
          Tell ol' Schmidt to settle up.
          With his heart condition, Farmer's
          is just itching to cancel. If they
          find out we paid, they'll cancel
          me.

                    IRENE
          Yes, sir. . . . Can I get some
          coffee from Rui?

                    DANNY
          We've got coffee.

                    IRENE
          I know, but Rui has the best
          coffee in Pittsburgh . . . and you
          know, his chili is the best in the
          country.

Danny nods as he removes his glasses and rubs his
eyes.

INT CLUB WITH SMALL DANCE FLOOR AND STAGE FRIDAY
EVENING

Danny's watching a 45ish singer (PatG). PatG finishes.

                    PATG
          Yes folks, don't forget. To stay
          ahead of trouble think Hubble. Our
          friend Danny Hubble serving
          Fineview and the Hill for forty
          years.

Danny looks at the obviously Irish guy (Kevin) next
to him.

                    DANNY
        I hate when he does this.

                    KEVIN
        I think that that's why he does
        it.

Kevin tilts his head and sips a beer.

                    DANNY
        Everyone here drinks . . . Even
        if they do remember, none of my
        carriers will want to insure them.

                    KEVIN
        It's Friday. Aren't you thirsty?

Danny rolls his eyes.

                    DANNY
        Get Kev another beer.

The bartender (Nick) uncaps a beer. PatG arrives
and puts his arms around Danny and Kevin.

                    PATG
        Hey, goombahs.

                    KEVIN
        I ain't your goombah, I'm Irish.

                    PATG
        Hey Nick, get these guys on me.

Nick looks over with a frown. PatG looks back.

                    PATG (CONT'D)
        Okay, you're right get them on you.

PatG breaks out in a song, "Tampa Day."

                         NICK
          You know, he's the only guy I know
          who pays to work.

Kevin tilts his beer.

                         KEVIN
          He buys a lot of drinks. Of
          course, we are his loyal fans—
          maybe his only—and loyalty has its
          rewards . . .

                         DANNY
          He's got a heart of gold.

                         NICK
          Hope so. That way at least I'll
          get his tab paid when he dies.

EXT IN FRONT OF THE CLUB LATER

     Danny's on the cell. Kevin walks out.

                         KEVIN
          What are you doing?

                         DANNY
          I'm going by Marla.

                         KEVIN
          I'm going by my Marla.

                         DANNY
          Do you ever get tired of hookers?

                         KEVIN
          Nope. I Couldn't get off if I
          didn't pay for it.

                         DANNY
          What's the going rate?

                    KEVIN
        Two bucks, a fin . . . I remember
        when they did it just to get
        something warm in their stomachs.

                    DANNY
        Nice.

                    KEVIN
        A few weeks ago, PatG had the
        prices jacked. He went with
        Cherry.

                    DANNY
        I don't need to hear this.

                    KEVIN
        Wait, Big shot finishes and gives
        her twenty. Word spread and they
        all thought that they were call
        girls . . . He better stay far
        away. I wouldn't pay more than a
        fin for Marilyn Monroe.

                    DANNY
        What if she's there when you get
        home?

                    KEVIN
        If she is, she'll get three bucks
        and a half of a Philly steak . . .
        That's all I got.

Danny smiles.

KEVIN'S BACK AS HE'S WALKING AWAY

                    DANNY
        See you Kev.

Kevin raises his hand without turning and continues to walk.

INT MARLA'S AVERAGE APARTMENT, SHORTLY AFTER

Danny's on the couch. A young woman's head is in his lap.

                    MARLA
          Danny, do you love me?

                    DANNY
          Watch the film.

                    MARLA
          Danny, what would you do if I left
          you?

Danny remains silent.

                    MARLA (CONT'D)
          Danny, what would you do if I left
          you?

                    DANNY
          I'd jump off a building. Now are
          you happy?

                    MARLA
          Yeah . . . but I'm also tired.
          Let's go to bed.

INT MARLA'S APARTMENT DARK

A couple are asleep in front of the TV set. Danny's at the door. Marla walks to him rubbing her eyes. She hugs him.

                    MARLA
          Bye, Danny.

                    DANNY
          Bye.

The girl on the floor stirs.

                    GIRL
     Bye, Danny.

                    DANNY
     Bye.

The girl turns over.

INT DANNY'S HOME SHORTLY AFTER

Danny enters. Ma's snoring. The TV's fuzzy. Danny
turns it off and covers his mother. She stirs.

                    MA
     Danny, leave money tomorrow.

                    DANNY
     Yeah, night, Ma.

INT PATG'S HOME FRONT ROOM SAME TIME

PatG enters. His mother's on couch with rosary in
her hands.

                    PATG'S MOTHER
     Find a nice girl so I can sleep.

                    PATG
     Ma, women use me for kicks.

PATG'S MOTHER You don' give them a chance.

PatG kisses her on the cheek and exits.

EXT FINEVIEW SUNDAY MORNING, LARRY'S HE'S NOT HERE
BAR

Larry's average, fifty-five with a cheap orangish
wig. He's holding the TV remote behind the bar.
Patrons are watching TV.

Danny walks in.

                    PAUL
          Hey Dan.

                    MARK
          Hey Danny boy.

                    DANNY
          Hey.

Danny sits down. Larry's looking at the TV.

                    LARRY
          A thousand channels and nothing on.

                    PAUL
          Go back to that girly film.

                    LARRY
          It's Sunday, have some respect.

                    PAUL
          Yeah.

Mark raises his beer.

                    MARK
          Praise the Lord. Put on rugby.

                    LARRY
          Don't Europeans play any real
          sports?

Larry wipes the counter in front of Danny.

                    LARRY (CONT'D)
          Hard-boiled egg, Danny?

                    DANNY
          Yeah. Give me a Slim Jim too.

                    PAUL
          Breakfast of champions.

                         LARRY
          Out of Slim Jims.

                         DANNY
          Give me a bag of bar-be-que chips.

                         MARK
          In training Danny?

Larry places the chips and egg in front of Danny.

                         LARRY
          I seen Ma at Schatzel's. I told her
          to quit or she'd end up like me.

Larry moves closer.

                    LARRY (CONT'D)
          (whisper) Damn chemo's a bitch.
          What do you think about the hair?

Larry rolls his eyes up. Danny smiles.

                         DANNY
          Rod Stewart . . . I like it.

Larry looks at mirror and raises closed fist to his
mouth.

                         LARRY
          Maggie, I think I got something to
          say to you!

                         MARK
          Rod, get me a beer.

EXT VICTORY PARK SUNDAY LATE MORNING

          Softball game. Danny's walking on the steel
          bleachers to PatG.

                         LADY 1
          Danny, they're hitting us like a
          mean stepmom.

                              LADY 2
                    Danny, get out there and pitch up
                    some Hubble Rubble.

Man turns to another.

                               MAN 1
                    Hubble's the best pitcher the hill
                    ever had. Shoots 'em out of the
                    ground . . . The batter doesn't
                    know if he should swing or duck.

Danny sits next to PatG.

                               PATG
                    How's Marla?

                              DANNY
                    Fine . . . What did you do?

                               PATG
                    Got a hummer in the parking lot.

                              DANNY
                    Judy?

                               PATG
                    Nah, she's chasing some rap
                    singer.

PatG looks at Danny, eyes cringed and tilts his
head.

                         PATG (CONT'D)
                    College girl.

                              DANNY
                    I remember when they taught
                    science at Pitt.

                               PATG
                    I prefer the modern courses.

                         DANNY
          Watch the game.

EXT VICTORY PARK AFTER

The park's emptying out.

                         LADY 1
          Danny, come out of retirement so
          we win a game.

Danny smiles and walks with PatG.

AN ELDERLY WOMAN PICKS UP A CUSHION FROM THE BENCH.

                    ELDERLY WOMAN
          Danny, how's Ma?

Danny holds onto the fence as he turns toward the
woman.
                         DANNY
          She's...

Danny falls to his knees and faints. The crowd
gathers.

                         PATG
          Give him room!

PatG kneels down. Danny's eyes are barely open.

                    PATG (CONT'D)
          Someone call an ambulance.

                         DANNY
          No, I'm fine, just slipped.

Danny starts to lift himself up.

                    DANNY (CONT'D)
          Get me home.

PatG helps Danny up.

                         PATG
          You sure?

Danny slowly winks.

INT. DANNY'S HOME SHORTLY AFTER

                         PATG
          I don't like the way you look.

                         DANNY
          I've never liked the way I look.

                         PATG
          (irritated) Cut it out.

Ma enters. Gives Danny cup. Cigarette ash falls
into it.

                         MA
          I'll get more.

Danny shakes his head, lays back. Ma enters the
kitchen.

                         MA (CONT'D)
          I got to go to Schatzels for
          Lipton tea.

Ma leaves. Danny stares away and rubs his cheek.

                         DANNY
          What's it all about, PatG?

                         PATG
          My ol' man came from Italy. He
          worked like a dog until the day
          he died. My family's scattered all
          over the country squeezing out a
          living. I wish I knew what it was
          all about.

                    DANNY
      I wish I had a family.

                    PATG
      You've got me . . . and Ma.

                    DANNY
      Sing me "Sweet Memories." I'm
      tired.

                    PATG
      Now?

DANNY'S FRONT AFTERNOON ROOM SHORTLY AFTER
PatG's singing. Danny sleeps.

                    PATG
      (sung) I don't know if you're that
      strong that . . . you can run from
      my thoughts all night long . . .

Doorbell rings. PatG opens window, looks out.

                    PATG (CONT'D)
      (mumbled) Marla? Damn.

INT DANNY'S HOUSE IN FRONT ROOM SHORTLY AFTER

Danny sleeps. Ma enters the house and goes to the
kitchen. She puts tea on shelf.
Marla nods. PatG and Marla walk into the kitchen.

                    PATG
      (whisper) Ma, this is Marla.
      Ma fills the teapot. Marla looks at
      PatG.

                    PATG (CONT'D)
      Ma, this is Danny's friend.

                    MA
      I have to make Danny's tea.

                         PATG
              He's sleeping Ma, make it later.

                          MA
              I'll make it now. Danny likes tea.

Ma turns to Marla.

                      MA (CONT'D)
              (Nasty) Who are you?

Marla's frozen.

                         PATG
              She's Danny's friend.

Ma fumbles for a cigarette, lights it, and inhales.

                          MA
              What do you want with my son?

Marla smiles timidly.

                        MARLA
              Hasn't Danny told you about us?

                          MA
              (Disgustedly) Who is she?

PatG looks to Marla.

                        MARLA
              I'm his girl, I love him very
              much.

Ma mechanically moves and looks at Marla.

                          MA
              I have to give Danny his tea.

Ma looks at PatG.

                    MA (CONT'D)
        You should be fixing cars. Your
        mother will die without peace. . . .

Ma looks at Marla.

                    MA (CONT'D)
        And you, I don't know what you
        should do. But whatever it is, you
        shouldn't be doing it with my son!

There's a soft knock. PatG opens the door. Irene
walks in.

                    IRENE
        I heard about Mr. Hubble.

                    MA
        He's fine. I'm making him tea.

Marla looks over PatG's shoulder at Danny.

                    DANNY
        What are you doing here?

Danny looks at his mother and rubs his hand over
his face.

                    DANNY (CONT'D)
        I want to die.

                    MA
        Danny, who is she?

                    DANNY
        PatG, sing.

Danny covers his face with the chair cover.

                    MA
        (forceful) Danny, who is this girl?

                         DANNY

         PatG, "Tampa Day." Now . . . sing.

Ma enters kitchen.

DANNY COVERED

INT. DANNY'S HOUSE IN KITCHEN SAME TIME

                         IRENE
         She's a pretty little thing.

                          MA
         She's not for Danny. Who is she?

                         IRENE
         She's very important . . . When
         she's at the office, I can't talk
         to Danny. . . . Did Danny drink
         his tea?

Ma passes PatG and Marla. She touches Danny.

                          MA
         Danny, Danny.

The blanket falls down, revealing Danny's pale face.

                         PATG
         Marla, call an ambulance.

INT HOSPITAL WAITING ROOM SHORTLY AFTER

Marla wipes her eyes. PatG's head is in his hands.
He raises his head and looks down the hall.

INT HOSPITAL EMERGENCY ROOM SAME TIME

Danny's in bed. Irene's on right holding his hand.
Ma's on left. His eyes open.

                         IRENE
          Oh Mr. Hubble.

INT. HOSPITAL EMERGENCY ROOM CORRIDOR SHORTLY
AFTER

Danny's on bed being wheeled by an average middle-aged
nurse. His mother and Irene are by his side.

                         MA
          Are you married?

                         NURSE
          Ma'am?

                         MA
          My son's an insurance executive.
          He's not married. Are you married?

DANNY OPENS HIS EYES, LISTENS AND CLOSES THEM AGAIN.

                         NURSE
          No ma'am, I'm not married.

                         IRENE
          Have you ever been married?

                         NURSE
          NO.

                         IRENE
          (spoken quietly) Mrs. Hubble, she's
          never been married.

Ma looks at Irene impatiently.

                         IRENE (CONT'D)
          I'm Mr. Hubble's private secretary.

                         NURSE
          Oh?

                         IRENE
          He's a fine man.

                          MA
          (low tone) Irene!

                         IRENE
          He knows how to use internet. He
          doesn't smoke and rarely drinks.

                         NURSE
          Sounds like a real catch.

                         IRENE
          He is (reaches into purse). Here's
          his card. Call or send a computer
          message. He gets loads of them.

                          MA
          (sternly) Irene!

Irene pulls her hand back.

                         IRENE
          Well, it's true. Some of them
          send pictures doing the craziest
          things.

The corridor ends at a double door.

                         NURSE
          Ladies, you'll have to wait here.
          I'll give you a minute.

The nurse takes clipboard and turns.

                          MA
          Danny, honey.

                         IRENE
          Danny, Mr. Hubble.

                    MA
    He knows his name.

               IRENE Oh.

Irene moves her finger to her lips. Danny's eyes
open.

                    DANNY
    You two are killing me . . . with
    embarrassment.

                    IRENE
    We're worried, Mr. Hubble . . .
    Danny. Aren't we, Mrs. Hubble?
    Bridget.

Ma looks at her sternly.

                    MA
    We'll be waiting.

INT DOCTOR'S OFFICE WEDNESDAY MORNING

Danny and Ma are sitting in front of a middle-aged
doctor with glasses and curly gray hair.

                    DOCTOR
    Is everyone comfortable?

                    MA
    I'm comfortable. Danny?

                    DANNY
    Oh yes, I'm comfortable.

                    DOCTOR
    Good. Do you smoke, Mr. Hubble?

                    DANNY
    Not directly.

Danny jerks.

                        DANNY (CONT'D)
              Ouch. What did you do that for?

                             MA
              Excuse me honey, it slipped.

                          DOCTOR
              I asked if you smoked, Mr. Hubble.

Danny glances at his mother.

                          DANNY
              No. But I'm around people who do.

                          DOCTOR
              I won't mince words. There's not
              time. You have a leukemia that
              normally afflicts heavy smokers.

Danny's mother covers her mouth with her handkerchief.

                             MA
              Leukemia?

                          DANNY
              Is it fatal?

                          DOCTOR
              Yes.

Danny looks to the side and shakes his head.

                          DANNY
              Will I be here for the hockey
              season? I've got season tickets.

                          DOCTOR
              That's hard to say. . . . We must
              start chemotherapy immediately.

                    DANNY
Doc, I'm an insurance man. I've
seen this all before. It's not my
choice to spend the last months of
my life in agony.

                    DOCTOR
(slightly irritated) That's up to
you. There are choices if you'd
give me a chance.

                    DANNY
You said fatal . . . How much
time?

                    DOCTOR
A month, two, six.

                    DANNY
What's the alternative to the
radiation elixir?

                    DOCTOR
A bone marrow transplant
maybe . . .

                    DANNY
And then what happens?

                    DOCTOR
(irritated) Then it's a dice roll.
You're healthy or you're not.

                    DANNY
You mean I'm healthy or I'm gone.

The doctor looks uncomfortably at Danny's mother.
Danny looks down and rubs his right hand over his
head.

DANNY (CONT'D)
This is tough. . . . She's my only
living relative. Is she too old?

DOCTOR
DNA compatibility is necessary.
We'll do a donor search. We could
get lucky.

Danny cups his right hand and shakes it. He blows
in it, pushes forward and opens it. Moves his head
to the right and left waiting for the imaginary
dice to land. The doctor looks down the desk. Then
he looks suddenly at Danny.

DOCTOR (CONT'D)
Mr. Hubble, I must go.

Ma covers her mouth with her handkerchief.

DANNY
Ma, it'll be all right. . . .
I promise.

INT DANNY'S KITCHEN EARLY MORNING

Ma's gazing out kitchen window as she prepares
Danny's tea. There's a squirrel hanging on to the
screen. Ma hesitates and then abruptly turns. She
pours them tea and sits at the table with Danny. Ma
is staring at the window.

DANNY
Ma, drink your tea.

MA
I have to tell you something . . .

The squirrel moves away.

INT DOCTOR'S OFFICE AFTERNOON

Danny and Ma are seated. The doctor enters.

> DOCTOR
> Mr. Hubble, Mrs. Hubble.

> DANNY
> (replicating tone) Doctor.

> DOCTOR
> (coldly) Your mother's not
> compatible.

> DANNY
> (sarcastically) Oh?

> DOCTOR
> You have a peculiar DNA.

> DANNY
> That's me, peculiar.

> DOCTOR
> Some DNA strands are clear and
> legible, others are light and . . .

> DANNY
> Bleached?

The doctor nods curtly. Danny smiles.

> DANNY (CONT'D)
> Faded genes.

> DOCTOR
> Do you refuse chemotherapy?

> DANNY
> I refuse.

                    DOCTOR
        Would you consider experimental
        nonconventional treatment?

                    DANNY
        The insurance won't cover it, and
        I'm not insane.

                    DOCTOR
        Your choice. Check with the
        hospital Friday morning to see
        what the search turns up.

Doctor stands. Danny and Ma quietly walk out of the
doctor's office.

INT PITTSBURGH UNIVERSITY HOSPITAL FRIDAY MORNING

Danny and PatG are in front of a smiling male
nurse.

                    NURSE

        We could check other donor centers.

                    DANNY
        At fifteen hundred a pop there
        won't be enough to bury me.

                    PATG
        Danny, I can get money.

Danny shakes his head and looks away.

                    NURSE
        Sorry, gentlemen.

INT RESTAURANT NOON

Danny and Ma enter. They follow Angie, a thin,
blonde out of a bottle woman who has only a
right hand, to a booth. Angie looks to the cook.

                    ANGIE
      Floyd, is that cheeseburger up?

                    FLOYD
      Any longer and you'll be able to
      stick it in his coke for ice.

Angie laughs.

                    ANGIE
      Give me a break, I've only got one
      hand.

Angie walks up to a patron at the bar. They high
five.

      INT RESTAURANT BOOTH MOMENTS LATER

                    DANNY
      Ma, what is it?

Two or three heads turn.

                    MA
      I don't want you to hate me.

                    DANNY
      I couldn't hate someone who's
      cooked for me for 47 years.

                    MA
      I'm a horrible cook.

                    DANNY
      It's the thought that counts.

Ma looks at her hands and back at the glass of
water.

                    MA
      Danny, your dad was not your
      father.

Heads turn as Ma continues to look at her glass.

                    DANNY
          (whisper) You watching Kardashians
          again?

Pause.

                    DANNY (CONT'D)
          How many Nicorettes did you take
          today?

                    MA
          He's Italian.

Pause.

                    DANNY
          That explains why I got this thing
          for pasta and clams . . .

Danny turns to the side and looks at the floor.

WOOD UNDER LINOLEUM OF CRACKED TILE

                    DANNY
          I'm 5'5. Dad was 6 foot.

                    MA
          I was pregnant when I married him.
          No one ever knew.

                    DANNY
          Are you sure you were pregnant?

                    MA
          I know when I'm pregnant.

Heads turn. Danny motions down with his hands.

                    DANNY
          Okay, okay. . . . They watch the
          Kardashians too.

                    MA
     We worked in Nap's bakery. He was
     stocky with dark puppy-dog eyes.

                  DANNY
     Like mine?

                    MA
     Exactly.

                  DANNY
     So you make bread and while it's
     in the oven he skates. . . .
     Sounds like a wonderful guy.

Angie brings their lunches and leaves.

               DANNY (CONT'D)
     What's his name?

                    MA
     Mimmo.

                  DANNY
     This may be hard to take . . .
     Neemo?

                    MA
     Mimmo (pronounced Mee-moh.) It's
     short for Dominick.

                  DANNY
     Mimmo is short for Dominick?

                    MA
     I'm going to ask Donald Nap where
     he lives, they're cousins.

His mother shakes her head.

                              MA (CONT'D)
                    (coldly) He didn't know. He ran
                    away but was deported and never
                    allowed to come back.

Pause.

                              DANNY
                    Ma, the ol' man's last wish was
                    that I keep Irene . . .

She gazes.

                              MA
                    He was a man . . .

                              DANNY
                    Let's go, PatG's taking me to my
                    pajama party. . . . Hmph . . .
                    Mee-moh.

Danny shakes his head and smiles.

Angie, bring the check!

EXT HOSPITAL PARKING LOT NEXT MORNING

                              DANNY
                    I'm not going to do this anymore.

                              PATG
                    No one can force you.

INT DANNY'S HOME AFTER

Danny's reading.

                              MA
                    I talked to Donny. Mimmo's in
                    Italy . . . in his town. You have
                    to go and find him.

                    DANNY
          Wouldn't it be easier to call?

                    MA
          No. . . . You must go.

Danny looks back into the book.

INT MARLA'S APARTMENT SATURDAY EVENING

Marla's dressing. Danny's leaned against a dresser
watching.

                    DANNY
          Enough, Marla.

Marla stops combing her hair and looks at Danny.

                    MARLA
          What?

                    DANNY
          Cut it out. We're not going
          anywhere. . . . We were never
          going anywhere. . . . And now,
          now . . .

                    MARLA

          Are you okay? We can stay home. . . .

                    DANNY
          Cut it out.

Marla moves her right hand to his arm.

                    MARLA
          PatG's waiting, he'll be
          disappointed.

Danny looks into her eyes.

DANNY
You tried an older guy . . . What
do you want now, a dying one?

Marla looks, tears well in her eyes.

MARLA
Danny.

Marla reaches down for his hand. He jerks it away
and walks out of her room. Moments later, the outer
door of the apartment is heard shutting.

INT NICK'S CLUB SATURDAY NIGHT

DANNY'S SITTING AT THE BAR

PatG walks over.

DANNY
I'm going to Italy.

PATG
Monday afternoon. Where's Marla?

DANNY
Monday? Really?

PatG nods, picks up the microphone, and winks.

AIRPORT MONDAY AFTERNOON CLOCK READS 3:05
An airline agent is watching Danny, Irene and Ma.

ATTENDANT
Sir, you'll miss your flight.

DANNY
Coming. . .

Danny looks at both of them.

                         MA
         Come back soon . . .

                       IRENE
         Come back soon, Mr. Hubble.

                       DANNY
         Yeah okay. Stop it.

He hugs them. Hat falls behind him. He breaks to
pick it up.

                  DANNY (CONT'D)
         Arrivederci.

He smiles and turns. PatG walks out from the bathroom
behind them. He's dressed like he's a disco mobster.

                       PATG
         Let's go, goombah.

                       DANNY
         Remember, Ma. Return the videos.

                       IRENE
         Danny, don't you have to remind me
         about something?

Danny looks and concentrates.

                       DANNY
         Yes Irene. Hold the fort down, at
         the office.

Irene turns to Ma.

                       IRENE
         Mr. Hubble told me to hold the
         fort down . . . at the office.

                         MA
         I heard.

                         DANNY
          And Irene, make sure she takes the
          DVDs back.

                         IRENE
          I have to make sure you take the
          DVDs back.

                          MA
          You can take them back for me.

                         IRENE
          But he told me to make sure that
          you take them back.

Ma shakes her head. They turn and look.

THE ATTENDANT IS CLOSING THE DOOR.

INT AMERICAN AIRPLANE MONDAY A FEW HOURS LATER

Plane's full. Danny's seated in the window seat.
PatG's on the aisle.

Where did you get the money?

                         PATG
          5 from Rui and 5 from Larry.

                         DANNY
          Great guys . . .

                         PATG
          Larry said he gave it to me
          because you're too short to be Rod
          Stewart.

PatG shrugs. Danny smiles and looks out the window.

INT. AIRPLANE LATER

Danny and PatG are watching a film.

                    PATG
          I got to leak.

                    DANNY
          (whispered) I got to go
          myself. . . . You ever take a dump
          on a plane?

                    PATG
          Yeah.

                    DANNY
          Is there any trick to it?

                    PATG
          No, I go first. I only got to leak.

INT AIRPLANE A FEW MOMENTS LATER

Danny's waiting by the bathroom. The door opens and PatG
steps out. Danny sniffs and looks strangely at PatG.

INT AIRPLANE BATHROOM A FEW MINUTES LATER

DANNY'S ON THE THRONE

There's a knock. Danny looks at the door and there's
another knock.

                    DANNY
          PatG?

                    VOICE
          Sir, open this door.

Danny cringes.

                    DANNY
          What?

Voices from outside. Danny fumbles. He breaks the
perfume bottle off the plastic stand and splashes
it all over.

                    STEWARDESS
          Sir, open this door immediately!

The door jiggles inward. Danny's buttoning his
pants. He opens the door. The stewardess is waiting
on the outside.

                 STEWARDESS (CONT'D)
          Sir, you've been smoking.

The male attendant sticks his nose in the cubicle.
He scrunches his eyes.

                      DANNY
          Yeah what do you smell like, Old
          Spice? . . . I don't smoke.

Danny looks at them.

                    STEWARDESS
          Sir, I want your name.

                      DANNY
          Why? Don't like your own?

                    STEWARDESS
          As an aviation representative, I'm
          an agent of the US government.

                      DANNY
          Give me a break. Today, who isn't?

                    STEWARDESS
          Sir, you're creating a disruption.

Danny looks up into her eyes.

          Well, I guess you have no
          choice. . . . Throw me off the
          plane.

Danny heads to his seat.

>   STEWARDESS
>   Mark his seat down.
>
>   MALE STEWARDESS
>   He says he didn't smoke . . . Will
>   they arrest him in Italy?
>
>   STEWARDESS
>   The Italians don't take anything
>   serious. When he returns to the
>   United States, he'll be in for a
>   big surprise.

INT AIRPLANE A FEW MOMENTS LATER

Danny arrives at his seat.

>   DANNY
>   I'm going to kill you.
>
>   PATG
>   I can't hear you. Headphones.

Danny looks at PatG sternly and sits down.

>   DANNY
>   Why didn't you tell me?

PatG faintly smiles.

>   DANNY (CONT'D)
>   Now I know why they search for
>   weapons in the airports.
>
>   PATG
>   Why?
>
>   DANNY
>   To protect the airline attendants.

PatG puts his headphones on and watches the film.

EXT BARI AIRPORT TUESDAY AFTERNOON

Danny and PatG are walking down the stairs of the airplane.

ON PLANE WRITTEN ITA AND SAN FRANCESCO D'ASSISI

About five feet off the stairs is a sleeping brown dog. The passengers all step around him. Danny removes his hat, wipes his brow, and looks at his watch.

HIS WATCH SIX FORTY-FIVE IN THE MORNING

Danny puts his hat back on and looks around.

ALMOST DESERT WITH THOUSANDS OF OLIVE TREES

A bus takes them to a five-hundred-foot-long termi- nal. Danny turns to PatG.

                    DANNY
          Kind of scary. What time is it?

                    PATG
          Add six hours.

                    DANNY
          Yeah and subtract forty years.

INT BARI AIRPORT TERMINAL SHORTLY AFTER

The luggage belt noisily starts. Danny looks out the window.

MAN THROWING BOX MARKED FRAGILE FROM THE BELT ONTO A CART

                    DANNY
          Fragile.

INT TERMINAL SHORTLY AFTER

While exiting, a man in a gray uniform points to
Danny's suitcases and then to a steel table in front
of him. Danny puts one on the table. Simultaneously, a sixty-ish man (Vito) arrives and whispers
into the ear of the agent. The agent waves Danny
on without the slightest change of expression. The
newly arrived man takes Danny's arm. The agent
signals PatG to place his luggage on the stainless
steel table.

                    VITO
          I am Vito.

Danny pulls his arm back

                    PATG
          What's going on?

Vito looks back at PatG.

                    VITO
          (Italian accent) Is he wit you?

Danny nods.

Vito nods to the official, PatG's waved through. Vito
takes a bag.

                    DANNY
          Who are you?

                    VITO
          I'ma Vito. You're Massimo coosin.
          You are Danny from Transylvania.

                    DANNY
          Who's Maximo?

                    VITO
          He's a my coosin.

They struggle to the exit. People are passing inside.
Women are waving handkerchiefs and yelling.

> VITO (CONT'D)
> Let's a go.

> DANNY
> Where are we going?

> VITO
> We gonna go toa your town.

> DANNY
> I'm from Pittsburgh.

> VITO
> I know Pittsburgh . . . Transylvania.

Danny rubs his head.

EXT BARI AIRPORT PARKING LOT SHORTLY AFTER

They're at a tiny car. Vito opens the trunk.

> VITO
> I gotta parenti a Chicago. Dey got
> parenti a Pittasburgh. And you
> are un coosin of my coosin . . .
> Transylvania's a beautiful place.

He starts to sing John Denver's song.

> VITO (CONT'D)
> Take me home toa de place I belong
> mountain Mamma Transylvania take
> me home . . . John Seattle, I cry
> when he die.

Vito smiles.

> DANNY
> What's parente?

                    PATG
Family relations.

                    VITO
You say family of my family.

                    DANNY
Where are we going?

                    VITO
Altamura, your family's-a town.

                    DANNY
Are you from there?

                    VITO
I wasa from dere but mia moglie,
my wifea she from Santeramo. My
fadder-in-law he givea me a job.
He sells a furniture. So when I
marry forty years ago I movea to
Grumo. My family is a Santeramo.

                    PATG
How do you speak English?

                    VITO
I don'a speak English. I wasa
never inna England. I speak-a
American. I was inna Norda
Carolina. Dey makea furniture
dere. I was dere for six years.
I teacha dem how you makea
furniture. Den I come home.

                    DANNY
It must have been tough on your
wife.

                    VITO
But tougher on my mudder too. I go
to de statesa for sixa years but I

go home. My mudder poor woman. I never move back to-a Altamura.

                    DANNY
          Too bad. How far's Santeramo from
          Altamura?

                    VITO
          About ten kilometers.

INT VITO'S CAR

TUESDAY SHORTLY AFTER

Danny's in front, PatG's crammed in the back with the luggage. The car arrives at a T in the road. There are blue signs outlined in white. Danny looks.

FIVE SIGNS STACKED WITH TOWN NAMES ON THEM WITH THE ARROW POINTED TO THE RIGHT. NEXT TO THEM FIVE IDEN-TICAL SIGNS WITH THE IDENTICAL TOWN NAMES POINTING TO THE LEFT.

Danny turns to speak but his head's blocked by a suitcase.

                    DANNY
          Hey PatG, look at that.

Vito nods his head.

                    VITO
          Italy's a country of choices.

The car sharply turns to the right. PatG grabs the ceiling.

                    PATG
          Whew, it's hot.

                    VITO
          Hot? It's April. This is a nottin'.

INT VITO'S CAR SHORTLY AFTER

THE CAR PASSES A SIGN WITH ALTAMURA WRITTEN ON IT

The streets are empty.

> DANNY
> Does anyone live here?

> VITO
> They a eatin'. Mangia.

Vito parks next to a stone building in an ancient enclave.

> DANNY
> Is this a hotel?

> VITO
> This is a home you gonna sleep.

> DANNY
> Who lives here?

> VITO
>
> My mudder. She take-a care of you.

Vito looks at PatG, who smiles.

> DANNY
>
> I don't want to put her out.

> VITO
> No problem. She like a company.
> She by herself. My sister she
> livesa wit her husband and
> children.

> DANNY
> Where do they live?

                         VITO
          Across da street.

TEN-FOOT-WIDE STREET, DANNY LOOKS

The door opens. A smiling old woman (Vito's Mother)
in black with a bandanna on her head smiles. Danny
and PatG smile back.

                         DANNY
          How old is your mother?

                         VITO
          She's ottanta-sei, scusa, I mean
          86.

                         DANNY
          And your father?

                         VITO
          Oh he diea young.

                         DANNY
          Oh?

                         VITO
          Yeah he was-a 82. My mudder
          she still weara black. She's a
          mourning.

                         PATG
          When did he die?

                         VITO
          '07' October 17. 17's a bad number.
          Every 17 I don'a drivea d' car.

                         PATG
          Did your father die in a car
          crash?

                         VITO
            No, he was too ol' to drive.

They move into the house. The table's set with wine,
cheeses, bread, and olives. The kitchen's decorated
with hanging peppers and garlic and pictures and
statues of saints.

                         DANNY
            How did your father die?

                         VITO
            He fall froma de tree. He was
            collectin' de olive. The olives.

Danny hesitates.

                         DANNY
            Why don't you drive on the 17th?

                         VITO
            17 unlucky number. Don'a you
            remember? I tole you.

Vito's mother opens a door. Inside are two small
beds and a closet.

CRUCIFIX OVER DOOR

                         VITO
            I sleep-a here when I was a boy.
            You gotta de name of who you gonna
            see?

                         DANNY
            Yeah, I got it here.

                         PATG
            I need to use the john.

                        VITO
        John?

                        PATG
        Banio.

                        VITO
        You call a de bagno john?

                        PATG
        Yeah, what do you call it?

                        VITO
        Bagno.

The mother takes PatG's hand. She opens a door.
PatG steps in. Danny hands a paper to Vito. In the
background PatG peeing is heard through a small
window-like opening in the wall.

                    VITO (CONT'D)
        Domenico Ciancia. Dey gotta a de
        bakery. How you know him?

                        DANNY
        He made bread with my mother.

                        VITO
        Your mudder she's bake a de bread.

                        DANNY
        She was the oven.

Vito looks curiously at Danny.

                        VITO
        I finda dis man. He know you here?

                        DANNY
        No.

                    VITO
          Oh it's a surprise? Italians love-a
          surprises.

                    DANNY
          (smiling) That's great.

INT VITO'S MOTHER'S BATHROOM.

PATG STANDING WITH HIS HANDS AGAINST THE WALL OF
THE TINY, COMPACT ROOM. HE'S LOOKING UP AT THE
CEILING

INT VITO'S MOTHER'S KITCHEN SHORTLY AFTER

The table's trashed. PatG smiles. Danny shakes his
head.

                    DANNY
          I'm beat.

                    PATG
          Dormo.

The mother gets up.

                    VITO
          She a make-a your bed.

                    DANNY
          No, no.

Danny gets up.

                    VITO
          Sit down my friend. You in Italy.
          My mudder pleasure to serve-a you.

Vito cuts a strawberry. He looks at PatG.

                        VITO (CONT'D)
        What do you do?

                        PATG
        I'm a performer.

Vito looks confused.

                        PATG (CONT'D)
        I sing.

Vito looks on in an impressed way.

                        VITO
        Tonight you sing-a for us.

                        PATG
        I don't have a band.

                        VITO
        Don' worry. I find it.

PatG shrugs.

                        PATG
        Okay.

                        VITO
        Da bed it's a ready.

                        DANNY
        What will you do?

Vito puts his two hands together and puts them up
against his right ear.

                        VITO
        Neenah nana. We take a de sack.

INT SPARE BEDROOM TUESDAY AFTERNOON

PatG and Danny are standing in the eight-by-eight
room. Vito's mother lowers the shutters and leaves.

BEDROOM IN THE DARK

                    PATG
        Hey Danny.

                    DANNY
        Yeah?

                    PATG
        What do you think?

                    DANNY
        I think that I like being Italian.

INT VITO'S MOTHER'S KITCHEN

TUESDAY EVENING

Danny's at the table. PatG walks in. Vito's ma's
making coffee.

                    DANNY
        Where did you go? I can't
        communicate. She tried to put my
        shoes on when I got out of bed.

                    PATG
        This place is great . . . and the
        women, oh the women.

INT BAR IN ALTAMURA TUESDAY EVENING

Danny and PatG walk in. Music's playing. Danny
looks at PatG.

                    DANNY
        Hey. That's you.

                    PATG
        I gave them a CD.

                    BARTENDER
        G, il caffè no fa lo raffreddare.
        (G, don't let the coffee get cold.)

                     PATG
          Sì, sì.

Danny sees the bartender and his assistant (FRAN-
CESCA). She's about twenty-five and scrumptious.
Danny looks back at PatG.

                    DANNY
        Hey, don't get too comfortable.

Vito looks at PatG and shakes his head.

                     VITO
        Friend in Italia. Watcha you step.

                     PATG
        What do you mean?

Vito pulls down the skin under his right eye.

                     VITO
        That's-a da bartender's
        granddaughter. Open your eyes.

Vito turns, slaps his hands together, and looks to
the door.

                VITO (CONT'D)
          Tommaso!

Everyone turns as a man with an accordion enters.

                   TOMMASO
        New York, New York, New York, New
        York, New York, New York . . .

INT BAR IN ALTAMURA LATER TUESDAY EVENING

Small crowd. Tommaso and PatG are performing 'Mala Femmina.'

THE BARTENDER'S GRANDDAUGHTER LOOKS AT PATG

EXT PARK IN CENTER OF ALTAMURA LATER

Danny's sitting. Vito stands and kisses a man on both cheeks.

                    VITO
          Don Antonio.

Don Antonio nods and walks on.

                    DANNY
          Who's that?

                    VITO
          A boss-a. It's time to eat.

INT VITO'S HOME IN GRUMO TUESDAY EVENING DINING

Danny, PatG, Vito, are seated at the table. Vito's wife (Luisa), and daughter are serving fruit. Danny gets up and takes a plate. Luisa smiles and takes the plate out of his hand.

                    VITO
          I found Mimmo Ciancia . . . He's
          a funny guy wit four kids and
          a bakery. Dey saya dat he go to
          America young and come back old.

Vito raises a strawberry.

                    VITO (CONT'D)
          Everyting in its season.

Vito hands a strawberry to Danny.

                    VITO (CONT'D)
He in America for a few week.
I tink maybe de food. All dose
chemicals. I don'a know. What you
wanna do?

                    DANNY
I need to ask him a favor.

                    VITO
A man like dat a favor?

Vito puts his right palm at eye level. He twists it.

                    DANNY
     Great.

Vito takes Danny's hand.

                    VITO
I gonna help you.

Danny looks at the carafe of wine.

                    DANNY
I don't know if you can help me.

PatG gets up.

                    PATG
I'll see you back in Altamura.

                    VITO
My son he drive a you G.

Vito pulls the skin down under his eye. PatG smiles
and leaves. Vito turns to Danny.

                    VITO (CONT'D)
Don'a worry . . . I help a lotta
people. I gotta my nephew he was a
goin' to jail for four years.

Vito sets a bottle of liquor on the table.

                    VITO (CONT'D)
He sella da cigarettes a un
police. De police he a yell. My
nephew he droppa de price. But de
police he a tired dat everyone
sells a de cigarettes and no a
follow da law. My nephew he in a
world of shit. . . . I get him-a
off.

                    DANNY
How did you do it?

                    VITO
I gave his boose 50 cartons of
cigarettes.

                    DANNY
Boss . . . That's bribery.

                    VITO
No, no. It was a gift.

                    DANNY
What happened to the policeman?

                    VITO
No one like a him. He make too
much noise. Dey take away his
sticker.

                    DANNY
Badge. My problem's medical.

                    VITO
I can help. My coosin's da
presidente of our hospital.

Danny nods.

                    VITO (CONT'D)
One time my anudder coosin he get
trouble. He no work. De trut, he
likea too much de women. He go and
go. You see de African girls on
the road from da airport?

                    DANNY
Yes.

                    VITO
Ita help you keepa de appetite.

Vito's wife walks in, he winks at her, she blushes.

                    VITO (CONT'D)
Luisa I gonna eatta you.

Danny becomes red and turns away from Luisa.

                    DANNY
(mumbled) Kiss you.

                    VITO
No eat her. Don'a worry she no
speak-a de English.

Vito yells in Italian. His wife blushes and smiles.

                    DANNY
What did you say?

                    VITO
I tell her in Italian. . . .
Anyway. My coosin who like a de
femmine. He missa de work. He
gotta pay de bills. He gotta wife
and a kids. He go to da dottore
and he say he no see. Dat way he
geta de pension. He go 1 time and
he bring a de doctor de fruit.
He go another time and he bringa

da doctor de vegetables. He go
anudder time and he bringa de
wine. But dis doctor he no wanna
do noting. He makea my coosin
poor.

                    DANNY
          Wait, wait. Your coosin. (Danny
          looks impatient.) Your cousin
          wanted disability so he could go
          with prostitutes?

Vito nonchalantly nods his head.

                    DANNY (CONT'D)
          He wanted disability because he
          was blind. But he was not blind?

                    VITO
          Aspetta, dat's a right. My coosin
          he bring-a wine, he bringa de
          vegetables, he bringa da frutta.

                    DANNY
          To the doctor who was going to say
          that he was blind.

Vito nods and winks.

                    DANNY (CONT'D)
          Yes, I understand.

                    VITO
          Well inna de end dis doctor say
          he gonna sign, che my coosin he
          a blind. My coosin hea happy. He
          goona getta de pension and dey
          gonna pay him back pay. Dis way he
          pay all a de bills.

Danny rubs his jaw.

                    DANNY
         What happened?

                    VITO
         I tell-a you. He bring all-a de
         wine and all de vegetables. And
         before he sign-a de papers . . .

Vito makes a sign of the cross and kisses his two
fingers on his right hand and he makes a small circle with them.

                    DANNY
         What?

                    VITO
         (voice raised) Hea die. After my
         coosin empty his house. He die.
         After my coosin he bring a de
         wine, fruit and de vegetable, he a
         die!

Danny rubs his eyes and looks to the side.

                    DANNY
         And so?

                    VITO
         And So? After my coosin hea
         bringa de wine and he bringa de
         vegetables and he bringa de fruit?
         He a clean his house for dat
         doctor! He a clean a de house!

                    DANNY
         I got that.

                    VITO
         My coosin he go to de son. De son
         takea de place ofa de papà. He
         say my coosin go to de specialist
         a San Giovanni. But my coosin he

explain dat he notta blind and de
son he say he no sign. My coosin
hea mad. I mean de son he atea de
frutta and he atea de vegetables
and he drinka de wine too!

                    DANNY
          Logical.

Vito nods contentedly.

                    VITO
          Bastardo! My coosin he tell de
          doctor he gonna kill him. Because
          it's-a his fault dat de family of
          my coosin no eat. I mean my coosin
          he gave de fadder de wine and...

                    DANNY
          Okay . . .

                    VITO
          I go and talk to him.

                    DANNY
          Did it help?

                    VITO
          I get my coosin a pension for the
          mentale, depression.

                    DANNY
          Oh . . . He was depressed?

Vito looks confused and indignant.

                    VITO
          No one in my family gotta
          depress . . . De father was a
          de bastard. Signor Benedica.
          (He crosses himself.) The law isa
          dat if you blind you gotta go to
          San Giovanni.

                    DANNY
          What's San Giovanni?

                    VITO
          It's a de hospital of Padre Pio.

                    DANNY
          I want to see their fruit.

                    VITO
          Me too.

                    DANNY
          So what did they do?

                    VITO
          I tol' you. I talk to de son. He
          feel bad dat his fadder take all de
          fruit, all of de vegetables . . .

                    DANNY
          Yeah, I got it.

                    VITO
          He feel responsabilla. He call
          a coosin dottor and we get a de
          pension per de mentale. He scrive
          che my coosin he's a crazy . . .
          I tell you he isa crazy. Dose
          African girls he know dem all by
          name. If I tell dem I his coosin
          dey make a discount. You wanna go
          tomorrow?

                    DANNY
          No. I'll pass. Thanks though.

                    VITO
          I gotta lotta coosins. What do you
          need?

          Danny sighs.

                    DANNY
        I need Mimmo Cha cha to take an
        HLA compatibility test for me.

                    VITO
        You canna find someone in America a
        takea de test? Youa smart man. You
        can'ta pass a de test yourself?

Danny looks to the side.

                    DANNY
        I'm sick. I need a bone marrow
        transplant. Because we're related
        he may be able to help me.

Vito scratches his jaw.

                    VITO
        I heard of dat. I gotta de coosin
        in Milano. All of de famiglia dey
        go to see if they could help him.
        But they don' give no test. They
        checka de blood.

                    DANNY
        That's what I need him to do.

                    VITO
        He do it. Are you hees coosin?

                    DANNY
        No.

                    VITO
        His nephew?

                    DANNY
        No.

                    VITO
        His brother? . . . No, you notta
        his brother. Aah.

Vito nods his head.

                    VITO (CONT'D)
          I getta de picture . . . Your
          mother she makea de bread with
          Mimmo.

Vito scratches his chin.

                    VITO (CONT'D)
          Dissa no gonna be simple. He gotta
          four kids. They can help you too?

                    DANNY
          Maybe.

                    VITO
          Hisa wifea Franca shea young. Hea
          sixty-four. Shea forty-three or
          forty-five or someting. It's a not
          easy witta de younga wife. You
          know. Someting like dis can give
          her to makea de . . .

Vito raises his right hand. He folds back all of
his fingers accept the baby finger and the finger
next to the thumb. Danny looks at Vito's hand.

                    DANNY
          What's that?

                    VITO
          I mean she maybe go crazy and . . .

Vito makes the sign again.

                    DANNY
          What's this?

Danny makes the sign.

                    VITO
          Datsa de corna.

Danny squints his eyes.

                    VITO (CONT'D)
          Qua in Eetaly we no kill. I mean
          Roma she a three million people dey
          kill sixty people a year. Napoli
          dere dey one million and dey kill a
          eighty. Dere dey gotta lotta.

Vito makes the sign with his hand again.

                    VITO (CONT'D)
          Half of all-a de murders in Italy,
          dey are from de corna. De resta
          dey de Mafia. But de Mafia dey don'
          wanna kill nobody.

                    DANNY
          Oh?

                    VITO
          No, eets a bad-a for beesiness. I
          mean if General Motors starta kill
          its workers . . .

                    DANNY
          Of course . . . But what is the
          corna?

Vito looks in the kitchen. He makes a fist with his
right hand. He grabs his upper right arm with his
left hand and begins to pump his fist up and down.
Danny watches closely.

                    VITO
          And den.

Vito makes his right hand flat and moves it across
his neck.

Danny scratches his head. Vito sees his confusion.

                    VITO (CONT'D)
          (whispered) Your papà.

                    DANNY
          He's not my papa.

                    VITO
          But he's not-a your coosin.

Danny nods.

                    VITO (CONT'D)
          He's not-a your uncle or your
          brudder . . .

Danny nods again and then catches himself.

                    DANNY
          Please just go ahead.

                    VITO
          Your papà, he got maybe fifteen,
          twenty years older den his wifea.
          Maybe he no likea before . . .

Vito makes the motion with his right fist up and
down.

                    VITO (CONT'D)
          Maybe she looka for reason to do
          le corne. He never tell her dat he
          got udder children, she makea de
          corna. He find out and he keel her.
          Everyone know dat he keel her but
          he no go to jail cause everyone
          know dat she . . .

Vito makes the sign with his fingers and rubs his
chin.

                    VITO (CONT'D)
We fix it. I talk to Don Antonio.
Dere's more den one way to drink a
cat.

EXT PARK IN CENTER OF ALTAMURA LATE EVENING

Danny and Vito watch PatG walk with Francesca.
Danny shrugs.

                    DANNY
          What's her story?

                    VITO
          She a nice a girl. She gotta sfiga.
          She unlucky. Her fidanzato, fiancee'
          he die in a car accidente.

                    DANNY
          How old is she?

                    VITO
          Francesca. Twenty-four, twenty-five.

                    DANNY
          My friend's forty-eight.

                    VITO
          If he's a gentleman, no problem.

Danny shrugs and rolls his eyes.

INT SPARE BEDROOM SEVEN THIRTY WEDNESDAY MORNING

Vito's mother walks in. PatG and Danny are up and
half nude. She picks up a pile of clothes. PatG
shrugs.

INT KITCHEN MOMENTS LATER

Danny and PatG walk out. Vito's waiting in the
kitchen.

204.

                         VITO
          Good morning. Good morning. We go
          to Mass and then you gonna see.

                         PATG
          Mass?

                         VITO
          Today's a May 1st. It's da feast of
          Saint Joseph de laborer. Everyone
          dey a go to Mass . . .

INT CHURCH WEDNESDAY SHORTLY AFTER PATG, VITO, AND
DANNY GOING FOR COMMUNION.

                         DANNY
          (whisper) This place is beautiful.

                         PATG
          (whisper) I ain't been to Mass in
          ten years. Hate to see it crumble.

EXT PARK IN CENTER OF ALTAMURA SHORTLY AFTER

Danny and PatG walking. People nod and wave to
them.

                         DANNY
          I wish I could talk to them.

                         PATG
          Just nod and smile.

INT BAR IN ALTAMURA WEDNESDAY MORNING

Bar's crowded with smiling and yelling people.

DANNY LOOKS IN THE MIRROR AT THEM, SMILES, AND
TURNS AWAY.

                         PATG
          Due caffè per favore.

                    PATRON
       Pago io.

                     PATG
       Grazie.

                    DANNY
       What's goin on?

                     PATG
       The guy paid for our coffee.

                    DANNY
       Should we accept?

                     PATG
       In Italy they say, "Se non accetti,
       non meriti."

                    DANNY
       What does that mean, professor?

                     PATG
       If you don't accept kindness, you
       don't deserve it.

EXT PARK IN CENTER OF ALTAMURA SHORTLY AFTER

PatG and Danny are walking. Vito's yelling. They
turn.

                    VITO
       Danny, G!

Vito's with a man of about twenty. They meet. The
man (Nicola) looks Danny up and down. He hugs and
kisses Danny.

VITO WIPES TEARS FROM HIS EYES

                    DANNY
       What's this?

                         VITO
           Danny, dis a you brother Nicola.

INT DANNY'S OFFICE WEDNESDAY NINE IN THE MORNING

Ma's at Irene's desk and Irene's sitting at Danny's
desk.

                         IRENE
           I wonder what Mr. Hubble's doing?

                         MA
           It's three in the afternoon. He's
           probably reading the paper.

                         IRENE
           In Italian?

                         MA
           Do you want tea?

INT RUI'S CHILI PARLOR

Rui's sitting on the inside of the bar. There are
three customers on the outside.

                         RUI
           Well, Danny Hubble's helped more
           people than anyone I know.

                         PATRON
           Before you canonize him, get me
           some coffee.

Rui stands up and gets the coffee pot.

                         RUI
           I know he's gonna be all right.

Ma and Irene are walking in.

                    PATRON
          Maybe Danny was Mother Teresa
          of the Hill, his old man was no
          prize.

Ma and Irene look at each other.

                     RUI
          (loud) Good morning, Ma Hubble,
          Irene. We were just talking about
          how we're all pulling for Danny.

                     MA
          I heard.

Ma looks over at the Patron, who gets up and leaves.

                     RUI
          I'll bet PatG's showing Danny a
          good time. Italy. Why Italy? They
          got something there for our Danny?

                    IRENE
          I certainly hope so.

INT CIANCIA BAKERY WEDNESDAY AFTERNOON

Nicola's speaking (in Italian) to his father, who
is short, bald, and muscular. Mimmo yells. Nicola
yells. The father slaps Nicola.

INT DANNY'S OFFICE LATER WEDNESDAY MORNING

Irene and Ma are sitting at the desks.

                     MA
          All of these people are late?

                              IRENE
                    No, some have paid.

                              MA
                    Did Schmidt pay?

                              IRENE
                    He'll never pay.

                              MA
                    He damn well better pay.

                              IRENE
                    Can't.

                              MA
                    Why?

                              IRENE
                    Died.

                              MA
                    What do we do about the money?

                              IRENE
                    It goes into the out bucket.

                              MA
                    What?

          Irene points to the wastepaper basket.

                              IRENE
                    We're out it.

                              MA
                    But it's so sloppy. Why wasn't
                    Schmidt current with his bills?

                              IRENE
                    No money.

                    MA
That's not our problem.

                    IRENE
Mr. Hubble didn't see it that way.

Irene stares out of the window.

                    IRENE (CONT'D)
Mrs. Hubble . . . Mrs. Hubble.

                    MA
Call me Bridget, for heaven's sake.

                    IRENE
Do you think Italy will help?

                    MA
He's searching for a donor.

                    IRENE
I know . . .

                    MA
How do you know?

                    IRENE
I added. Bridget, I added.

Ma looks hard at Irene.

                    MA
What are you saying?

                    IRENE
I know that Mr. Hubble could not
sire children.

                    MA
Just what else did you know about
my husband?

Irene closes her mouth and touches her hand to it.

INT BAR IN ALTAMURA SIX THIRTY WEDNESDAY EVENING

Danny, PatG, Vito, and Nicola are at a tiny table
having coffee. In the background men are arguing.

                    DANNY
          How is it that you speak English?

                    NICOLA
          We take a foreign language from
          the second grade. . . . I like U2
          so I translate. They're Irish, but
          they speak English.

                    DANNY
          You speak well.

                    VITO
          Your father, he is a hard head.

Vito raps on his forehead as he would on a door.

                    VITO (CONT'D)
          Nicola thinks his mother can help.

                    DANNY
          I don't want to create problems.

                    VITO
          Your fadder say he no remember
          nottin'. You know . . .

Vito makes his right hand into a fist and pumps it.

                    DANNY
          My mother says that I'm his son.

                    VITO
          You are.

Danny and PatG stare at Vito

                    DANNY
          How do you know?

                    VITO
          Nicola say dat you de twin.

                    NICOLA
          My mother will see too. She's
          wise.

                    DANNY
          I should just go home.

                    PATG
          Bull. These hardheaded DP's . . .

                    VITO
          Are you sure it's your only
          chance?

                    DANNY
          (mumble) Faded genes.

                    NICOLA
          Listen. . . . We gonna help you.

                    DANNY
          It's crazy. Why should he care?

Danny stares.

                    NICOLA
          You're family . . . Sangue tira.

                    DANNY
          What's that?

                    VITO
          It means dat da blood in your
          veins pulls da blood in his veins.

INT BEDROOM WEDNESDAY EVENING

Danny's packing his bags. PatG's sitting on his bed.

                    PATG
          You'll go home to die.

                    DANNY
          The olive does not curse the tree
          as it falls. . . . Nicola.

                    PATG
          Passion dies, love is. . . .
          Francesca.

                    DANNY
          Romeo, don't get yourself killed
          over it.

                    PATG
          Love's the only thing worth
          getting yourself killed for.

Danny stares at the wall. Silence.

CRUCIFIX

He then takes a folded shirt in his hands.

                    DANNY
          I feel at home here.

                    PATG
          Give it a chance. The kid would do
          anything for you. . . .

                    DANNY
          That's why I'm going to leave.

The door opens, Vito's mother walks in. She takes
the shirt out of Danny's hands and starts unpacking
his suitcase. PatG laughs.

                    PATG
          Woman doesn't need to act like a
          man. . . . She's a woman. ~
          Francesca.

                    DANNY
          (laughing) A woman could pull a
          bus with one of her pubes. ~ Vito.

They both laugh. Vito's mother finishes unpacking
and exits.

EXT VITO'S MOTHER'S HOUSE

PatG and Danny are against the wall. Vito and
Nicola drive up.

                    VITO
          Get in.

Danny and PatG get in.

WOMAN IN WOODEN CHAIR RISES TO MAKE ROOM FOR THE
CAR TO PASS

                    PATG
          Where are we going?

                    VITO
          It's ricci season.

                    DANNY
          Ricci?

                    PATG
          I think that they're sea urchins.

                    DANNY
          You eat 'em?

EXT ON THE SEA WEDNESDAY LATE EVENING

The walkway is jammed. PatG, Danny, and Vito sit on a breaker wall eating sea urchins with bread. Nicola takes pictures.

DANNY RAISES A RICCIO TO HIS LIPS, STICKS HIS TONGUE IN IT, LOWERS IT, AND SMILES. NICOLA SNAPS A PICTURE.

> VITO
> Don Antonio speaka to your father.

> PATG
> Who is he? Is he a mafioso?

> VITO
> Dere's Don Antonios in all towns.
> Some are good, some are not.

Vito nods his head.

> VITO (CONT'D)
> Italy isa free because de
> government, de church, and de
> Mafia coexist. We not aworry about
> getting beat up by de police.
> Our government cannot become too
> powerful. De church, de Mafia.

> DANNY
> What does "Don" refer to?

> NICOLA
> We call priest and big men "Don."

> PATG
> So does Don Antonio run the town?

> VITO
> He's a like a de king. A just king
> is de best form of government.
> Today capitalism wears-a da face

of-a democracy. In a monarchy
people are-a eaten by a lion, in
democracy they're-a eaten by a
pack of rats.

Danny has a clam in his hand.

                    VITO
          Italy has de greatest country in
          de world and we are de greatest
          lovers.

                    DANNY
          Oh, the greatest lovers? Just how
          do you prove that?

                    VITO
          I no prove dis. You prove it.

Danny stares.

                    VITO
     Who was the greatest queen of all times?

                    DANNY
          Cleopatra?

                    VITO
          Precisely. And Cleopatra could
          have had de best lovers from all
          of Africa or anywhere in de world.

                    DANNY
          Okay?

                    VITO
          She marry Egyptians because she
          was forced to, but her two lovers,
          she could have had lovers from all
          over Africa, all over de world.
          Who were her lovers?

Danny stares, genuinely entertained.

                         VITO
              But who were her lovers?

                         DANNY
              Her lovers?

                         VITO
              Yes, de men she cheat on her
              husband.

                         DANNY
              Mark Antony and Caesar?

Vito nods.

                         VITO
              Dat's why Italy is part of de
              greatest race on de planet . . .

Danny stares.

                         VITO
              We are Latins.

                         DANNY
              But you're Europeans.

                         VITO
              Precisely. We are Latin Europeans,
              like our brothers, the Latin
              Americans. And our race and our
              society is the best on de planet.

                         DANNY
              Hey this thing is still moving.

                         NICOLA
              It's fresh.

                         DANNY
              What should I do with it?

                    VITO
          Eat it. It's a fresh. All food
          should be eaten fresh. . . .

Vito takes one and sucks it off the shell.

INT LARRY'S BAR WEDNESDAY AFTERNOON

Kevin's drinking with three guys.

                   LARRY
          Ol' Danny may come home in a box.

                   KEVIN
          Have you heard from him?

                   LARRY
          Nah . . . I hope he's getting to
          some of those churches. . . .
          Italy ought to be a nice place to
          see the Lord.

                   KEVIN
          I saw the Lord clearer in a bar
          than in a hundred churches.

Kevin downs the rest of his beer and walks out.

                   PATRON
          If he talks about the Lord like
          that again I'll sock him.

                   LARRY
          That would make the Lord
          happy . . .

INT VITO'S CAR WEDNESDAY EVENING

CARS ARE ZOOMING BY ON THE RIGHT AND LEFT

                    VITO
          I hope Papà listen to Don Antonio.

                              PATG
                 Doesn't he have to listen?

                              VITO
                 Not even Don Antonio can interfere
                 wit a man's a family.

INT DANNY'S HOUSE IN KITCHEN WEDNESDAY EVENING

Ma and Irene are looking at pictures.

                              MA
                 This is Danny when he was seven.

                              IRENE
                 I wish we could have been closer.

                              MA
                 We were close enough.

                              IRENE
                 Mr. Hubble was a fine man.

                              MA
                 Drink your rum.

INT BAR IN ALTAMURA LATE WEDNESDAY EVENING

PatG and Tommaso are singing "Al di là" to a crowd.

PATG REALLY GIVING IT ALL

                              PATG
                 Ci sei tu, ci sei tu per me . . .
                 la la la la . . . la la la la. La
                 la la laaa.

FRANCESCA STARING AT HIM

EXT SIDE STREET IN ALTAMURA AN HOUR LATER

PatG's under a streetlamp. Francesca comes, kisses
his cheek.

INT CIANCIA HOME SAME TIME

Nicola and father are screaming. The father slaps
Nicola's face hard. The mother comes running in.

                    FRANCA
          Basta! Basta!

Mimmo stares at his wife. His wife remains staunchly
calm.

INT BAR IN ALTAMURA EARLY THURSDAY MORNING

Francesca brings coffee and rolls to G, Vito, and
Danny.

AN ENVELOPE BETWEEN PATG'S COFFEE CUP AND SAUCER.

PatG takes the envelope, walks outside. Vito shakes
his head. Danny smiles. A pause.

                    PATG
          (heard from outside) Yahoo!

INT DANNY'S FRONT ROOM THURSDAY NIGHT CLOCK READS
2:10

MA IS SNORING ON THE COUCH. IRENE'S SLEEPING ON THE
CHAIR

The doorbell rings. Irene stirs, walks to Ma and
shakes her.

                    IRENE
          There's someone at the door.

                    MA
          It's PatG. He's here for Danny.

Irene walks and looks at the door handle, then she
looks up.

                         IRENE
              Bridget. PatG's in Italy.

Irene looks at Bridget. Bridget continues to snore.

INT BAR THURSDAY MORNING SAME TIME IN ITALY

As PatG walks in he puts the envelope in his back
pocket. PatG looks at Vito. Vito looks sternly back,
then smiles.

                         PATG
              Italy's the most beautiful place
              on earth.

Vito shakes his head, looks at Francesca and raises
his cup.

                         VITO
              To the beauty of Italy.

FRANCESCA SMILING FROM BEHIND THE BAR

INT DANNY'S HOUSE IN KITCHEN SHORTLY AFTER

Marla's sipping tea with Irene.

                         IRENE
              I'm sorry about your parents.

                         MARLA
              People say I'm with him trying to
              replace my father. They're wrong.

                         IRENE
              I know, honey.

                         MARLA
              I love that half-pint to death.
              I don't know what I'd do if
              something happened to him.

                    IRENE
        I know, honey.

                    MARLA
        Danny says that he's just my
        experiment. He's so childish.

                    IRENE
        All men are, honey.

Ma gets up off the couch and walks into the kitchen.

                    MA
        I said to stay away from my son! I
        want this girl out of here!

Ma walks into the bathroom slamming the door behind
her.

INT BAR IN ALTAMURA SHORTLY AFTERNOON

Nicola walks in. Joins PatG, Vito, and Danny.

                    VITO
        Any news with Papà?

Nicola points to his bruised face.

                    NICOLA
        He's not in a real good mood.

Danny gets up and leaves.

INT THE CIANCIA BAKERY LATER THURSDAY MORNING

PatG, Vito, and Nicola are waiting. Mimmo's serving
customers.

                    PATG
        (whispered) They're twins.

The last customer leaves. Mimmo picks up a bread
knife.

                         MIMMO
              Non sono fatti tuoi! (This is none
              of your business!)

PatG moves behind Vito.

                          PATG
              Guy's a little emotional.

                          VITO
              Signor Ciancia, ti prego di
              ragionare. (Mr. Ciancia, I beg you
              to be rational.)

                         MIMMO
              Ti prego di andarsene o morire!
              (And I beg you to leave or die!)

                         NICOLA
              Papa, papà . . .

                         MIMMO
              A casa! A casa! (Go home now!)

Nicola, angered, rushes out the door.

                     MIMMO (CONT'D)
              E voi due, via! (And you, leave!)

                          PATG
              (smiling) I don't stay where I'm
              not welcome.

Mimmo comes around with the knife. PatG and Vito
leave.

EXT PARK IN CENTER OF ALTAMURA LATER THURSDAY

Danny and PatG are sitting feeding pigeons. Nicola
approaches.

                         NICOLA
              Danny, my mamma wants a to know
              you.

DANNY
To know me?

PATG
If she means the biblical sense,
this could become interesting.

DANNY
Cut it out.

NICOLA
She says that she must see you . . .

EXT MIMMO'S HOUSE SHORTLY AFTER

THE OLIVE TREES THAT SURROUND THE HOUSE

Danny, Nicola, and Vito sneaking up stairs. Nicola
enters.

NICOLA
(whispers) Mamma . . . Mamma.

His mother arrives at the door

NICOLA (CONT'D)
(continuing to whisper) E Papà?

MAMMA
Entra. Entra. (Come in, come
in . . .)

They enter. The mother looks at Danny. She hugs him.

MAMMA (CONT'D)
(crying) Sangue del mio sangue.
(blood of my blood.) Parlo io con
lui. (I'll talk to him.)

DANNY
What's she saying?

>   VITO
>   Blood of my blood. You gotta de
>   same blood as her children.

Nicola takes Danny's arm and pulls him toward the
door.

>   VITO (CONT'D)
>   Let's a-go. She'll talk a-to her
>   husband for you.

Vito winks at Danny.

>   VITO (CONT'D)
>   No one has a de power over a man
>   dat his a wife has.

Vito smiles.

>   VITO (CONT'D)
>   Even Don Antonio has a to pay
>   attention to his a wife.

Danny heads down the stairs. He holds his chest.
Nicola and Vito notice. They each take an arm.

>   VITO (CONT'D)
>   Take it easy Danny. Take it easy.
>   Tutto apposta. (Everything's fine.)

DANNY COUGHS, HOLDS HIS CHEST. TEARS COME TO NICO-
LA'S EYES.

>   NICOLA
>   Let's go to the hospital.

They move Danny into the car as he clutches his
chest.

EXT HOSPITAL SHORTLY AFTER

A SQUALID THREE-STORY BUILDING WITH A LARGE STATUE
OF THE MADONNA OVER THE ENTRANCE.

They escort Danny and meet a cigarette-smoking male nurse dressed in white. Danny looks down.

CIGARETTE BUTTS ALL OVER THE FLOOR, DINGY WALLS MISSING PAINT.

The nurse puffs a cigarette, puts it out on the floor in front of Danny. Vito, Nicola, and Danny sit in tiny chairs.

                    VITO
          Questo ha leukemia. (He has
          leukemia.)

The nurse disappears into a doorway in front of them.

INT BAR IN ALTAMURA THURSDAY SAME TIME

Francesca answers the phone. Her face turns to fear.

                  FRANCESCA
          Bene . . . Bene . . .

She turns to her grandfather.

               FRANCESCA (CONT'D)
          Devo trovare l'Americano. (I must
          find the American.)

Her grandfather looks sternly.

               FRANCESCA (CONT'D)
          Nonno . . . nonno . . . per
          piacere.

          (Grandfather, grandfather, please.)

He nods. Francesca kisses him, removes apron, and exits.

EXT PARK IN CENTER OF ALTAMURA SHORTLY AFTER

PATG'S STANDING. A TABLE OF OLD MEN PLAYING ITALIAN
CARDS.

Francesca runs up from behind him.

> FRANCESCA
> Patrizio, Danny sta al'ospedale.
> (Patrick, Danny's in the hospital.)

A MAN LOOKS AT FRANCESCA, HIS PARTNER LOOKS BACK
AND NODS

INT HOSPITAL EMERGENCY ROOM SHORTLY AFTER THURSDAY
AFTERNOON

The nurse comes with another man. He's wearing a
white smock and a stethoscope and has a cigarette
hanging from his mouth.

> VITO
> It's a de doctor.

Noise comes from outside. The doors open. A young
girl walks in with a towel wrapped around her hand.
A crying man, a hysterical woman, and four other
people enter. The doctor takes Danny's arm. They
follow the screamers.

INT HOSPITAL EMERGENCY ROOM MINUTES LATER

The family's yelling and crying. The doctor unwraps
the girl's hand, exposing a gashed finger.

> DOCTOR
> Metti tre punti. (Put in three
> stitches.)

The nurse nods and coaxes the family to leave.
The mother and father remain. The nurse prepares
a steel platter with thread and needle. The door
bursts open. In rush Francesca and PatG.

                    PATG
          Danny, Danny, are you all right?

                    DANNY
          Still kickin'. . .

The doctor approaches Danny with a cigarette in his
mouth.

                    DOCTOR
          No good a de smoking.

He grins, walks to the girl, examines her finger,
takes her arm, and waves her and her parents out
with his right hand.

               FATHER OF GIRL Grazie
          Dottore . . . Grazie.

The doctor nods kindly and returns to Danny. The
doctor puts the cigarette out on the floor. He
motions with his hands.

                    DOCTOR
          Takea offa your clothes.

DANNY STARES

                    DOCTOR
          Takea offa your pants

DANNY STARES

                    DOCTOR
          Takea offa your shirt.

                    DANNY
          Now we're getting somewhere.

Danny removes his shirt. Doctor places his hand on
his back and thumps it with a knuckle. He repeats
this on the chest.

DOCTOR NODS

                     DOCTOR
         Leukemia. I tink you might gotta
         leukemia.

                     DANNY
         Yeah, I know.

                     DOCTOR
         Dat's no good.

                     DANNY
         That's what they say.

                     DOCTOR
         Why you comea to Italy witta
         leukemia?

Danny looks at Vito. Vito addresses the doctor in
Italian.

                     VITO
         Lui è figlio di Ciancia u fornaio.
         (He's Ciancia the baker's son.)
         É qua per vedere se il padre può
         aiutare. (He's here to ask his
         father for help)

The doctor looks and knocks his head with his
knuckles.

                     DANNY
         Well?

                     VITO
         He say you father is a hardhead.

                     DOCTOR
         You must a go home. . . . If you
         getta bad here. . . . Dat's a not
         good.

DANNY LOOKS DOWN AND OPENS AND CLOSES HIS LEFT HAND

                    DANNY
          I have to die somewhere.

                    DOCTOR
          Me and your father are fra cugini?

                    DANNY
          Fra cugini?

                    NICOLA
          They're not cousins but their
          cousins are cousins. They're . . .

Vito makes a ball of his hands then he reopens
them, clasping the fingers together.

                    VITO
          Dey're between coosins.

                    DANNY
          Are you related?

Vito looks and shrugs.

                    VITO
          Gesù say we all brudders . . . da
          closer da blood, da stronger de rope.

Vito makes his fist into the form of a rope and
tugs.

                    DOCTOR
          You go home a domani tomorrow.

                    DANNY
          My ticket's for Tuesday.

                    DOCTOR
          You come wit ITA Airline?

Danny nods.

                         DANNY
               Part of the way.

The doctor pushes his finger up and dials his cell
phone.

                         DOCTOR
               Cugi . . . come stai? E la
               signora, i bambini? Bene bene
               bene. Senti ho un problema.
               (Cousin, how are you? And the
               missus, the kids? Listen, I have a
               problem.)

The doctor looks at Danny.

                    DOCTOR (CONT'D)
               What's a your name?

                         DANNY
               Doc, without a transplant I'm dead
               and in no rush to go home.

                         DOCTOR
               Don'a worry. What's a your name? My
               coosin he do it all. Don'a worry.

The doctor speaks into the phone.

                    DOCTOR (CONT'D)
               Ciancia.

The doctor looks at Danny.

                    DOCTOR (CONT'D)
               What's a you name?

                         DANNY
               Danny Hubble.

The doctor looks confused. He speaks in the phone.

                         DOCTOR
            Cugi . . . ti chiamo più tardi.
            (Cousin, I'll call you later.)

Vito looks at the doctor and winks.

                         VITO
            Grazie Dottore. Ci pensiamo noi.
            (Thanks. We'll take care of it.)

The doctor nods.

                         DOCTOR
            Infermiere, ossigena.

The nurse wheels a green tank over to Danny.

                    DOCTOR (CONT'D)
            Take a dis wit you. If you feel
            pain or trouble breathing, take
            it.

The doctor breathes loudly in and out. He puts a
plastic mask on. He attaches a tube. He turns a
handle and oxygen exits.

                    DOCTOR (CONT'D)
            You take dis and you be okay. I will
            talk a to Signor Ciancia. . . .

The doctor winks.

                         DANNY
            Thank you. What do I owe you?

The doctor is puzzled.

                         DOCTOR
            Owe?

Danny looks at Vito. PatG is concentrating to hear.

                    VITO
          Don'a worry about it.

                    DANNY
          But what about the oxygen tank?

                    VITO
          I bring it back when you done. Is
          it different in America?

INT CIANCIA HOME LATER

The doctor's drinking coffee. Mimmo's fidgeting nervously.

                    DOCTOR
          E se è veramente fig? (And if he is
          your son?)

Mimmo slams his hand on the table.

                    MIMMO
          No! Non è! (He's not!)

Doctor puts his cup down and raises his hands.

                    DOCTOR
          Bene.

INT VITO'S MOTHER'S KITCHEN SAME TIME

Nicola and Danny are sitting. Danny has the oxygen
mask on.

                    DANNY
          They serve McDonald's in American
          children's hospitals. . . . Who
          can prove what kills you faster?

                    NICOLA
          Someday I want to go to America.

                    DANNY
          Why?

                    NICOLA
          Everyone's rich. The women are
          beautiful. The streets are safe.
          Here, everyone does as they please.

Danny gazes.

                    DANNY
          Want to get a caffè?

                    NICOLA
          Are you okay?

                    DANNY
          I'm fine.

Danny takes the mask off.

INT BAR IN ALTAMURA THURSDAY EVENING

Danny and Nicola walk in. Patrons greet them.

                    PATRON 1
          Ciao Danny.

                    PATRON 2
          Way! Danny.

                    PATRON 3
          Danny, vuoi un caffè?

PatG's sitting at a side table. He gets up and hugs
Danny.

                    PATG
          My friend, come and sit down . . .

The two sit, and Francesca brings them coffee.

                    PATG (CONT'D)
        He doesn't leave your side.

                     DANNY
        He's a good kid. I'll miss him.

DANNY STARES. NICOLA SMILES.

INT DANNY'S OFFICE THURSDAY SAME TIME

Irene's pushing buttons on the phone.

                     IRENE
        I can't get through. . . . I hope
        he's okay. It's strange he doesn't
        call.

                      MA
        Life's strange, Irene.

INT BAR THURSDAY LATE AFTERNOON

Nicola, PatG, and Danny are seated. Mimmo enters.

                    MIMMO
        Fuori Nicola! (Nicola, get out!)

Nicola looks from his coffee to his father. His
eyes tear up.

                 MIMMO (CONT'D)
        Fuori! (I said to get out!)

Mimmo walks out. Nicola follows with his head faced
down.

                     DANNY
        Who was that?

                     PATG
        Your father.

INT VITO'S MOTHER'S SPARE BEDROOM SHORTLY AFTER

Danny's sitting on his bed. PatG's watching.

                    DANNY
          I caused enough trouble. When it's
          time to check out, you check out.

INT DANNY'S OFFICE THURSDAY SAME TIME

Ma's at Irene's desk. Irene's standing over her with
a paper in her hands. Ma's banging the buttons of
the telephone.

                    MA
          It's useless!

                    IRENE
          Calm Bridget . . . Calm.

                    MA
          Easy for you, he's not your son.

She throws the phone on the floor, rests her arm and
head on the desk, and sobs.

INT VITO'S MOTHER'S SPARE BEDROOM THURSDAY AFTERNOON

Danny and PatG sitting on the bed. Nicola walks in.

                    NICOLA
          I will take the exam.

                    DANNY
          I'd rather it be me dead than you.

                    NICOLA
          We're brothers. I must help you.

Nicola smiles. His eyes are glassy. The brothers
hug.

                    PATG
        I'll let you settle family matters.

PatG leaves.

                    NICOLA
        The fox jumps one hundred times
        for the grape. But he can't reach,
        so he convinces himself that the
        grape's sour. The fox forgets.

                NICOLA (CONT'D)
        Papà does not. The sour lives
        inside him. His grape was America.

EXT BAR ALTAMURA SHORTLY AFTER

Nicola and Danny pass arm in arm. PatG's talking
to Francesca.

                    PATG
        Hey, wait up you guys.

PatG wraps Danny's arm. The three walk the park arm
in arm.

                PATG (CONT'D)
        Where are you going?

                    NICOLA
        Home. I have an exam.

                    DANNY
        I'm going to the park.

                    PATG
        I'll come with. We need to talk.

Nicola waves. PatG looks at Danny.

                PATG (CONT'D)
        I want to marry Francesca.

                    DANNY
        I know.

                    PATG
        How do you know?

                    DANNY
        You say you want to marry every
        girl after a week.

INT BAR THURSDAY AFTERNOON

Danny and PatG are sitting. One of the town police
walk in.

                    POLICEMAN
        Caffè.

Another Patron enters.

                    PATRON
        Un affogato.

FRANCESCA MAKES DRINK WITH ICE, WHIPPED CREAM, AND
SEVEN LIQUORS

Policeman sips coffee. Patron takes affogato,
removes the policeman's hat, and pours the dessert
over the policeman's head.

THE DRINK RUNS DOWN THE POLICEMAN'S FACE. HE LICKS
HIS MOUSTACHE.

                    PATRON
        Dalle multe a uno che può pagare.
        (Write tickets to the people that
        can afford them.)

The Patron exits. Policeman pushes ice cream onto
the floor.

The grandfather offers a rag, he cleans himself off.

                    POLICEMAN
          Acqua.

Francesca brings water. He drinks and leaves.

                    PATG
          I'm moving here.

EXT A STREET IN ALTAMURA THURSDAY LATE EVENING
DARK

THE BACKS OF PATG AND FRANCESCA WALKING HAND IN
HAND

INT BAR IN ALTAMURA FRIDAY MORNING

                    DANNY
          I feel comfortable here.

                    VITO
          It's-a where da souls of your
          people are . . . It's-a your home.

                    DANNY
          It's a strange place.

                    VITO
          Italy's de home of the family, de
          Renaissance, de Mafia, and freedom.

Patron makes duck quack with his hand. Vito smiles.

                    VITO (CONT'D)
          We find-a order in disorder. Da
          government, church, and de Mafia fight
          for power, and de people breathe da
          freedom left by the holes dat dey
          make in da fabric of our nation.

                    DANNY
          But your young people listen to
          English music and dream of the
          American way of life.

                         VITO
          The youth is-a spoiled by quick-a
          richness. But dey are Italian.

Vito raises his hand and finger to make a point.

                       VITO (CONT'D)
          Southern Italians are-a Arabic
          Europeans who have-a more in common
          wit de Tunisia than wit Milano.

Danny sips from his water glass.

                       VITO (CONT'D)
          Italy speaks hundreds of a
          dialects. We have different foods.
          It's a quilted fabric made of five
          hundred pieces. There's no udder
          place like it.

Nicola walks in.

                        NICOLA
          (breathless) Danny. My mother she
          say you eat with us today.

                        DANNY
          (shocked) What about your father?

Nicola shrugs his shoulders.

                         VITO
          Ma tuo padre lui può uccidere
          questo. (But your father will kill
          him.)

Vito waves to Danny.

                       VITO (CONT'D)
          Come on.

                        DANNY
          Where are we going?

                         VITO
           To pay respect to your family.

Danny, Vito, and Nicola drive through tiny streets.

EXT CEMETERY SHORTLY AFTER

The cemetery is surrounded by a ten-foot-high wall.

FIFTEEN-FOOT CRUCIFIX IN THE INSIDE

They enter.

                         DANNY
           It's beautiful. I've never . . .

Nicola leads the way. The tombs are in walls that
are about ten feet tall and have pictures of the
deceased on the front.

CIANCIA LEONARDO 1883-1984 BOUQUET OF FLOWERS ON
HIS TOMB

Nicola kisses the photo.

                         NICOLA
           This is grandfather and his
           parents.

Danny looks up.

CIANCIA

INT ALTAMURA CEMETERY FRIDAY SHORTLY AFTER

Nicola's pointing to a tomb stone on the wall.

                         NICOLA
           That's Zio Michele. He was crazy.
           One day his donkey kicked him. He
           punched it in the head. It died.

Nicola walks along and points to the next stone.

                    NICOLA (CONT'D)
          This is his wife. She hit him over
          the head with a pot and told him
          to go with his donkey.

Nicola continues to walk.

                    NICOLA (CONT'D)
          This is our cousin Giovanni.
          He died when he was 7.

Nicola rubbed his hand over the laminated photo of
the boy.

                    NICOLA (CONT'D)
          This is his mother. She killed
          herself over the pain.

                    DANNY
          She's beautiful.

INT BAR IN ALTAMURA FRIDAY LATE MORNING

Danny's stuffing money into the phone.

                    DANNY
          Yeah Ma . . . oh Irene. What are
          you doing there?

                    DANNY (CONT'D)
          Good. Take care of her . . .
          Everything's fine. Tell her that I
          need some time. I got to go.

Danny hangs up.

INT SAINT ALCUIN SEVEN IN THE MORNING, FRIDAY

Irene and Ma are two of ten people in the church
for Mass.

                    IRENE
          (whisper) I feel good after Mass.

                         MA
          (whisper) Nothing can make me feel
          good.

The priest exits onto the altar and genuflects.

INT VITO'S MOTHER'S SPARE BEDROOM EARLY AFTERNOON

PatG's tying Danny's tie.

                         DANNY
          I feel like I'm going to my
          communion . . . to be assassinated.

                         PATG
          It'll be okay.

                         DANNY
          Where will you eat?

                         PATG
          Don't worry. Enjoy yourself.

                         DANNY
          Enjoy my own hanging?

THE SOUND OF A HORN.

                         PATG
          Vito's here . . . How do you feel?

                         DANNY
          Okay.

                         PATG
          Bring the oxygen just in case?

                         DANNY
          No. I don't . . .

EXT THE CIANCIA RESIDENCE FRIDAY LUNCHTIME

Vito kisses Danny. PatG waves from the car. Vito wipes under Danny's left eye with his handkerchief. Danny turns to walk.

                    PATG
          Wait a minute Danny.

PatG exits the car, runs to Danny, kisses him on both cheeks. They hug.

                    PATG (CONT'D)
          Be calm . . . Everything will be
          all right. I love you Danny.

EXT OUTSIDE VITO'S HOUSE

PatG's driving. Vito opens his door.

                    VITO
          You sure you a wanna to do deese?

PatG smiles and nods.

                    VITO (CONT'D)
          Dere could be trouble.

PatG rolls his eyes.

                    VITO (CONT'D)
          You know de street?

PatG nods and smiles.

                    VITO (CONT'D)
          Don'a smile. It's a not funny.

PatG nods.

                    VITO (CONT'D)
          You eat al L'Ancora, dey wait.

PatG nods.

                    VITO (CONT'D)
          You no gonna say not'ing?

                    PATG
          Grazie.

EXT SAINT ALCUIN FRIDAY SAME TIME

Irene and Ma are walking out of the church.

                    IRENE
          Do you feel better?

                    MA
          I feel . . .

                    IRENE
          There's Kevin.

Irene points up the street. Kevin's a bit wobbly.

                    MA
          Going out for the day?

                    KEVIN
          Coming home from the night. Ladies.

Kevin takes his hat off and puts it to his chest.

                    IRENE
          We went to church.

                    KEVIN
          Oh, and what did you do there?

                    IRENE
          (hesitated) Why, we prayed.

                    KEVIN
        For who?

                    IRENE
        Why, we pray for everyone. Don't
        we, Bridget?

                    KEVIN
        Do you pray for me?

Pause. Irene looks at Bridget.

                    IRENE
        We pray for all of Danny's friends.

                    KEVIN
        Well stop it! Last time someone
        prayed for me, I broke a leg.

Kevin tilts his hat and smiles.

                  KEVIN (CONT'D)
        (Irish accent) Top o' the morning.

EXT CORNER AT OUTSKIRTS OF ALTAMURA

FRANCESCA IS ENTERING VITO'S CAR

INT THE CIANCIA RESIDENCE FRIDAY SAME TIME

Danny and Nicola are together at the dining room
table.

                    NICOLA
        He'll be home soon.

NICOLA PATS DANNY'S HAND

INT VITO'S CAR SHORTLY AFTER

Francesca's head's on PatG's shoulder. A car zooms
by.

                         PATG
          (singing) *And I love that girl,*
          yes I love that girl, oh I love
          that girl and someday, she'll be
          mine!

Francesca looks at him and smiles.

INT THE CIANCIA RESIDENCE FRIDAY SHORTLY AFTER

DANNY'S ROLLING THE PLASTIC FACE OF HIS WRISTWATCH.

INT L'ARAGOSTA RESTAURANT SHORTLY AFTER

A man escorts PatG and Francesca into the restaurant.

                         HOST
          (loud) This is PatG de American
          singer.

Everyone in the restaurant looks as they walk to
the veranda.

                    HOST (CONT'D)
          The best people eat here, Mr. G.

He pulls out a chair for Francesca and then PatG.

                    HOST (CONT'D)
          Mr. G, you must sing for us. We
          gotta de accordion player.

PatG smiles and nods. The host walks quickly away.

                         PATG
          Io sono nervoso per Danny. (I am
          nervous for Danny.)

Francesca touches PatG's his hand and smiles.

                    FRANCESCA
        Non ti preoccuparti. (Don't worry.)

A waiter arrives.

                    WAITER
        Mr. G you wanna de wine?

                    PATG
        Sì.

The waiter hands PatG a wine book.

                    PATG (CONT'D)
        Beh.

                    FRANCESCA
        Patrizio prendi bianco per il pesce.
        (Patrizio, get white for the fish.)

                    PATG
        Sono morti che se n'importa?
        (They're dead, what do they care?)

The waiter smiles, Francesca laughs.

                    WAITER
        I'll bring you a nice Locorotondo.

PatG winks.

INT THE CIANCIA RESIDENCE SHORTLY AFTER Danny looks
up from his watch.

EXT STREET ON THE WAY HOME FROM CHURCH SAME TIME

Ma and Irene are walking.

                    MA
        Without a transplant, Danny dies.

                         IRENE
          I know.

                          MA
          It's a lost cause.

                         IRENE
          They're the only ones worth
          fighting for.

EXT L'ARAGOSTA RESTAURANT ON VERANDA SHORTLY AFTER

The accordion player's a serious, chubby boy. He's
playing.

                         PATG
          (singing) *Strangers in the night*
          exchanging glances wondering in
          the night what were the chances we
          could fall in love . . .

PatG stops. He walks over to Francesca.

                     PATG (CONT'D)
          Fammi mangiare con quella che
          amo. (Let me eat with the one I
          love.)

The other tables clap. A man stands and toasts.

                          MAN
          All'americano. (To the American.)

INT THE CIANCIA RESIDENCE SHORTLY AFTER

The mother and daughters enter with food. Nicola
stands.

                         NICOLA
          This is Maria. She's almost thirty.

Maria bows her head.

> NICOLA (CONT'D)
> This is Anna. She's twenty-four
> years old.

Danny smiles and Anna bows her head. Noise from a door opening is heard. The house is silent. A thirty-ish man walks in. He looks into the dining room and yells at his mother.

> NICOLA (CONT'D)
> That's Antonio. He's the rooster.

Nicola makes like a rooster with his arms. His sisters laugh. Antonio walks in. He notices that he's being mocked.

> ANTONIO
> Non sarà da ridere per papà!
> (It will not be funny to father!)

Antonio looks at Danny. They both smile tightly. The door opens in the kitchen. Everyone runs to their seats.

EXT L'ARAGOSTA RESTAURANT SHORTLY AFTER

> PATG
> I'd like to move here. Stare qua.

> FRANCESCA
> America's big and rich. Italy is
> piccola e povera.

> PATG
> Vuoi stare cumme? (Would you like
> to be with me?)

INT THE CIANCIA RESIDENCE SHORTLY AFTER

Mimmo and the mother are standing. The others are sitting.

250.

                    MIMMO
          Non lo voglio do! (He's not welcome
          here!)

Danny looks at Nicola.

NICOLA HOLDS DANNY'S HAND UNDER THE TABLE

Danny tries to stand up and Nicola holds him down.

                    MIMMO
          Questi sono i miei figli! Questa
          è la mia famiglia. (These are my
          children! This is my family.)

Mimmo passes his hand with his palm up in front of
his kids.

                    FRANCA
          Mangiamo.

The husband looks sternly. She looks back sternly.

                    FRANCA (CONT'D)
          Mangiamo?

Mimmo grunts and sits.

                    NICOLA
          Caro Gesù benedici questo cibo
          . . . e aiuta tutti malati della
          nostra famiglia. Amen. (Dear
          Jesus, bless this food . . . and
          help all of the sick and all of
          our family. Amen.)

Everyone bows.

ANNA AND MIMMO LOOK AT DANNY. MIMMO LOOKS AT ANNA
AND LOOKS AWAY QUICKLY

The father's mumbling.

                    DANNY
          I don't want to make problems
          here.

                    NICOLA
          Shh. My mother will handle him.

                    FRANCA
          Se qualcuno deve stare male, sono
          io. (It's me who should be upset.)
          Io accetto tuo sangue. E tu? (I
          accept your blood? And you?)

                    NICOLA
          My mother says that blood is
          blood.

                    MIMMO
          Basta! Mangiamo!

                    NICOLA
          My father wants to eat, not talk.

The women serve. Mimmo's served, then Danny.

                    NICOLA (CONT'D)
          (whispering) My mother served you
          after my father, this says that
          you're not a guest. She served you
          before the rooster. This says that
          you're the oldest brother.

Nicola looks around the table. The family starts
to eat.

                    MARIA
          Perché c'è la sedia elettrica in
          America?

                    NICOLA
          Maria wants to know why there's
          the electric chair in America.

                         DANNY
              To stop the killing.

Nicola doesn't bother to translate. He looks confused.

                         NICOLA
              You kill people to stop killing?

Danny shrugs.

                    NICOLA (CONT'D)
              Anna wants to know if you like
              Lady Gaga?

Danny's face twists.

                         DANNY
                   No.

Franca speaks to Nicola who turns to Danny.

                         NICOLA
              My mother wants to know when you
              go home.

                         DANNY
              Martedì. (Tuesday.)

Danny smiles. Franca smiles back.

THE FATHER HAS HIS HEAD BURIED IN HIS PLATE

Franca speaks to Nicola.

                         NICOLA
              My mother wants a to know when you
              come back?

                         DANNY
              Tell your mother that I hope to
              live long enough to come back.

Nicola explains, and the whole table sounds like a
beehive.

                    NICOLA
          Danny, they want to know about
          your sickness, your disease.

                    DANNY
          I have leukemia.

                    ANNA
          (slowly) But you have to do
          something so you live.

                    DANNY
          I need a bone marrow transplant.

                    ANNA
          My mother says that you are my
          brother. Is this true?

Danny looks to Mimmo, who's wearing a stone face.

                    DANNY
          I don't know. I don't know . . .
          Nicola, can you take me home?

                    NICOLA
          But we're eating. It's okay.

                    DANNY
          I know, I don't feel well.

                    NICOLA
          Danny deve andare. (Danny must leave.)

THE FATHER HAS AN ANGERED FACE. THEIR FACES LOOK
CONCERNED.

                    MIMMO
          Nessuno parte finché siamo finiti.
          (No one leaves until we're finished.)

The father looks sternly. The mother looks away submissively.

                    NICOLA
          Danny, it's offensive to leave
          before we're finished.

                    DANNY
          Tell your father that I will leave
          when I please.

Danny stands up. Mimmo yells. Franca yells and the whole family begins to scream. Mimmo goes to the door.

DANNY STARES IN MIMMO'S EYES, OPENS THE DOOR, AND LEAVES

EXT BACK ROAD NEAR ALTAMURA

LATE AFTERNOON

PatG and Francesca are parked in the middle of olive trees. PatG's shirt's off. Francesca's kissing him from above.

                    FRANCESCA
          Ti amo.

EXT STREET TO VITO'S MOTHER'S FROM CIANCIA'S, SAME TIME

Danny's walking slowly in the direction of home.

INT THE CIANCIA RESIDENCE SHORTLY AFTER

NICOLA LOOKS ALL OVER THE ROOM

Nicola attempts to leave. Mimmo shoves Franca, grabs Nicola. Franca attacks Mimmo. Others rush. Nicola cries, breaks his father's hold and exits. Mimmo's blocked by the family. He spits.

                    MIMMO
Sulla tomba della mia madre, avrò
niente da fare con questo uomo!
(On my mother's grave, I will have
nothing to do with that man!)

EXT VITO'S CAR FRIDAY SAME TIME

PatG and Francesca are embraced.

                  FRANCESCA
We love, but we're afraid to lose.

                    PATG
Tell me something about love.

                  FRANCESCA
If love finds you worthy it will
direct its own course.

INT DON ANTONIO'S HOME

Vito's sitting with Don Antonio.

                    VITO
Don Antonio. È una situazione
pazzo. (It's a crazy situation.)

                 DON ANTONIO
Ciancia è stato diportato. C'è
odio per la vita che voleva fare.
(Ciancia was deported. He is angry
about the life he wanted.)

                    VITO
Ha una famiglia e una bella vita.
(He has a good family and a good
life.)

                 DON ANTONIO
Amico, l'uomo è insaziabile.
(My friend, men are never satisfied.)

> VITO
>
> Don Antonio, puoi provare un'altra
> volta? (Don Antonio, can you try
> to help again?)

> DON ANTONIO
>
> Sì. Provo. (Yes I will try.)

Vito stands up. He takes Don Antonio's hand.

> VITO
>
> Grazie Don Antonio.

Vito's leaving.

> DON ANTONIO
>
> Amico. Il mio potere è limitato
> quando l'uomo non è ragionevole.
> (Friend. My power is limited when
> man is irrational.)

Don Antonio smiles.

> DON ANTONIO (CONT'D)
>
> Ci sono poche scelte con un
> testardo. E poi si distrugge ogni
> speranza. (The way to deal with a
> hard head would destroy all hope.)

Vito nods.

> VITO
>
> Grazie Don Antonio.

VITO EXITS. THE DOOR CLOSING

> DON ANTONIO
>
> Mangiamo. Ho fame. (Let's eat. I'm
> hungry.)

His wife nods from the kitchen doorway.

EXT STREET IN FRONT OF CIANCIA HOME

NICOLA'S DESPERATE FACE AS HE LOOKS UP THE EMPTY
STREET

EXT STREET ON THE WAY TO VITO'S HOUSE SHORTLY
AFTER

PatG's heading up the street in Vito's car.

DANNY'S LYING ON THE STREET.

PatG swerves to a stop.

NICOLA'S RUNNING

They put Danny into the car.

INT VITO'S MOTHER'S KITCHEN FRIDAY EVENING

The doctor, PatG, and Nicola with Danny, who's taking oxygen.

> DOCTOR
> My son. You may not make it. I
> have a coosin, he's a doctor in
> Rome.

> DANNY
> (slowly) How did I know he was
> going to say that?

The doctor looks at Vito.

> DOCTOR
> Did you talk to Don Antonio?

Vito makes a pistol of his right hand, twists it,
and frowns.

> VITO
> But he will try again.

                         DOCTOR
              Nicola, e Papà?

                         NICOLA
              My brother and sisters and I will
              take the exam.

                         DOCTOR
              And your father?

Nicola makes a pistol of his right hand and twists
it.

                         DOCTOR (CONT'D)
              Will Papà allow this?

                         NICOLA
              No one can stop us.

The door opens. Maria and Anna enter. Anna kneels
next to Danny. She cries and kisses his hand.

                         DOCTOR
              You take de plane Tuesaday. I come
              later . . . You're in good hands.

                         DANNY
              Doc. If I don't make it until
              Tuesday, what will happen?

The doctor looks to the side and grins.

                         DOCTOR
              Whatta you mean? People, dey must
              die at home.

Danny waves, the doctor puts his ear next to Danny.
He nods strangely at Danny and stands up.

                         DANNY
              Promise?

The doctor looks, purses his lips closed and nods.

                    DOCTOR
        I call my coosin at Bari so you
        all can takea de test Monday
        morning.

He shakes his head.

                    DANNY
        (slowly and faintly) America is de
        land of de dollar. Italy is the
        land of the coosin.

The doctor smiles.

                    DOCTOR
        Non mangiare prima dei esammi. (No
        one can eat before the exams.)

Anna and Maria nod. The doctor walks out.

                    DANNY
        I'm so sorry.

                    NICOLA
        For what? You found your family.

Nicola rubs Danny's head. There's a knock at the
door. Francesca's holding a tray.

                    FRANCESCA
        My nonno say a drinka dis, Danny.
        It a help you respirare.

Danny removes the mask and sips it.

                    DANNY
        What is it?

                    FRANCESCA
        La menta calda. (Hot mint.)

Danny nods his head and smiles.

INT DANNY'S OFFICE LATE FRIDAY MORNING

Ma's reading a magazine. Irene's filing. Marla walks in.

                    IRENE
          Hi Marla.

                    MARLA
          News?

                    IRENE
          He called and talked for a moment.

Irene looks in Ma's direction.

                    MARLA
          Hello Mrs. Hubble.

Irene ignores her.

                    MARLA (CONT'D)
          Do you have a number for him?

                    IRENE
          The number we have doesn't work.

                    MARLA
          Where is it?

Irene hands Marla the paper.

INT VITO'S MOTHER'S KITCHEN FRIDAY EVENING

Maria, Anna, and Vito's mother with Danny. Laughter. Anna's leaning with her hand on Danny's head. He's looking up at her from the corner of his eyes. PatG walks in.

                    PATG
          How you doing, partner?

                    DANNY
          Good . . . better.

                    PATG
          Wanna take a walk? It's beautiful.

Anna looks at PatG.

                    ANNA
          No. He's a not well.

                    DANNY
          No, look I wanna get some air.

                    MARIA
          Danny.

                    DANNY
          Please. I'll be right back.

                    PATG
          Are you his sisters or something?

EXT THE STREET IN FRONT OF VITO'S MOTHER'S HOUSE

                    DANNY
          Hurry.

                    PATG
          Feeling bad again?

                    DANNY
          Horrible. I gotta take a leak.

PatG smiles.
                    PATG
          That would've been rough.

                    DANNY
          If I'd have taken a leak there, I
          wouldn't have to worry about my
          leukemia any more.

                    PATG
          Why's that?

                    DANNY
          They'd have heard it all. I'd have
          died of embarrassment.

INT THE BAR FRIDAY EVENING

Danny and PatG are seated.

                    PATG
          I'm going home Tuesday, fix some
          things and come back.

                    DANNY
          You're what?

                    PATG
          I'm coming back here.

                    DANNY
          For the summer? Anna comes
          running in.

                    ANNA
          (breathless) Danny, it's your lover
          on the phone.

                    PATRON
          What's a dat?

                    ANNA
          Danny hurry, your lover from
          America.

                    PATRON
          (Loudly) È la sua amante. (His
          lover's on the phone.)

                    PATRON
          Bravo Danny. Bravo.

                    PATRON 2
          Forza Ciancia. (Go get her
          Ciancia.)

The patron makes a kissing sound. Everyone laughs.
A few people pat Danny's back and clap as he leaves.

INT VITO'S MOTHER'S KITCHEN SHORTLY AFTER

Danny has the antique gray phone in his hand.

                    DANNY
          Ma, what's going on? Why did you
          say you were my lover?

Voice of Bridget comes through loud and clear.

                    MA
          I said no such thing. I said I was
          your mother.

                    DANNY
          Oh I get it. Lover, mother.

                    MA
          Danny, come home. Irene says
          hello. . . . And someone wants to
          talk to you. I'll put them on.

                    MARLA
          Danny, It's Marla.

                    DANNY
          Hi.

                    MARLA
          You never called. How are you?
          What are you doing?

                    DANNY
          Dying. What are you doing there?

Marla looks at Danny's mother and Irene. They both turn their backs. Marla talks softly in the phone.

> MARLA
> Danny, I miss you. I want you to come home.

> DANNY
> Don't do this. Marla, wake up . . .

> MARLA
> But Danny, I need . . .

> DANNY
> Marla, I can't fill your needs.

INT DANNY'S OFFICE SAME TIME

MARLA'S FACE AS SHE HEARS A CLICK AND A DIAL TONE

Danny hits the wall with his hand.

INT BEDROOM SATURDAY MORNING

Danny's sleeping with oxygen. Anna's sitting. Danny rolls over. His back's to Anna. He throws off the blankets, stands bare chest and underwear, puts on slippers and turns.

ANNA'S SMILING FACE

> DANNY
> Oh jeez.

Danny grabs his blanket and covers himself.

> DANNY (CONT'D)
> Oh sorry, scusa, scusa.

Anna walks out of the room laughing.

INT DANNY'S HOUSE IN FRONT ROOM SATURDAY EARLY MORNING

MA'S SITTING IN THE KITCHEN WITH A CUP AND A CIG-
ARETTE

Irene walks in.

                    IRENE
          You promised Danny not to smoke.

                    MA
          Yes, and he promised that
          everything would be fine. We're
          even.

                    IRENE
          It's not his fault, Bridget.

Bridget looks crossly at Irene.

                    MA
          Whose fault is it?

Bridget inhales and blows smoke in Irene's direction.

                    MA (CONT'D)
          You and my husband both thought
          that I was so stupid.

                    IRENE
          That's not true.

                    MA
          Well what is true?

                    IRENE
          Bridget, we're family.

                    MA
          I'm not a Muslim.

Irene solemnly gazes into Bridget's eyes.

266.

IRENE
The two most important people in
my life are the most important
people in your life.

INT VITO'S MOTHER'S KITCHEN TUESDAY MORNING

The doctor's testing Danny's blood pressure. A cigarette is hanging from his mouth.

DOCTOR
Danny, will you do me a favor?

DANNY
Sure. I don't know what a forty-
seven-year-old bald, short, fat
man dying of leukemia could do for
anyone but...

DOCTOR
Calla your doctor. I'm a family
doctor. I'm not qualified.

Danny looks at the doctor. He takes a deep breath
and shows discomfort. He nods his head.

DOCTOR (CONT'D)
I'll leave you in the good care of
your sister Anna.

Anna smiles and turns holding a tray of coffee and
cookies.

ANNA
Mangia, Danny.

DANNY
You know, a guy could get used to
this. . . .

DANNY SMILES WARMLY. HIS FACE IS THAT OF DEATH

EXT PARK IN ALTAMURA LATER SATURDAY MORNING

PatG and Vito are seated on a bench.

                    VITO
          Americans always bring change. Be
          careful witta that girl. Dose you
          leave behind pay for-a your sins.

                    PATG
          What do you mean?

                    VITO
          Francesca's family trust me . . .
          What are your intentions?

PatG looks at Vito seriously.

                    PATG
          Intentions . . . what if I told
          you that my intentions were
          serious?

Vito nods and smiles.

                    VITO
          If you leave a de mess here, I'm
          responsible also. You usea my car.

                    PATG
          Why did you help me?

                    VITO
          I love Americans.

                    PATG
          It seems that all Italians do.

                    VITO
          You saved us in da war . . . I
          hope we can save-a ourselves from
          you . . . da television, de
          music, da fast food and a de fast
          life. De tings dat have made de

American family broken and de
American people sick wit diabetes
and cancer.

> PATG
> It'll never come here.

> VITO
> I hope the youth resists-a.

> PATG
> They're Italian. I see it.

> VITO
> What do you see-a?

> PATG
> I see culture, love, and
> commitment.

> VITO
> And Danny. Whatsa he see?

> PATG
> I don't know what he sees.

> VITO
> Da doctor wantsa him to leave.

> PATG
> I don't know if Danny does . . .
> Maria's taking him to school
> today.

> VITO
> What does he-a have to go home to?

PATG GAZING

INT SCHOOL IN ALTAMURA SATURDAY SAME TIME

Maria is in front of the class.

THE CRUCIFIX ON THE MIDDLE OF THE FRONT WALL.

>   MARIA
>   Danny è un agente di
>   assicurazione. (He's an insurance
>   man.)

Danny nods and bows nervously. A boy blurts out.

>   BOY
>   Be a good boy.

>   MARIA
>   Gennaro!

>   DANNY
>   That's okay.

Danny raises his hand and smiles tightly.

>   DANNY
>   I am fine.

Danny gazes over the class.

>   DANNY
>   My name is Danny. I am from
>   Fineview, part of Pittsburgh,
>   Pennsylvania in the United States.

A girl raises her hand. Danny points to her.

>   GIRL
>   Is it cold in Pittsburgh?

Danny rubs his palms together.

>   DANNY
>   It can be very cold in the
>   winter. We get lots of snow and
>   temperatures hit minus 30, meno
>   trenta.

                    GENNARO
        Meno trenta?! My balls would freeze!
        The class erupts into laughter.

                    MARIA
        Gennaro! Continui e ti butto
        fuori. (If you do not stop, I will
        throw you out of the classroom.)
        Another girl raises her hand.
        Danny points to her.

                    GIRL 2
        How is the food?

Danny smiles.

                    DANNY
            Interesting.

                    GIRL 2
        McDonald's came to Altamura 20
        years ago and was shut down in a
        few months. They made a film about
        it called *Focaccia Blues*.

                    DANNY
        That's a wonderful thing. I'll have
        to see the film.

A boy with glasses raises his hand. Danny points
to him.

                    BOY
        Why did America invade Iraq and
        Afghanistan?

Danny's face shows a bit of difficulty. Danny clears
his throat.

                    DANNY
        I'm not sure why we invaded Iraq
        and Afghanistan, and today, more

than ever, the American people are
against the decision to do so.

Gennaro raises his hand.

> GENNARO
> Why don't American presidents
> go to jail for invading their
> neighbor's country?

Danny pauses and then contritely responds.

> DANNY
> We have the strongest military
> in the world. The president is in
> charge of the military. Who would
> throw him in jail?

> GENNARO
> You are saying, Mr. Danny, that the
> United States is above the law?

> DANNY
> No. I am not saying that.

Danny points at another girl who raises her hand.

> GIRL 3
> Why is America so dangerous? You
> have a five times better chance of
> getting murdered there than in
> Italy, and a three times better
> chance of committing suicide, per
> capita.

Maria stares at Danny. His face demonstrates discomfort.

> MARIA
> Okay, okay, can we change the
> subject? Mr. Danny is not an
> expert in everything American.

He is an insurance man. Ask him
about things that he would be more
familiar with.

Another girl raises her hand. Danny points.

                    GIRL 4
          Mr. Danny, do you like Rihanna?

Danny smiles.

                    DANNY
          My favorite American performers
          are Boz Skaggs and Al Green.

Danny smiles.

                    DANNY
          And PatG.

A boy raises his hand. Danny points. The boy stands.

                    BOY 2
          I'm Francesca's cousin. I have
          heard PatG sing. I like it. I like
          it when he sings in Italian—his
          accent is funny. Do you think he
          loves my cousin?

Maria covers her smile. Danny clears his throat.

                    DANNY
          Your cousin is a very nice woman. I
          think that PatG likes her very much.

                    MASSIMO
          My father says that if PatG's not
          respectful, he will break his leg
          caps.

                    MARIA
          Massimo!

                    MASSIMO
          Scusa. I mean kneecaps.

Danny raises his hand, palm down.

                    DANNY
          That's all right, Massimo. PatG's
          heard similar things many times
          in his life.

Danny's face is a bit easy. He points to the door.

                    DANNY
          Con permesso. (With your
          permission I will leave.)

                    MARIA
          Bravo Danny, bravo.

Maria looks at the class.

                    MARIA (CONT'D)
          È vero, ragazzi? (Is it true, class?)

                    CLASS
          (The class yells) Bravo!

Danny walks out and Maria follows him.

                    MARIA
          Do you like the school?

                    DANNY
          Very much.

                    MARIA
          Where will you go?

                    DANNY
          I'm going to find PatG.

Maria kisses him on the cheek.

                    DANNY (CONT'D)
          Thanks.

Danny smiles and turns away.

EXT RESTAURANT ON SEA ON THE VERANDA SATURDAY
AFTERNOON

PatG, Danny, and Vito are at a table.

THE OXYGEN TANK

                    PATG
          What are they called?

                    VITO
          Tartufi.

PatG grabs one and a piece of bread. He dips the
bread into the soft tartufo shell. He bites the
bread and looks at Vito.

                    PATG
          Interesting. I don't know if
          I like it, but it's definitely
          interesting.

Danny takes a tartufo, dips bread into it, and eats it.

                    DANNY
          I like it. I've never tasted
          anything like it, but I like it.

                    PATG
          Vito, why do you think the food
          tastes so different here? We
          import Italian oil and wines and
          stuff.

                    VITO
          De apple tastes best eaten under-a
          da tree.

Shipped five thousand kilometers it can never taste
the same.

                    PATG
          That's why I'm moving here.

                    DANNY
          Sure.

                    PATG
          Besides. I don't want Vito's life
          on my conscience.

                    VITO
          Follow your heart. I take care-a
          of myself.

                    DANNY
          You'd never leave America.

                    PATG
          You're right but sometimes I feel
          like America's left me.

Vito waves to the waiter to bring another bottle
of wine.

                    DANNY
          Vito, are Italians patriotic?

Vito shrugs his shoulders.

                    PATG
          Vito, what's patriotism mean to
          you?

                    VITO
          Disliking all-a countries except
          your own.

276.

EXT THE RESTAURANT ON VERANDA A FEW HOURS LATER

PatG's singing with the accompaniment of the accordion player.

                    PATG
          (singing) *Anna mai core* . . .

The tables clap. PatG takes his wineglass in his hand.

                    PATG (CONT'D)
          All'Italia. (To Italy.)

                    VITO
          A Francesca. (To Francesca.)

The three toast.

INT A BARI APARTMENT SATURDAY LATE AFTERNOON

Danny, PatG, and Vito are sitting with drinks in their hands. A woman walks in. She's in her forties. She rubs Vito's face.

                    VITO
          There's a nottin' like an Italian
          woman . . . nottin'

                    DANNY
          What are we doing here?

                    VITO
          I'm-a come once a month for ten-a
          years.

A bell rings. A dark-skinned girl enters. She's greeted at the door by the madam. They kiss. They walk in to the men.

                    WOMAN
          Questa è Antonella.

Antonella walks in and smiles.

                    WOMAN (CONT'D)
          Chi lo vuole? (Who wants her?)

Danny looks strangely at PatG and Vito. The bell
rings. Another woman enters.

                    WOMAN (CONT'D)
              Questa è Filippa.

Filippa kisses the three men on each cheek.

                    WOMAN (CONT'D)
          Chi lo vuole? (Who wants her?)

                    VITO
          Ci sono tutte e due per Danny.
          (They're both for Danny.)

PatG laughs. Danny looks terrified.

                    DANNY
          Hey, I ain't.

                    PATG
          Danny, pretend you're back in the
          United States, in Las Vegas and
          have a good, no, a great time.

Vito winks. The woman prods the girls at Danny.
Each of them take an arm and pull him into a room.

INT BARI APARTMENT AN HOUR LATER

PatG and Vito are sitting with drinks in front of
them. A woman is on Vito's lap with her arm around
him.

                    VITO
          Jesus's best friend was a
          prostituta.

                         PATG
          Yeah . . . but she repented.

                         VITO
          So dey say . . .

Vito pushes the woman off his lap. He gives her his
empty glass. She goes to refill it.

                    VITO (CONT'D)
          Life-a comes from-a da woman. For
          four million, nine hundred, and
          seventy-five tousand years man,
          he was a warrior and-a hunter.
          He was-a kill off like-a de flies.
          He had two, three, four wifes.
          The stronger he-a was, da more
          wifes he had. He was a lion and
          da woman lioness protect-a her-a
          cubs often from-a him. Twenty-five
          tousand years ago woman, dey learn
          agriculture.

                         PATG
          Why woman?

                         VITO
          She was-a at home. She see a tree
          sprout or someting. Man he too
          selfish to-a worry bout fighting.

                         PATG
          Okay.

                         VITO
          About fifteen thousand years she
          teach-a man. Den she try to-a
          domesticate man like she did-a dog
          and cat.

                         PATG
          Oh this is good.

                    VITO
     Good but not-ta easy. Man's a lion.
     He wanta more women and he wanta
     young woman. In Italia we say a
     lion always want-a fresh meat.
     That'sa why older men crave-a
     younger women.

PatG starts laughing and the woman walks in with
fresh drinks.

                    VITO (CONT'D)
     In America you take-a tree wives
     like-a de Arab. You divorce and
     protect de individual. Or so you
     tink. America is too much about-a
     selfishness. I wanna do dis. I
     feel like dat. My feeling and
     what I wanna is more important
     den my wife, chil'ren, husband,
     even parents! Sickness passes for
     healty . . .

PatG continues to laugh.

                    VITO (CONT'D)
     In Italia we try to protect-a da
     family. So de man he gotta one
     wife. But he have a de adventure.
     But he no breaka da family.

                    PATG
     You think that's right?

                    VITO
     Look, at de suicides of American
     chil'ren and de shooting in-a
     schools. Do you tink dat's right?

                    PATG
     We're a strong religious country.

                    VITO
You were John Wayne in da 60's.
Twenty years later you're de
country of gay San Francisco. Your
priests-a molest a da children is
a sign that your society is not-ta
well. You spread a de disease over
de planet wit your marketing and
TV shows.

PATG RAISES HIS DRINK TO HIS LIPS

                    PATG
That's a bit harsh.

                    VITO
It is-a true. When my wants and
desires are-a more important to
me den dose of odders. . . I am
a selfish . . . dere are no tings
worse den selfish peoples.

INT BARI APARTMENT SATURDAY SHORTLY LATER

Everyone kisses as PatG, Danny, and Vito exit.

INT BAR IN ALTAMURA SATURDAY EVENING
Danny, Vito, and PatG enter. Francesca looks at
PatG. A few people come and greet them. PatG speaks
in a low voice.

                    PATG
Something's wrong. Did you see how
she looked at me?

                    VITO
She know.

                    PATG
What do you mean?

                    VITO
     She know.

                    PATG
          Impossible.

                    VITO
     Not for de Italian woman.

Danny starts to laugh. Vito Pats him on the back.

INT CHURCH ALTAMURA SUNDAY MORNING

Nicola, Maria, Anna, Franca, Danny, PatG, and Francesca seated.

THE PRIEST IS RAISING THE EUCHARIST

EXT STREET IN ALTAMURA SUNDAY AFTER MASS

The group is walking away from the church.

                    NICOLA
     You leave the day after tomorrow.

                    DANNY
          Yes. I leave . . . (quietly) but
          I'll never leave here.

INT BAR IN ALTAMURA SUNDAY EVENING

PatG's singing "Volare." Danny's sitting with his oxygen mask. Francesca brings a cup of tea. She touches Danny's face.

                    PATG
          Hey. Hey.

PatG waves a finger at Francesca. A few people laugh. PatG sees Francesca's grandfather and turns away.

PATG (CONT'D)
Oops.

EXT STREET IN FINEVIEW

EMPTY STREET WITH A SQUEAKY NOISE IN THE BACKGROUND
IRENE'S PULLING A LAUNDRY CART. A MAN IS WALKING
HER WAY

The man's closer.

KEVIN
Hello Irene! Goin' to the
laundromat?

IRENE
No.

KEVIN
Oh . . . Honeymoon's over?

IRENE
Danny comes home tomorrow.

KEVIN
I see . . . Irene, do you know the
two best words that I never said?

IRENE
No.

Irene looks confused.

KEVIN
I do.

Irene looks strangely.

KEVIN (CONT'D)
And top of the morning to ya.

Kevin bows. Irene continues on.

INT VITO'S MOTHER'S SPARE BEDROOM MONDAY MORNING EARLY

Maria wakes on a chair. She gently pushes Danny's arm.

> MARIA
> Danny . . . Danny . . .

Danny turns over and smiles.

> DANNY
> Today's the day.

> MARIA
> Yes Danny, today is the day.

Danny puts his hands together and shoos Maria.

> DANNY
> Vestire. (I must get dressed.)

MARIA'S SOFT GENTLE FACE

> MARIA
> You no wanna no help?

> DANNY
> If you help me I would die.

Maria smiles and walks out.

INT VITO'S MOTHER'S KITCHEN SHORTLY AFTER

Maria, Danny, and Vito's mother are seated. A horn beeps.

DANNY LOOKS AT THE OLD WOMAN. SHE SMILES AND NODS

EXT THE STREET IN FRONT OF VITO'S MOTHER'S HOUSE

THE BACK OF THE CAR. PEOPLE ARE ALL CRUNCHED TOGETHER

284.

EXT STREET ON THE WAY TO BARI HOSPITAL

Antonio's driving. He and Nicola are in suits. A man cleans the stopped car window. Antonio hands him some change. By Vito's side a boy's selling packs of tissues. Vito gives him some change. Antonio looks over at Vito and smiles.

                    ANTONIO
          Mangia e fa mangiare. (Eat and
          help others eat.)

Danny smiles.

INT BARI'S HOSPITAL SHORTLY AFTER

The hospital is dingy and unclean. The five siblings and the Altamurano doctor are waiting.

A SIGN (TEN FEET TALL) "PRIMARIO TROCCOLI GIUSEPPE"

A man in a white smock opens the door, smiles, and waves the doctor from Altamura in.

INT THE HOSPITAL HALL SHORTLY AFTER

The door opens, and the doctor from Altamura exits.

                    DOCTOR
          Danny, you first.

INT DOCTOR TROCCOLI'S OFFICE

A nurse assisting taking blood from Antonio.

INT DOCTOR TROCCOLI'S OFFICE SHORTLY AFTER

A nurse assisting taking blood from Nicola.

INT DOCTOR TROCCOLI'S OFFICE SHORTLY AFTER

A nurse assisting taking blood from Maria.

INT DOCTOR TROCCOLI'S OFFICE SHORTLY AFTER

A nurse assisting taking blood from Anna.

INT DOCTOR TROCCOLI'S OFFICE SHORTLY AFTER

All seven are in Doctor Troccoli's office. The doctor's smiling. The nurse puts tubes of blood together.

> DOCTOR TROCCOLI
> We'll know in less than a week.

> NICOLA
> I hope it's me.

ANTONIO SMILES AT DANNY

The nurse exits and reenters.

> NURSE
> Dottore c'è un'altro Ciancia. Lo faccio entrare? (Doctor, there is another Ciancia. Should I let him come in?)

The doctor curiously nods. Mimmo Ciancia walks in with his hat in his hand. He's dressed in a suit. The room's quiet.

> DOCTOR TROCCOLI
> Sì?

> MIMMO
> Sono qua per fare l'esame per aiutare il mio figlio. (I'm here to take the test to help my son.)

Mimmo bows reverently.

> DOCTOR TROCCOLI
> Bene bene.

The doctor shakes Danny's hand.

                    DOCTOR TROCCOLI (CONT'D)
          Buona fortuna.

                         DANNY
          Thank you, Doctor.

                    DOCTOR TROCCOLI
          Thanks is appreciated. If anything
          can be done, it'll be His doing.

Doctor Troccoli points up behind Danny's head.

AN OIL PAINTING OF CHRIST ON THE CRUCIFIX

The doctor from Altamura opens the door to the
hall.

DON ANTONIO'S SITTING ON THE BENCH

                         DOCTOR
          Don Antonio.

The two embrace.

INT THE CIANCIA RESIDENCE MONDAY AFTERNOON

The room's packed. Fruit's on the table. PatG, Francesca, and the doctor are present as well as Danny
and his family.

THE OXYGEN TANK

The doctor stands up.

                         DOCTOR
          Alla famiglia Ciancia. (To the
          Ciancia family.)

He hands a glass to Danny. The table stands up one
by one.

A TEAR RUNS DOWN DANNY'S FACE

He breaks down crying, and his head falls to the
table.

HIS HEAD BURIED IN HIS ARMS

INT VITO'S MOTHER'S SPARE BEDROOM SHORTLY AFTER

Danny's head is buried in his arms so you don't
know exactly where the scene opens.

                    DOCTOR
          You not make de choice to live
          here. You make a de choice to die
          here. This is not America.

                    DANNY
          I'll wait on the results. If
          there's no compatibility, there's
          nothing for me in America.

                    DOCTOR
          And your friend?

Danny smiles.

                    DANNY
          (weakly) PatG will do as he pleases.

Danny reaches out to shake the doctor's hand.

                    DANNY (CONT'D)
          Grazie dottore.

THEIR HANDS CLASP

INT THE CIANCIA HOME A MONTH LATER

REOPENS WITH A HAND CLASP

Antonio clasping Danny's hands helping him out of a wheelchair. Danny's lips are closed tight in a smile.

> ANTONIO
> Vieni, ti porto a letto. (Come, I bring you to bed.)

INT DANNY'S BEDROOM IN THE CIANCIA HOME

PatG walks in and looks at the plastic-covered oxygen tent.

CIANCIA DANNY CAC DNL 57 S 24 Z 404 H

PatG smiles.

> PATG
> What's this?

> DANNY
> (weak) The old man had to raise hell at the hospital.

Danny fights laughter. He speaks almost in a whisper.

> DANNY (CONT'D)
> Antonio and Mimmo almost threw a guy out the window to get me government coverage. It's for my son! He yelled my son's entitled!

Danny fights laughter.

> DANNY (CONT'D)
> (whisper) First the guy don't want to know me, then he wants to throw someone out the window to help me.

> PATG
> We should've ask Don Antonio to find you a donor.

                    DANNY
          It's okay like this, PatG. It's
          okay. . . .
          It's a dream to check out this
          way.

Danny coughs. The door opens. Franca and Anna
enter. Danny raises his hand.

                    DANNY (CONT'D)
          Sto bene. Sto bene. (I'm okay.)

The two sisters leave.

                    PATG
          Your Italian's getting good.

Danny points to a book on the desk.

                    DANNY
          I'm studying. I write letters to Ma
          and study Italian. Mimmo gave me a
          Bible. . . . I can't make heads or
          tails out of it.

PatG smiles.

                    DANNY (CONT'D)
          Live like you'll die tomorrow.
          Learn like you'll live forever.

PatG takes his friend's hand. Danny nods and winks.

INT. DANNY'S OFFICE MONDAY MORNING A WEEK LATER

Irene's speaking with a young man.

                    IRENE
          Sir, we have no bills, and our
          clients are very loyal. They love
          Mr. Hubble. He was good to them.

                        MR. SPARKS
            I'm sure . . . I'm sure . . .

                          IRENE
            I must talk to Mrs. Hubble and her
            son before I can decide.

                        MR. SPARKS
            But of course.

There's a noise behind them. They turn.

BRIDGET'S FACE. SHE HAS AN ENVELOPE IN HER HAND

                           MA
            He's not coming home. Not tomorrow
            or next week or ever. (she cries.)

                        MR. SPARKS
            I'll come back later.

Mr. Sparks walks out. Ma reads from Danny's letter.

                           MA
            Ma, life's about dying. It's
            beautiful. I'll write you soon.

Ma stares.

                       MA (CONT'D)
            He's delirious. He sleeps with a
            Bible that he can't read . . .
            What are those Eyetalians doing to
            him?

Irene looks and smiles.

                          IRENE
            A Bible can't be bad, Bridget,
            even an Eyetalian Bible.

                    MA
He's still waiting on the results.
What are those Eyetalians doing?
You know they kidnap people . . .

                    IRENE
Why would they kidnap Danny?

                    MA
Why were you talking to Mr. Sparks?

                    IRENE
Nothing important.

                    MA
PatG's mother's going crazy.
There's a rumor that he's going to
marry one of those Eyetalians.

                    IRENE
Impossible. They don't shave their
armpits.

INT DANNY'S BEDROOM IN THE CIANCIA HOME.

PatG, the doctor, Mimmo, and Franca. Danny's asleep
under the tent.

                    PATG
Shouldn't he be in the hospital?

The doctor shakes his head and waves them out of
the room.

INT THE CIANCIA RESIDENCE OUTSIDE DANNY'S ROOM.

                    DOCTOR
Ho mandato i raggi al professore
di Bari e mio cugino a Pavia. C'è
niente da fare. (I sent his X-rays
to Bari and my cousin in Pavia.
There's nothing left to do.)

                              PATG
              But in America?

                              DOCTOR
              Do you remember when Danny
              whisper to me? When he eat by his
              father and he come back here by
              himself?

PatG looks strangely.

                              PATG
              The day I found him on the street?

                              DOCTOR
              Yes. He say dat if dere is a no
              match he wanna die here. . . . He
              tell me dat day. I promise him.

They hear coughing and run back into the room.

                              DANNY
              (whispered) PatG.

Danny feebly raises his arm and waves PatG over.

                              DANNY (CONT'D)
              I told Irene to sell Sparks the
              business and to pay Larry and Rui.

                              PATG
              Danny.

                              DANNY
              It's a present. . . . In my drawer
              is a letter to my mother. It
              explains many things. . . . I want
              to sleep. . . .

PatG turns to leave. He hears a whisper. He turns
back.

                    DANNY (CONT'D)
        And PatG. Figli maschi. (May your
        children be male.)

PatG smiles and quietly closes the door.

EXT THE CIANCIA RESIDENCE THE NEXT MORNING

PatG approaches. Deranged yelling and screaming
come from the house. He opens the door. There's a
crowd in Danny's room.

DANNY'S WHITE AND HALF-NAKED. MIMMO AND ANTONIO
ARE STRUGGLING TO GET HIS SHIRT ON.

PatG grabs Nicola.

                    PATG
        What are they doing?

                    NICOLA
        (crying) They musta dress him
        before he gets a stiff.

                    PATG
        Oh no. Danny! Danny!

PatG breaks through and hugs the dead body of his
friend.

                    PATG (CONT'D)
        Ahhhhhhhhh!

HIS HEAD GOES BACK IN ANGUISH WHEN IT COMES BACK
DOWN HE'S TEN YEARS OLDER AND BEHIND THE BAR SERV-
ING A COFFEE

Francesca walks in holding the hand of an eight-
year-old boy.

                    FRANCESCA
          Patrizio, il cimitero chiude a
          l'una. (Patrick, the cemetery
          closes at one.)

PatG takes his apron off and hands it to the grandfather.

                     PATG
          U nonn, me ne vado. (Grandfather,
          I'm going.)

The old grandfather nods.

INT THE CEMETERY

FROM BEHIND, PATG AND FRANCESCA ARE WALKING HAND
IN HAND. THE BOY IS RUNNING AHEAD WITH A BOUQUET OF
FLOWERS

                     PATG
          Qua Danny.

The boy turns back.

THE WALL OF TOMBS, CIANCIA MICHELE

PatG picks Danny up.

                     PATG
          Qua è Zio Danny. (Here's Uncle
          Danny.) Dangin un muerss. (Give
          him a kiss.)

Francesca arranges the flowers to the side of Danny's stone.

LITTLE DANNY KISSES DANNY'S PICTURE

DANNY'S SMILING FACE FROM THE PICTURE TAKEN AT THE
RESTAURANT

DANNY HUBBLE CIANCIA

Francesca kisses her hand and then touches Danny's picture.

                    LITTLE DANNY
          Papà mi avevi detto che mi insegna
          baseball come lo zio. Possiamo
          oggi dopo che mangiamo? (Papà,
          you told me that you'd teach me to
          throw a baseball like Uncle Danny.
          Can you teach me today after we
          eat?)

                    FRANCESCA
          Devi mangiare tutto. (You must eat
          everything.)

                    DANNY
          Sì Mamma.

INT DANNY'S HOUSE IN FRONT ROOM THAT DAY

Ma and Irene are watching TV. Irene's knitting. Ma's
watching wrestling and suddenly turns to Irene.

                    MA
          Danny just came to me.

Irene stops. She raises her finger to her mouth.

                    IRENE
          It's the anniversary of when Danny
          left for Italy. It's ten years
          today.

Irene holds the sweater up.

                    IRENE (CONT'D)
          This will fit you fine, Bridget.

The screen freezes, and PatG's music comes on singing

*It's your time, it can't be wrong,
better learn to sing that song,
been hurt before, we all have you
see, stung before but still want
honey . . .*

Images one by one click onto the screen.

IMAGE OF OLD MEN PLAYING CARDS IN THE PARK

IMAGE OF DANNY, PATG, AND VITO AT THE RESTAURANT

IMAGE OF PROSTITUTES BRINGING DANNY INTO BEDROOM

IMAGE OF BOY IN SCHOOL TELLING DANNY TO BE A GOOD BOY

IMAGE OF DANNY'S TOMB WITH HIS SMILING FACE IN A
PICTURE ON THE FRONT OF IT

CLOSES ON DANNY'S FACE

THE BEGINNING